THERE WILL YOUR HEART BE ALSO

BY CHIP DANGELMAJER

To Maria,

... aka Mrs. Donatello

(minus the perfume)

Preface

There Will Your Heart be Also was originally written for our grandchildren and future grandchildren. When holding an infant grandchild in my arms, I wonder how their life will manifest. Will they live a happy, satisfying life? How do I advise them if I am not there to do so?

There Will Your Heart Be Also is a powerful story told through the lives of real, yet fictionalized, people who have lived deeply satisfying lives. They face daunting challenges with courage, a heart full of love, and hope for a better future. Ultimately it is their faith in God, and love of neighbor, that delivers them to the place of peace that surpasses all understanding.

I hope you enjoy this story and may we all arrive at that place of peace.

Chip Dangelmajer
9/3/2019

Chapter 1

Early September, 1969
Lawrence, Massachusetts

Father Peter Ryan leaned back in his chair and smiled at the pile of mail on his metal desk. Like every other piece of furniture in his cramped office, his desk was cluttered with paperwork, knickknacks, and the tools of the trade. A black desk phone and an overstuffed pencil holder competed for space with framed photos and loose-leaf papers. As for the mail, no doubt most of it had been opened already by someone in the outer office. He was well aware of his staff's determination to keep the chaos in his office from spreading beyond his door, which, in a symbolic gesture, was always left open. If something important was in that mail, he'd hear about it before he got around to actually reading it.

It was the first day of school. Peter, in his fourth year as principal of St. James High School, felt blessed to be beginning another academic year at such a venerable institution. Neither new nor particularly impressive, St. James nevertheless boasted a storied history in the community, and he was delighted to be part of it. Teachers, students, coaches, parents—everyone contributed to the lore, which, year after year, grew richer and more varied. To be part of the experience was equally thrilling and sobering.

Peter straightened in his chair the moment he caught whiff of the scent. Sweet and pungent, like a heady bouquet of peonies, the smell of

1

her perfume always preceded Mrs. Maria Donatello, the school's financial officer and administrator.

Maria's face appeared in the doorway just seconds later. "Do you have a moment, Father?" she asked in a way that suggested he had no choice.

"Of course," he said, gesturing toward the chair across from his desk. "Please have a seat."

Instead of heading for the chair, Maria paused to close the door behind her, signaling she was planning to do more than offer first-day-of-school pleasantries. An attractive woman in her early forties, Maria moved with grace and poise. Her long brunette hair, pulled back into a bun, was just beginning to show a few strands of gray. Her confidence and competence, as palpable as her perfume, had always impressed Peter. He never hesitated to explain to newcomers who kept St. James running day after day. The wall clock behind her showed they had fifteen minutes before the early staff meeting was scheduled to begin.

"We have a problem," Maria said as she lowered herself into the wooden chair.

Peter's own chair squeaked as he leaned back and lifted his eyebrows. "We do?"

Maria's eyes lingered a moment on the mess of his desk, and a barely suppressed smile tugged at the corners of her coral-colored lips. She didn't seem annoyed as much as amused by his absentminded housekeeping. She'd been tolerant of his eccentricities since his first day on the job.

"My cousin Gayle," she began, "you've met her, I think."

Peter searched his memory, then nodded. Gayle Fallows was a secretary at the diocese. He was fairly certain she was a few years younger than Maria. "Yes, I met her once outside Bishop Woodbury's office. A fine young lady. She strikes me as a sharp thinker. Must run in the family."

"You're too kind," Maria said, impatience creeping into her voice. "Anyway, I just got a call from her that I think you should know about."

"Oh?"

"She wanted to let me know that you'll be getting a letter today from the diocese."

Peter furrowed his brow. It wasn't uncommon to receive a letter from the diocese. It was, however, uncommon to be warned of it. "Did she say what the letter would be about?"

Maria hardly let Peter finish his question. "Our financial situation."

"Ah."

Peter had never focused much on the school's finances, but he wasn't surprised that they'd become an issue. The land acquisition, construction costs, and endowment for St. James had relied largely upon a local family that owned several textile and paper mills. Arthur York, a St. James graduate whose children also had attended the school, had carried on the tradition of generosity begun by his grandfather. Unfortunately, Mr. York had died the previous fall when he lost control of his automobile while driving in a downpour. His widow had promised to continue her late husband's charitable work, but not long afterward, an audit of the company had revealed it was barely profitable. Thus, Mrs. York had been forced to break up the company and sell its assets to several international firms. None of those firms was inclined to continue supporting St. James.

Peter had already reached the conclusion that plans for a new art building would have to be put on hold, and he knew he'd eventually have to find a way to replace the Yorks' funding. He'd assumed he'd have a while to sort out the details. But the worry lines on Maria's forehead suggested the news was much worse than the loss of the new art building.

He drew a breath and released it in a sigh. "Okay," he replied. "Tell me what's going to be in the letter."

"They want to merge St. James with Notre Dame and create a regional high school. The building and land that St. James currently occupies will be sold off, and the proceeds will be invested in the new high school. Since Notre Dame already has a lot of land, they feel that they can expand it to accommodate our students."

Peter stared at her in disbelief. "Sell the school? What about our faculty and administrators?"

"I don't know. I suppose a few will be needed, but not many."

Peter shook his head as though trying to shake off a bad dream. Sell the land? Merge with Notre Dame? The news felt like a hammer blow. "But how will the students get there? Notre Dame is across town."

"By bus. The diocese promises a smooth transition."

"How sure is Gayle about all of this?"

"She typed the letter herself. And she's overheard several conversations between the bishop and others. They're concerned that if they keep St. James open, it will become a financial drain."

"Does she know when this will happen?"

Maria tilted her head and gave him a worried frown. "As far as she can tell, they haven't settled on a timetable yet."

Peter pushed himself back from his desk. The first day of school was usually his favorite day of the year, but this one was quickly deteriorating into something else entirely. He thought of the people who'd be affected by such a change, and shuddered. He couldn't imagine the harm that would be caused by breaking up the faculty and disrupting the students' lives.

The more he meditated on the potential fallout, the more desperate for a solution he became. Yes, he loved his job as principal of St. James High School, but it was more than that. The phenomenal staff, the dedicated faculty, the exuberant student body—St. James was a pillar of the community, a longstanding institution that connected the past to the present, individuals to the community. To sell off the school and its property struck him as not just shortsighted, but injurious, a heartless concession to financial priorities.

"There must be something that can be done to preserve St. James," he exclaimed, throwing up his hands in desperation. "What can we do?"

Maria didn't waste time. It was obvious she'd mulled over the problem already. An accountant by trade, she had a gift for solving complex issues and accomplishing daunting administrative feats. Thus, most of the school's clerical, financial, administrative, and even legal challenges were directed toward her.

"We need a cash infusion," she said. "A *large* infusion."

"How large?"

Her eyes shifted away from his for a moment, then returned. "Half a million dollars."

His jaw dropped. "Half a . . . *million*?"

"I'm afraid so. I've run through the cash flow projections several times under differing scenarios. That's how much we need to keep St. James open. And it's clear we don't have much time. Once they settle on a timeline and begin moving forward, the plan will take on a momentum of its own."

Peter thought more about his beloved school. The synergy and intimacy at St. James couldn't possibly be replicated at a sprawling regional high school. The structures in place and the intricate relationships involved enabled the school to function smoothly. He glanced past Maria at the wall clock and saw that the faculty meeting was about to begin.

"Maria," he said as he returned his gaze to her. "I hate to add to your burden, but please don't tell anyone about this just yet. I'd like to sit with this awhile before we share it with anyone else."

"Of course." Maria stood, pausing to straighten her long skirt. The streaks of gray in her hair suddenly looked more pronounced, and her coral-colored lipstick, so bright when she'd entered Peter's office, appeared faded.

Chapter 2

Peter's mind was still reeling from the news of the school's financial troubles when, perspiring and out of breath, he arrived at the faculty lounge. Low-pile carpet. The faint odor of cigarette smoke. A long bank of squat, rectangular windows along the far wall that looked out at the brick and mortar of the school auditorium. It wasn't the most inspirational place to gather, but the faculty lounge always cultivated in Peter a feeling of gratitude and communal joy. This was where he lived, in the back-and-forth between colleagues, the sharing of stories, the delight of human contact. In his short time at St. James, he'd come to appreciate not only the bright minds of the students but the persistent dedication of the pedagogues who delivered their education. Day after day, week after week, month after month, teachers and coaches poured themselves into their work, which, in Peter's mind, was nothing short of heroic, even if it sometimes went unnoticed in the broader community.

"Good morning, Father." The first person to greet Peter was Vice Principal JD Long. At six feet, eight inches and three hundred pounds, the man was hard to miss. He rose from one of the couches clustered in the middle of the room and offered his hand.

Peter took it and smiled up at him as his hand disappeared inside the big man's meaty paw. "Good morning to you, Mr. Vice Principal. I can't tell you how happy I am to see you."

Indeed, there was something comforting about retreating to the safety of the faculty lounge and gathering with some of his favorite people in the world. Perhaps St. James was on the verge of being shuttered forever, but here, in the presence of the school's lively faculty, Peter drew strength from the familiar faces smiling back at him.

JD ran a hand through his flattop—an unconscious tick, Peter assumed, given how often he did it—and retook his seat on the couch. Had there ever been a vice principal who so looked the part? It seemed doubtful. With his square jaw and broad shoulders, JD evinced the kind of authority no one dared question. He'd come to St. James from the Massachusetts Department of Corrections, having earned his credentials before retiring a captain, and had quickly asserted himself at the school. Yet despite his forceful persona and towering presence, he contained a quiet, mysterious depth, or so it seemed to Peter. The man was intimidating on the outside, but something else entirely on the inside. A tender soul, perhaps?

Seated beside JD was Roger Dean, the portly baseball coach. Fifty-two, blunt, and rough-edged, the coach had a great sense of humor—no doubt useful when the team struggled, which wasn't very often. "You sure you're ready for the first day of school, Father?" he asked without getting up. "You look like you just ran a marathon."

"I was held up back at the office," Peter replied with a chuckle that he hoped concealed his state of near-panic. He exchanged smiles and nods with the others in the room.

"Is that all?" Coach Dean asked, raising an eyebrow. "If I didn't know better, I'd think someone chased you here. You look like my dog after a tussle with the neighborhood tomcat."

The room erupted with laughter, and Peter heard his own guffaw above the rest. Sometimes laughter was the best medicine. And nobody elicited it more often than Coach Dean, who balanced wisecracks with a directness that sometimes offended his colleagues. He had no time for flattery or diplomacy, but Peter appreciated his bluntness. At an institution where decorum and deference usually prevailed, Coach Dean provided a breath of fresh air.

As soon as everyone quieted, Peter addressed the group. "I know you've all got places to be shortly, but I just want to take a moment to thank each one of you for bringing your unique talents to St. James." He made eye contact with Ed Kowalski, the forty-six-year-old football coach charged with turning around a program that historically had been anything but a powerhouse, and then Father Kovacs, the thoughtful and soft-spoken mathematics and science chair. Next, he smiled at Mathilde Weaver, a Juilliard-trained pianist and the school's music educator, followed by Laurel Nord, St. James's talented art teacher. "The parents in this community entrust you with their children's education, and you prepare our students—body, mind, and soul—for the world that awaits them. It's nothing short of a miracle what you do. When I think back to the day . . ."

Coach Dean caught Peter's eye and pointed at his watch, offering a not-so-subtle hint to wrap up his remarks.

"Right. We don't have much time. Before you go, I believe we have someone new on our faculty. I'd like to introduce you to . . ." Peter searched the room. "She must be here somewhere."

Sister Consuela Alvarez, thirty-one and in charge of girl's athletics, sat near the long bank of windows in an overstuffed chair, from where she was signaling Peter. Dressed in her usual nun's habit, she beamed back at him and then, with a dramatic flair, leaned to her right, revealing the newest faculty member behind her.

Silhouetted by the bright morning sunlight pouring in through the windows, a beautiful young woman stood. "Hello," she said with an infectious smile.

"Yes," Peter stammered. "Hello. This is Alessandra Alvarez, our new English teacher. She recently graduated from Boston College with a bachelor's degree in English and a minor in dance."

"Alvarez?" Laurel Nord asked and turned to get a look at the new arrival. "Are you related to Sister Consuela?"

9

"She's my kid sister," Sister Consuela responded in a tone that conveyed amusement as well as perhaps a touch of jealousy.

"Please," Alessandra said. "Call me Sandra."

A hush fell over the room as the others took in the stunning beauty. Even Peter, not usually one to be stymied by physical beauty, found himself briefly tongue-tied. Perhaps it was the bright sunlight that framed Sandra—or the effects of learning of St. James's financial peril. He was on edge, after all. Regardless, he felt a strange combination of admiration and embarrassment, as though the mere act of looking upon such a lovely young woman somehow made him smaller by comparison.

For once, Coach Dean also appeared speechless.

Sandra, with her dark hair and deep blue eyes, seemed unfazed by the collective response. She waved at her colleagues, revealing a slender arm and wrist, and then dropped her hand to her side. "I'm honored to join this faculty. My sister has told me wonderful things about all of you. Thank you, Father Ryan, for this opportunity."

Peter glanced at the others and noticed smiles forming on their faces. They saw it too. Yes, Sandra was stunning, the embodiment of grace, but she also glowed with something else: kindness. Better still, she exuded competence. He knew at that moment that she would do more than turn heads at St. James; she would engage minds and touch hearts.

His fears about the school's uncertain future, so prominent in his mind only moments earlier, were replaced by a determination to do right by his faculty and the institution he so cherished.

Chapter 3

Sandra Alvarez was seated at her desk, praying over her rosary beads, when her first student entered the classroom. Head down, books pressed against her chest, the girl looked up long enough to acknowledge Sandra with a shy smile. Then she continued toward the back of the class, where she found a seat against the wall.

"Good morning," Sandra said cheerfully.

"Good morning," the girl replied with an awkward nod as she retrieved a Bic ballpoint pen from her bag. Her whole body, from her slumped shoulders to her pigeon-toed feet, appeared to be frowning. She wore the standard Catholic school uniform for girls at St. James: an oversized navy-blue blazer over a white blouse, a dark plaid skirt, and knee-high, navy-blue socks.

This one, Sandra thought, would need some coaxing to come out of her shell. As the room filled with more students, Sandra noticed two distinct patterns. While the girls gazed at her with something between admiration and envy, the boys, wide-eyed and slack-jawed, stumbled to their seats like drunken barflies trying to find their stools.

Sandra had grown accustomed to such reactions, although, admittedly, she'd hoped her students would behave differently than her peers and professors back at Boston College. Her conservative outfit, from her loose-fitting blouse to her long wool skirt, was designed to hide the curves on her five-foot-six frame. She wore only a hint of makeup and had pulled her long, dark hair into a bun.

She realized she'd have to prove herself, just as she'd done in Boston, and the effort would require the same patience, humility, and humor. Patience, to wait for her students to recognize in her the same humanity everyone shared; humility, to acknowledge that the spell she seemed to cast wherever she went was a blessing as much as a curse and did not belong to her; and humor, to remind herself that every awkward moment had the potential to provoke laughter, though sometimes only after the fact.

As soon as the bell rang, Sandra took attendance. The awkward girl at the back of the room? That was Jenny O'Donnell. The too-smooth-for-his-own-good boy at the front currently giving her the once-over? Danny Corvino. The students in her first-period English class, all juniors, boasted a full range of personalities, from jocks to jokers.

A perpetual early bird, Sandra had arrived an hour earlier to clean the blackboard, run through her roster, and take one last look at her notes. Her life had been characterized by success built upon success. She learned early on that discipline ultimately brought freedom.

"Good morning, everyone," she said as she took a piece of chalk in her hand. "My name is Alessandra Alvarez. You may call me Miss Alvarez. Today I'm going to give you a short preview of what you'll be studying this semester. Vocabulary. Reading comprehension. Grammar. Articulation." She wrote each word on the blackboard as she said it. "You won't be able to pass my class without mastering these fundamentals." She pointed at Danny, who was smiling at her but seemed to be undressing her with his eyes. "Mr. Corvino, can you tell the class what a homonym is?"

He ran a hand through his short-cropped blond hair and glanced side to side, clearly startled. "A what?"

The students around him giggled.

"A homonym," Sandra repeated.

He straightened in his chair. "Oh, yeah. It's, ah, a word that sounds like another word but has a different meaning."

Sandra raised an eyebrow. "Very good. Can you give me an example?"

The young man's forehead gave way to a sea of wrinkles as he thought about the question. He opened his mouth, grasping for a response, then finally threw up his hands in defeat, eliciting more tittering from fellow students.

Sandra wrote two words side-by-side on the blackboard: *cell* and *sell*.

Danny, looking like someone struggling to shake off the effects of anesthesia, stared at the words without comprehending them.

Sandra turned to the rest of the class. "Can someone else give me another example?"

Seated behind Danny, Erin Manning, a bookish girl with glasses and braces, raised her hand enthusiastically. "Pair and pear!"

"Yes, thank you. Homonyms also can share the same spelling. The word *fair*, for example, can describe a community gathering or something that's just." Sandra eyed the others. "Anyone else?"

As Sandra led the class through a quick survey of the semester's workload, her mind raced. It was obvious that she'd entered a perilous teaching environment. Too many of her students, especially the boys like Danny, appeared transfixed by her beauty. How would she be able to reach them if they were mentally proposing to her? How could she be taken seriously if she was seen only as a romantic object?

Unfortunately, the problem was even more complicated due to the transformation already underway in classrooms all over the country. Toward the end of her senior year at Boston College, a professor had warned her that students wouldn't view her as an authority figure but as more-or-less an equal. The subject matter of her lectures, he'd said, would hold limited value for many of her students. Although only a few years older than her students, she could sense the differences between them. Something was happening with today's youth. They appeared to value individual expression over societal norms, change over tradition. Some kind of social revolution was going on, and she wondered if she was the last of the old guard, someone who would be left behind in the coming years.

Sandra, though, wasn't one to give up easily, and as she thought about the way her male students regarded her and the way students in general were changing, she stumbled upon a potential solution. She'd speak to them in their own language. More specifically, she'd use their youthful thirst for romantic love to fuel their academic pursuits. Such a teaching method was dubious, she conceded, and entirely unorthodox. But if the times were changing, she'd be better served by flexibility and spontaneity—two qualities today's youth cherished—than by the rigid methods she preferred.

When it came time to introduce articulation, the last of the four categories she'd written on the blackboard, she decided to take the leap.

"There are moments in life when accurate articulation and nuance are important," she began. "Such as dating." She pivoted toward the young man gazing up at her in awestruck silence. "Danny, if you were deeply in love, how would you articulate this to your beloved?"

The young man blushed and once again was at a loss for words. After an uncomfortable silence, he sputtered, "You know, uh, like, uh, I think you're outta sight. Like, you know what I'm saying?"

The girls in the class squealed with laughter, and the boys, perhaps sensing that the most promising among them had just bombed, grimaced in disgust.

Sandra studied Danny for a moment and then addressed the girls. "Ladies, pretend you're Danny's beloved. Are you impressed with the way he's articulated his love?"

The girls, most of whom were smirking, shook their heads in

unison, and chatter erupted among the students. While the boys chided Danny for such a lame attempt, the girls talked excitedly about what he *should* have said.

Sandra let them voice their opinions for a minute or two and then silenced them with her hand. It was time to tend to Danny's badly bruised ego. Publicly humiliating a student, even one as self-assured as Danny, constituted a risk. But she was willing to take that risk if she could turn his humiliation into an eagerness to learn.

"Danny," she said warmly, "can we work together to more accurately express your passion and love for a most fortunate woman in your future?"

He cocked his head slightly, and a smile formed on his face, which had been red with shame just seconds earlier. "Sure. Let's do it!"

Sandra returned his smile and then clasped her hands as she addressed the whole class. "Shakespeare. Whitman. Dickinson. Along with learning the fundamentals of English this semester, you'll be studying some of the greatest authors to have ever put pen to paper. And everything you learn will help you along your quest, which is to perfect the art of self-expression. Mastering the English language isn't just about memorizing rules and learning the difference between a homonym and a homophone. It's about learning to articulate your thoughts, about sharing your deepest feelings. Your first assignment is to write a poem for your beloved."

Jenny O'Donnell, still slumped silently against the back wall, raised her hand just high enough to capture Sandra's attention.

"Yes, Miss O'Donnell?"

Jenny stared at her desk as she spoke, her face ashen. "What if we don't have a beloved?"

A few of the other students nodded empathetically.

"Ah, but you do." Sandra was determined to squelch Jenny's doubt before it could take root. "That beloved need not be anyone you know, or even a person. Perhaps your beloved is a place, or a memory, or a song. The only requirement is that you write a poem expressing your love for it."

Jenny smiled weakly, just enough to suggest she was satisfied with the answer. As Sandra continued to answer questions and explain the assignment, the atmosphere in the classroom became electric. The students were excited to express themselves with the written word. Better still, and to Sandra's great relief, they were focused on something besides their new teacher.

~~~

Just as Maria had predicted, Bishop Woodbury's letter arrived that afternoon. Peter struggled for a moment to find his letter opener on his desk, then opened the letter and read every sentence, his heart in his throat. It was just as Maria's cousin had said: because St. James had lost its primary funding source, it was on the chopping block.

Peter set down the letter and dialed Bishop Woodbury's direct number at the diocese.

The bishop picked up on the second ring. "This is Bishop Woodbury."

"Hello, Bishop," Peter answered. "This is Father Ryan. I just received your letter."

Bishop Woodbury's voice, a deep, melodious baritone, paused briefly. "I'm sorry to be the bearer of such bad news. I wish we could fund the shortfall. But even the Catholic Church has to pay its bills."

"I understand," Peter said. "But we've been looking at the problem. Mrs. Donatello has put together some cash flow projections. We feel that St. James can be self-sustaining with an infusion of cash."

"Of course. But as I said, the diocese isn't in a position to do that."

"I'm talking about an *outside* source."

"If you're talking about a loan of some kind . . ." The bishop's words trailed off.

"Not at all. I'm talking about a lump sum cash contribution."

"Of how much?"

Peter tried to sound casual as he said, "Five-hundred-thousand dollars."

After a pause, the bishop said, "Well, that's just about what our own projections show. But, Peter, how in the world would you be able to come up with that much money?"

"I haven't worked out all the details," Peter said in what must have been the biggest understatement of his life. "But what if I can come up with a plan to raise the money?"

Bishop Woodbury cleared his throat. "I don't have the final say. Ultimately, it's the archbishop's decision."

"I understand that," Peter said. "Will you make a case for us?"

"I suppose I could." The bishop didn't sound very convincing. "But, Father, you still haven't answered my question. How will you find those funds?"

Peter took a deep breath. He'd never been much of a gambler, but St. James, it seemed to him, was worth the risk. "I'll find a way, Bishop. You just buy me some time."

Chapter 4

The doorbell rang just as Peter sat down to dinner that evening. He lived alone in St. James's rectory, a tidy, two-story brick Tudor situated beneath a canopy of old hickory trees, just a stone's throw from the chapel. Visitors were frequent, but most came before the dinner hour.

He left his plate of leftover spaghetti on the dining room table, which was cluttered like his desk and had room for only one place setting, and passed through the parlor on his way to the front door. He was surprised to find his sister, Susan Jones, standing on the front stoop. Four years his senior, she had his same dark brown hair, although hers was shaped into an attractive pixie cut, and the same greenish-blue eyes. Like him, she'd also put on a pound or two since their youth. But the tiny bit of extra weight became her, for she'd always been, in their father's words, a beanpole.

She smiled broadly. "Hello, little brother."

He gave her a warm hug and invited her inside. "What brings you to town?"

Susan and her husband lived in Boston and rarely visited Lawrence on weekdays. "I'd love to say I was just in the neighborhood, but I was hoping you and I could talk."

Peter led her to an old sofa in the parlor. "Take a seat."

Susan plopped down on the lumpy piece of Victorian furniture and placed her small handbag beside her.

"Is it Bobby?" Peter asked.

He already knew the answer. Bobby Jones, Susan's only son,

was a brilliant young tenor who had become guarded and withdrawn since returning home from his service with the US Army's 1st Cavalry Division in Vietnam. Susan had been calling Peter regularly for several months, desperate for some insight on how to help her son.

She pursed her lips and nodded worriedly. "I'm at my wit's end. He won't return my letters. He won't pick up the phone." Her shoulders shook as she wiped a tear from her cheek. "I feel like we're losing him."

Peter sat quietly as he tried to absorb the news. He and Bobby had always been close—until Bobby had left to join the fighting in Vietnam soon after his graduation from Boston College. Peter had tried to talk him out of the decision, and Bobby had bristled at the intrusion. Chastened, Peter had eventually thrown his support behind his nephew, telling the young man that he admired his resolve. The alternative—letting Bobby ship off to Officer Candidate School at Fort Benning in Georgia with the tension still simmering between them—had been unthinkable.

To everyone's relief, Bobby had come home in one piece. But it seemed he'd sustained his share of wounds, after all—all of them psychological.

"Do you think he'd take his own life?" Peter asked.

Susan looked away. "I don't know."

"There would be signs. A tidying of affairs. A sudden projection of serenity."

"Again, I don't know! I haven't seen him in weeks."

"Do you know if he's been drinking?"

Susan shook her head. "I don't think so. He can be sullen and bitter. He can be mean. But he's never been the self-destructive type."

"When you say mean . . ."

"Not abusive or anything like that, just prickly. He tends to lash out when he's feeling cornered."

This much was true, Peter thought. Bobby was kind-hearted and

19

not inclined to hurt others, which quite possibly was at least part of what was troubling him. By all accounts, he'd served admirably as a 2nd lieutenant during his tour in Vietnam. Perhaps he was haunted by what he'd seen, by what he'd had no choice to do, while wearing the uniform of an American soldier.

"What can I do?" Peter finally asked.

"Talk to him. Engage him. Anything! He obviously doesn't want to talk to me. But I need to know he's not alone in all of this."

Peter, who had been seated opposite his sister in a matching loveseat with frayed upholstery, got up and joined her on the sofa. "I will," he said and wrapped his arm around her. How he was going to find time to rescue St. James *and* help his nephew fight off his demons was a mystery, but such a quandary was nothing new to Peter. If his own experiences had taught him anything, it was that, with a little faith, anything was possible.

"Thank you." Susan wiped her eyes, cleared her throat, and sniffed at the air. "Is that spaghetti?"

~~~

Peter sat on the end of his bed, removed his slippers, and rubbed the tension from his feet. It had been a long, eventful day. Before he could pull back the comforter and slip into bed, he heard the phone ring downstairs. Much of the rectory's second story was devoted to storage, but his living quarters were at the end of the hallway, which made answering the phone a chore.

By the time he reached the first-floor parlor, the old black phone on the end table had stopped ringing. He frowned and turned to leave. It rang again. This time he caught it on the second ring.

"Hello?" He eyed the clock above the mantle. It was just after nine o'clock—a little late for a phone call. Susan had called a half hour earlier to let him know she'd made it home safely, so it couldn't be her. His mind raced straight to the bishop. Was he already getting back to

Peter with news?

"Peter, it's Jonathan. I hope I'm not disturbing you."

Peter tried not to sound disappointed. "Not at all, old friend, although another minute and I'd have been counting sheep."

Peter had known Jonathan Bloom for four decades. He'd been only four years old when, in 1927, his family had moved into the farmhouse next to Jonathan's on the outskirts of Lawrence. The two boys, one Catholic and one Jewish, had become fast friends while playing in the Bloom family's orchard. Their families vacationed together at Cape Cod every summer, and had remained close all the way through high school. Both had joined the war effort not long after America entered World War II, with Peter serving in the navy in the Pacific and Jonathan, a mathematics whiz and gifted musician, flying to Bletchley Park in England to join the British codebreakers.

After the war, Peter had answered the call of the priesthood, while Jonathan had gone on to study mechanical engineering at MIT followed by music at the New England Conservatory of Music, where his scintillating performances on the piano had kept him in high demand as a professional musician. Still inseparable after all these years, they remained in regular contact.

"I won't keep you long," Jonathan promised. "I just wanted to share some wonderful news."

"Oh?" Peter replied, sensing excitement in Jonathan's tone.

"I've discovered an opportunity for Bobby that could be of immense help to him, both professionally and . . . emotionally."

Peter sat on the plush leather wingback chair next to the end table. A gift from a generous parishioner, the chair was the only nice piece of furniture in the parlor—or the rectory, for that matter. "Susan just left an hour ago. She's frantic about him. Your timing couldn't be better. Please, tell me everything."

"I had dinner tonight with Greg Bergmann. You might have

21

heard of him. He's a conductor of several famous orchestras in the United States and currently the guest conductor with the Boston Symphony Orchestra."

"I have indeed," Peter said and switched the phone to his other ear. "I think I've even seen him in action."

"Well, Mr. Bergmann needs a tenor to perform Handel's *Messiah* this Christmas season. He's looking for someone young and vibrant who can communicate the intense spirituality of the piece. I suggested he audition Bobby, who, as far as I'm concerned, is tailor-made for the part. I mean, think about it! He's young, a virtuoso, and can easily communicate the spiritual values contained in the libretto."

Peter frowned. He loved listening to Jonathan talk about music, but he felt uneasy about where their conversation was going. "What did he say?"

"He said he remembers Bobby! He met Bobby in his youth and worked with him several times while Bobby was at Boston College. He said Bobby has 'a commanding stage presence' and 'striking good looks.' He even—"

"Jonathan, hold on. Does Mr. Bergmann want to audition Bobby?"

"Yes! Can you believe it?"

"I can, actually. But do you really think now is such a good time? The boy hasn't spoken with his mother for weeks. No one's seen hide nor hair of him. For all we know, he hasn't sung a note since he joined the army."

Jonathan was unfazed. "He's probably a little rusty, but trust me, this is right in his wheelhouse."

"But what about his mental state? Susan says he spends all day holed up in his cycle shop—at least that's what he was doing the last she heard from him. Throwing him into the fire like this could be a risk." Peter scrambled to explain himself. "It's not that I don't think

22

he's talented. I do. But think of the kind of pressure he must be under already. To give him such a high-stakes role—"

"It's the opportunity of a lifetime," Jonathan countered. "Peter, it could open doors for him. It could change everything."

Peter thought for a moment. "Okay. But won't more parts like this come along in the future? And wouldn't it be smarter to ease him back into civilization first? Maybe he could join a choir. I'm sure there are churches all over town that would love to have him."

"Peter." Jonathan's tone was taking on an edge of impatience. "The Bobby I know is a star-in-the-making, not a faceless member of some volunteer choir. He can do this. And, no, parts like this don't just come along every day. This is a once-in-a-lifetime opportunity, especially for someone who left the music world to become an infantry officer."

Peter sighed. "I keep coming back to Bobby's mental state. If he succeeds, this could bring him back to us. But if he fails . . ."

"I told Bergmann all about Bobby, his service in Vietnam, everything he's been through since. The man was sympathetic. He comes from a large Lutheran family. Apparently two of his nephews are serving in Vietnam right now. He's appreciative of their service, of course, but doesn't understand why we're fighting a war in Southeast Asia. If anyone can extend Bobby some sympathy, it's him."

Peter stood to pace. He wanted to be excited for Bobby, but the best he could do was feel guardedly optimistic. "Is he a kind man? Will he be patient?"

Jonathan laughed. It was clear he sensed he was winning the argument. "I wouldn't use either word to describe Mr. Bergmann. But if you've seen him conduct, then you know he's magnificent. He's not only an amazing conductor, he's also a superb pianist. The way he engages an audience—it's pure magic. Between pieces he'll talk about a composer or the history behind the piece. People who have never been to a concert before walk away knowing volumes more about music. He makes them feel valued and intelligent and a part of the event. But he's demanding, too, at least where the orchestra, choir, and soloists are concerned. He expects excellence from everyone, and has no problem firing anyone who's unable to meet his standards. I think that's why everything he touches is so sensational. He brings out the best in everyone."

Peter came to a stop in the middle of the room with the receiver to his ear. He was finished pacing. "So who's going to talk to Bobby?"

"We *both* will."

Peter smiled to himself. "Of course."

"Do you think he'll do it?" Jonathan asked, the optimism in his voice waning for the first time.

"I don't know," Peter answered. "But if everything is as you say it is, we'd be fools not to do everything in our power to convince him that this is a golden opportunity. Sometimes you have to take a leap of faith, whether you're ready or not."

~~~

Peter often had trouble sleeping, and that night was no exception. He'd been delivered two stunning pieces of information—one troubling, one promising—and as he lay in bed and stared at the ceiling, he felt certain that his fifth year at St. James would be, if nothing else, an interesting one.

Chapter 5

Vice Principal JD Long had just returned from lunch the next day when he heard a knock on his office door.

"Come in," he said.

The door swung open, and Phil Major, a senior who had made multiple visits to JD's office over the past few years, appeared with Janet Miller, the school secretary, behind him.

"Picking up right where you left off last year, I see," JD said. "Second day of school. Even for you, Phil, that might be a record." He turned to Janet. "What is it this time?"

"Smoking on campus, sir," Janet said with an eye-roll. She turned to leave and disappeared into the outer office.

JD sighed and motioned for Phil to close the door and take a seat.

Phil, a wiry kid who, at five feet, eleven inches, might have weighed one hundred and forty-five pounds soaking wet, did as he was instructed. Even in his gray slacks, white Oxford dress shirt, and sweater vest, he looked disheveled. His sandy blond hair was threatening to grow over his ears, which was against the school dress code, and his footwear, far from the usual patent leather dress shoes, consisted of a pair of dirty Chuck Taylor canvas high-tops that had been white at one time but now resembled a pair of used dish rags.

JD said nothing, opting instead to let the boy stew in his own juices.

Phil squirmed in his seat, pausing to glance at his Spartan surroundings. Framed on either side by JD's well-kept office, which was largely empty, save for a bookshelf that contained only a smattering of books and one lonely houseplant, Phil looked small and out of his element. He finally spoke, but did so while avoiding eye contact. "Detention, sir?"

"Detention," JD repeated.

Phil started to rise from his chair, but JD motioned for him to stay put. It was time to set Phil straight. JD had mastered the core principles of discipline as a corrections officer, but knew he had to tread lightly. Phil wasn't a bad kid, far from it. He was a people person, warm, outgoing, and fun-loving. Everyone at St. James liked him, from the students to the teachers and administrators. But he had yet to find his niche at the school. Academics. Athletics. Phil excelled at neither. He had reached a dangerous juncture in his life and, like a skittish animal, shouldn't be frightened lest he bolt in the wrong direction.

JD had shown even less promise in his youth. The son of divorced parents, he'd been left to his own devices after his father left and his mother went to work as a Linotype operator at the local printer. Unsupervised and undirected for most of the day, he'd taken up with a band of troublemakers. Only a reprimand from a police officer had rescued him from oblivion. After scolding JD and his friends, the officer had taken JD aside and told him something remarkable: "You remind me of myself when I was your age." JD immediately took a liking to the officer, and when the officer gave him a brand new basketball and told him to find new friends, JD took the message to heart. He was indeed "better than that." JD could still remember the officer's last words, which were spoken in a confident baritone: "I want to read about you in the sports section."

If there was one thing JD had learned in his previous line of work, it was that only a small segment of the population was truly evil. When he encountered such students at St. James—rarely, thank God— he promptly removed them from the school. Nothing could be done for them. They were best sent packing and, if necessary, locked away. But most people had good in them, and Phil was no exception.

JD leaned back in his chair with his hands behind his head and studied Phil. "What do you like to do in your spare time, son?"

Phil, clearly caught off guard by the question, seemed to shrink in his chair. He offered a meek shrug.

"What are you good at?"

Phil's answer sounded more like a question. "I don't know?"

JD chuckled. This kid was going to be a challenge. But JD knew that all young men and women yearned for knowledge and accomplishment. Every student wanted to prove his or her worth. "You like music?"

"Sure, I guess."

"Art?"

Phil offered another shrug.

JD figured the trick was to funnel Phil into some kind of pursuit that could simultaneously pique his curiosity and engage his aptitudes, whatever they might be. Everybody was gifted in some way, but discovering a student's strengths wasn't always easy. Some knew exactly who they wanted to be, but some, like Phil, were still groping for an identity. Maybe he didn't have any support at home. Maybe nobody had ever encouraged him. Whatever the case, JD was determined to give Phil a gentle push toward something that would challenge and eventually reward him.

"Son, you may not know it yet, but you're a genius."

Phil's sleepy brown eyes widened. "A genius, sir?"

"You bet. Every student in this high school possesses a unique gift, something they can do better than anyone else. But it's not always easy to figure out what that unique gift is. And as important as a high school education is, the academic life is not for everyone." JD raised an eyebrow at Phil. "There's a whole world outside these walls. The marketplace offers limitless opportunities for a person's individual talents."

Phil furrowed his brow in confusion. "Are you saying I should quit high school?"

"No. I'm saying do your best here, and keep searching for your calling. You'll know it when you find it." JD threw Phil a sober look. "Where were you supposed to be when you were caught smoking?"

"Precalculus," Phil mumbled with a frown.

JD nodded knowingly. He, too, had struggled with math. It was just a hunch, but he had a feeling Phil's time would be better spent elsewhere, at least for the moment. "I tell you what, son. Drop precalculus. You can always take it next semester. In the meantime, I've got a class that might be just right for you."

"A class, sir?" Phil repeated as his prominent Adam's apple bobbed in his throat. Was he nervous or excited? It was impossible to tell.

"Some students are destined for the industrial arts. I think you might be one of them."

JD could pick out a mechanically inclined future tradesman without too much difficulty. The typical candidate was quiet and did poorly in academics. Many had difficulty fitting in socially. All were introduced to Thomas Harraka, the shop teacher and a retired commercial contractor who often placed his students in high-paying jobs in the construction industry after they graduated. The abundance of success stories among Harraka's graduates ensured that the industrial arts was competitive at St. James.

Phil, though, wasn't a typical candidate. He was more outgoing, breezier. Still, there was something about him that suggested he might benefit more than most from Harraka's class. Regardless, it was obvious JD was going to have to sell him on the idea.

"You ever been in the woodshop?"

"No, sir."

"Well, it just happens to be my favorite place on campus. The second you walk through the door, it hits you."

Phil leaned forward expectantly. "What, sir?"

"The smell of the place. Red cedar. Mahogany. Maple. Each has a distinct fragrance, you know. Each has its own look too. After you've studied a few pieces of lumber, you can start to tell the differences between the woods. And these kids who work with them, they're artists. Maybe they don't use a canvas or an easel, but Mr. Harraka teaches them how to turn blocks of wood into chests, toys, guitars, you name it. You'll learn how to work with planes and chisels and all kinds of saws. Ever cut a mortise and tenon joint?"

Phil shook his head.

"How about a dovetail?"

Another shake of the head. By now the boy's mouth was hanging open, his eyes threatening to glaze over.

JD straightened in his chair. "I didn't know much about woodworking either until Mr. Harraka invited me to sit in on his class a few years ago. Now I drop in whenever I can. When the students get those saws and sanders going, it sounds like a symphony. Music to my ears. Anyway, son, it sure beats precalculus, which I gather isn't your favorite subject."

"No, sir."

Finally, a definitive response from the kid. It would have to do.

"Then it's settled, Mr. Major." JD stood and offered his hand across the desk, well aware that his meaty paw dwarfed the kid's. "You're taking woodshop."

Phil gulped. "Yes, sir."

~~~

A few doors down, Peter was on the phone with Bishop Woodbury, who seemed determined to keep Peter in suspense regarding the future of St. James. Rather than share the details of his discussion, now apparently a few hours old, with the archbishop, the bishop was rambling on about a recent fishing trip with his young nephew.

"The boy's twelve years old and had never seen a fishing pole before," Bishop Woodbury said. "Can you imagine?"

"That's unusual," Peter said, trying his best to sound interested.

"He's a city boy. Born and raised in Boston. But even so. I can't believe his father has never taken him fishing."

"Perhaps he's too busy."

"Oh, I'm sure he is. He's an attorney at a big law firm in downtown Boston. Thing is, I wouldn't be surprised if *he's* never been fishing. Not exactly an outdoorsman."

Peter got the distinct feeling Bishop Woodbury didn't like his brother-in-law. "Well, we all have our predilections. Some people thrive in the hustle and bustle of a big city. I'm sure his father has taught him a thing or two that only someone versed in law could know."

"Yes, I suppose you're right."

Peter didn't want to continue exploring the subject, which meant drifting further afield of St. James's future, but common courtesy dictated that he see it through to a satisfying conclusion. "So how was the trip? Did you catch anything?"

"We just went pond fishing. Nothing fancy. I figured he'd enjoy dropping some bait in the water and see what comes up. But that boy!" Bishop Woodbury's voice, normally so musical, cracked as he burst into wheezy laughter. "When he found out he had to put a worm on a hook, he became as stubborn as an old mule." The bishop cackled again. "We ended up 'liberating' the worms and taking a stroll around the pond instead."

Peter chuckled. "So, he's a sensitive soul."

"He sure is." The bishop sighed loud enough for Peter to hear it on his end of the line. "Ah, but I suppose it's all for the best. At least he has the courage of his convictions. He wasn't going to let me boss him around, that's for sure."

Peter thought of Bobby and their argument before the young man signed up for the US Army's Officer Candidate School. "That quality will take him far in this world."

"Agreed. Well, enough with my stories. Let's get down to business. The archbishop has agreed to give you a reprieve. St. James will remain open if—and it's a big if—you can find a way to make up the shortfall and keep it funded."

Peter was thrilled at the news, but something in the bishop's voice curbed his excitement. Perhaps he was reading too much into the man's tone, but Bishop Woodbury sounded skeptical that St. James could be saved. Did he even *want* it to be saved? Peter wasn't so sure. But he knew it was wise to simply thank him for his efforts.

"Thank you, Bishop Woodbury. I appreciate your help."

"Don't thank me yet. You still need to find a way to raise a half million dollars. If we reach the end of June and you still haven't found funding, the merger will go forward over the summer."

"I understand." Peter couldn't think that far ahead. All he knew was that, just as he'd hoped, the bishop had bought him some time. Somehow, someway they'd find a way to raise the necessary funds. "Please thank the archbishop for me."

"I will," the bishop said. "But, Father, I put my neck out for you. Don't make a fool out of me."

Chapter 6

Peter watched from the bleachers that afternoon as Coach Kowalski ran the football team through a series of drills on the second day of school. Another New England fall was just around the corner, and the deep blue sky seemed to beckon everyone to the outdoors. The air was still warm, but the days were growing shorter, sunlight more precious. Every glorious September day felt like a gift to Peter, who was determined to spend as much time as he could outdoors.

As far as Peter could tell, Coach Kowalski was a details-oriented coach. While Peter looked on from the bleachers, the gruff, middle-aged coach instructed his players on the intricacies of smash-mouth football. He seemed keenly aware that his rugged, husky players had been little boys just a few years ago, but any patience he exhibited was offset by his insistence on proper technique—and his blue-collar vernacular.

"Execute, dadgummit!" he hollered after an offensive lineman missed a block.

When the player made the same mistake again, Ed shoved him aside and proceeded to show him how to come off his stance and gain leverage on the opposing player. The unsuspecting kid playing on the defensive side of the ball ended up on his backside, earning a smattering of laughs from his teammates.

Peter winced. Football definitely wasn't for the meek.

Coach Kowalski gathered the team at the fifty-yard line. "Listen up!" he barked as the players closed ranks around him. "You boys better not bore easily, because we're gonna practice the same thing

32

every day until you get it right. And then we're going to practice it some more. Got that? This ain't rocket science. It's football. You execute, you win. You gotta learn these techniques inside and out, because when the whistle blows and bodies start flying, you ain't gonna have time to think, understand? You just *do*. But that's the beauty of executing properly. Once the repetition sinks in, you can let your training take over. Won't matter if it's the first quarter or the fourth, if we're up by three or down by thirty. Proper technique never changes. And let me tell you another thing: you learn how to execute on the field, and that discipline will serve you off the field. In class. On the job. You're not just learning how to play football, fellas. You're learning how to succeed in life."

A good lesson, Peter thought. He was so engrossed in Coach Kowalski's words that he didn't notice Maria Donatello's presence until he was engulfed by her heady perfume. A second later, she was clambering up the noisy bleachers toward him.

He shielded his eyes from the sun as he smiled at her. "Good afternoon, Maria. I didn't know you were a football fan."

Maria, dressed in a long skirt and long-sleeved blouse, looked out of place outside, if only because Peter was used to seeing her in the sterile fluorescent lighting of the office.

She lowered herself to the aluminum bleachers and stared out at the field. "Can't say that I am, although I've been to my share of games. My husband is a big Patriots fan."

Peter nodded. "I prefer the college game, although, honestly, I don't know much about either."

"So, what brings you out here?" Maria asked.

Peter motioned to a narrow greenbelt behind the field. Tall sugar maples flickered in the afternoon sun, their leaves dancing in the breeze. "Just soaking it all in before the weather changes. I figure we'll be huddled beneath blankets and drinking hot cider before too long."

He let go a contented sigh. "Mostly I just come out here to think."

Maria nodded understandingly. "Have you thought much more about the school's financial situation?"

Peter perked up at the question. "I have. In fact, I've been talking with Bishop Woodbury. I spoke with him yesterday and I just got off the phone with him an hour ago. We've been granted a reprieve."

"A reprieve?"

"Well, sort of. He had to clear it with the archbishop this morning, but Bishop Woodbury says the diocese will put the plans to close St. James on hold for now. If we can find a way to cover the shortfall by June, St. James will remain open."

"Great," Maria said, nodding. "That's a good first step. Now all we have to do is find half a million dollars by then."

"Right. I'll admit I'm still at a loss. I don't know where to start."

Maria had a ready-made response. "The main thing is that we *start.*"

That was just like Maria, Peter thought. He'd heard her lecture others in the office on the difficulty of thinking clearly. Her contention—that too many people were lazy and didn't want to think hard—rubbed some the wrong way, but Peter was sympathetic to the notion. People had to be held accountable not just for their actions but for their thought processes, especially since the latter often informed the former. If people were laboring under false assumptions, there was no telling what they might do.

Of course, Maria's insistence on logic and disciplined thinking sometimes resulted in newer staff members bringing their most difficult-to-solve problems directly to her, rather than wrestling with them individually. But Maria typically responded by turning them around and sending them back the way they'd come. The message was clear: until they'd explored potential solutions on their own—and thus had endured the discomfort associated with problem-solving—they had

34

no business approaching her. Peter appreciated the result, which was an office full of competent, confident workers.

Now Maria was directing her exacting expectations at him. He didn't mind the challenge, but he'd have been lying had he said he wasn't a little intimidated by it.

"It seems clear that we'll have to search for outside help," he said.

"You sound reluctant. Do you think there's a problem with that?"

"Not necessarily." He leaned forward slightly and propped his chin on his fists. "We belong to a community. Far from being independent, we're connected with and beholden to that community." He drew in a breath and released it in a sigh. "Still . . ."

"Still? As I said, you seem reluctant to ask for outside help. Is it pride, Father?"

Peter frowned. "I hope not. I'd prefer to think of it as a preference for self-reliance."

"Nothing wrong with that," Maria said. "But self-reliance might not be enough in this case. I think we should be open to all of our options."

"So you think we should go in search of a few wealthy benefactors?"

"If that's what it takes."

Peter thought some more. Plenty of affluent parishioners had contributed to the school during his time at St. James. Their largesse often meant the difference between funding a new project or putting it off a year. But to ask for help merely to keep the doors open—the idea was mortifying.

As Peter culled his memory, he could think of only one potential donor who might have the capital *and* the generosity to fund such an effort. "What about Mr. Federici?" he asked. "You know him and his wife, if I'm not mistaken."

"I do." Maria nodded and fell silent, her face thoughtful.

Although Peter had met him only casually a couple of times and didn't really know the man, Antonio Federici was known as a legendary philanthropist. Indeed, with the York family out of the picture, it was difficult to imagine anyone else in the diocese with Federici's financial clout. His wife, Kathleen, regularly volunteered at the parish elementary school. As Peter understood it, they weren't able to have children, and that deprivation served as the motivation for the couple's philanthropic work.

"They adore St. James," Maria said. "And Mr. Federici has contributed greatly in the past. But I don't think this is a good time to ask him for a large donation."

Peter drew his head back in confusion. "What do you mean?"

"They left for Italy last week," Maria said. "Mr. Federici is attending to his recently departed mother's estate. From the sounds of it, she owned many properties and investments, but never bothered to finish her will. There may be some conflict among siblings about how to handle the estate. I doubt Mr. and Mrs. Federici will be back anytime soon."

"Getting something like that sorted out could take weeks," Peter muttered.

"Or months," Maria said. "Even if they were to return soon, approaching them about our problem would be a delicate matter."

Peter nodded. So sorry for your loss, Mr. Federici, he could imagine saying. Now, can we have half a million dollars?

Down on the field, the offense had just botched a routine play, prompting Coach Kowalski to throw up his hands in disgust. Once again, he gathered the team around him and launched another speech. Peter had found the last one inspirational, but this one quickly devolved into a blue-streaked harangue. The more the coach spoke, the angrier

36

he became. Even from the bleachers, Peter could see his face turning beet red under the afternoon sun.

Finally, the rant reached a deafening crescendo. "I teach yous guys everything I know," Coach Kowalski fumed, "and yous still don't know nothin'!"

Peter found himself smiling. He traded glances with Maria, who, like him, was suppressing a laugh, and then returned his attention to the field. The players, too, were doing their best to maintain their composure, but soon a wave of mirth rose through the ranks, and before Coach Kowalski could protest, the players were doubled over in laughter.

I'll find a way to save this school, Peter promised himself. I just need to have faith.

Chapter 7

Less than an hour later, Peter and his old friend Jonathan Bloom were trundling down a largely abandoned street in Lawrence's industrial sector. The engine in Peter's Mercury Comet purred as they rolled past dilapidated brick buildings that long ago had constituted a textile factory. As he eyed broken windows and graffiti-covered walls, Peter felt a sense of loss. A place that had once hummed with activity now lay silent. Weeds grew between cracks in the sidewalks. Wrecked machinery rusted in forgotten loading docks.

Jonathan pointed at one of the buildings, a small red-brick edifice no less shabby than the rest, and Peter parked next to a large motorcycle with a big engine, lots of chrome, and high handlebars. It was the only vehicle in the small lot.

They entered the building through a side door and found themselves in a musty, cavernous space. Peter's nephew Bobby, taking advantage of the dirt-cheap rent, had chosen this location for his burgeoning cycle shop. An accomplished airbrush artist, Bobby painted his customers' gas tanks, fenders, and helmets. His work was stark and often portrayed violent scenes of mythical combat juxtaposed against modern warfare. Red and white tracers. Angels and demons. Lifeless bodies with souls guided by beautiful angels toward heaven. Every piece explored light and darkness, good and evil. The souls of the slain were depicted as being drawn toward a bright, enticing light.

Jonathan side-stepped a pile of broken glass on the cement floor, his lanky frame bisecting the natural light pouring in through a row of broken windows, and threw Peter a knowing look. They followed the sound of an air compressor down a long corridor that eventually opened into another cavernous room, where they found Bobby seated on a wooden crate with his bare back to them.

The steady chugging of the air compressor and the hiss of the airbrush masked their approach. Bobby, engrossed in his work, remained bent over his creation as they neared him. Dirty and shirtless, he labored beneath the names of eight men, all of them memorialized in tattoos on his back—four on the left shoulder blade and four on the right. Peter recognized one of the names: Lamar Jackson, Bobby's beloved NCO and right-hand man as they navigated the hostile jungles of Vietnam.

Unable to stand the sight any longer, Peter lifted his voice above the cacophony of his nephew's work. "Bobby!"

It took several more tries before Bobby finally turned and acknowledged them with a faint smile. His dark hair had grown several inches since Peter had last seen him, and his once-boyish face now sported bushy sideburns and a thick mustache. He offered a nod and a quiet hello. "Uncle Peter. Jonathan. I didn't hear you come in."

"Good to see you, Bobby," Peter replied.

Jonathan followed with, "Hi, Bobby."

Bobby gently set down his airbrush and stood to shake their hands. His grip was strong, and his hand covered in grit. As he walked over to shut off the air compressor, he left a trail of musky body odor.

"What brings you by?" Bobby asked.

Peter had long since mastered the art of small talk. In his line of work, he regularly engaged parishioners on everything from the weather to sports and local news. Recipes, gardening tips, the finer points of auto maintenance or macramé—all were fair game when speaking to his flock. But as he and Jonathan engaged Bobby in the harmless banter, he longed to ask about Bobby's time in Vietnam.

Peter and Bobby had been close since Bobby's youth, when the two had spent summers boating and fishing off Cape Cod. A relationship of mutual admiration had been forged while observing passing humpback whales and hiking and camping in the mountains of New Hampshire every autumn. Along with attending Bobby's high school cross-country and track meets, Peter had watched the young man develop into a talented tenor. Admittedly, Peter had needed Jonathan's help in recognizing Bobby's extraordinary talent. It was Jonathan who had called Bobby's vocal abilities unsurpassed. Jonathan had taken Bobby under his wing and become like a second father to the boy.

But the war had damaged those relationships. Bobby, by then majoring in international studies and minoring in music at Boston College, had become fixated on the fighting in Southeast Asia. Upon graduation—and against Peter's vehement protests—he'd signed up for OCS and ranger training, and was assigned to the 1st Cavalry Division at Fort Hood, Texas, as a 2nd lieutenant. Peter, no stranger to war, had eventually made peace with his nephew's decision.

Now, as Bobby fielded questions, head down, voice subdued, Peter ached for the young man. When he'd left for Vietnam, Bobby had been a firm believer in the domino theory, and the necessity of fighting communism in Asia before it could spread elsewhere. But he'd returned home a shell of his former self, an old man inside a young man's body, a broken soldier haunted by what he'd witnessed. Peter suspected Bobby's undoing had occurred when his platoon walked into an NVA ambush On October 7, 1967. But Bobby had yet to share the details of the encounter.

"So what's on your mind, Uncle Peter?" Bobby finally asked as he reached for a rag to dab at the sweat on his forehead. "I know you didn't come here to talk about the weather."

"Right," Peter said with an uncomfortable laugh. "Jonathan here has stumbled upon a unique opportunity for you. I'll let him explain."

Jonathan's eyes twinkled as he spelled out the details. "The Boston Symphony Orchestra is looking for an emerging young tenor soloist to perform Handel's *Messiah* this Christmas season. My colleague of many years, Greg Bergmann, would like to meet with you. He's interested in having you audition."

Peter studied Bobby's face. Did the news make him happy? Nervous? Angry?

Bobby stared at the dusty cement floor. "I remember him. The great maestro Greg Bergmann." His response teetered on the edge of disdain. "What made him think of me? He hasn't heard me sing in a long time."

"A little birdie reminded him of how talented you are," Jonathan said with a wink. "I told him about your educational and military experience, and said you'd be a perfect fit. And he agreed to audition you." When Bobby didn't immediately respond, Jonathan added, "Look, Bobby, I think this could be a wonderful opportunity for you."

Peter felt his muscles tighten as the cavernous room fell silent. He cherished Jonathan's enthusiasm, but that kind of energy aimed at someone as troubled as Bobby could backfire. The last thing they needed to do was make the young man feel pressured.

But much to Peter's relief, Bobby looked up from the floor and made eye contact first with Jonathan and then Peter. In his gaze, Peter caught a fleeting glimpse of the young nephew he remembered, the one who had never gone to Vietnam—innocent, warmhearted, eager to experience the world.

"Sure," Bobby said, his face brightening ever so slightly. "Why not?"

Chapter 8

Sandra Alvarez entered the faculty lounge Wednesday at the noon hour and wrinkled her nose at the cloud of cigarette smoke hovering above the couches and chairs. The foam ceiling tiles, a dingy shade of yellow, had no doubt been white once upon a time.

After pouring herself a cup of coffee at the small counter in the attached kitchenette, she found a seat at one of the tables in the dining area and began to unwrap a pastrami sandwich she'd packed in her briefcase.

She was soon joined by Laurel Nord, the art teacher, and Mathilde Weaver, the music instructor. Both looked glum.

"Something bad happen?" Sandra asked.

Laurel, who appeared to be in her early forties, was a natural beauty with a subtle elegance. She wore her straight blond hair pulled back in a French braid. "We just learned that Mrs. O'Donnell has passed away."

"Mrs. O'Donnell?" Sandra asked. Then she made the connection. "Jenny O'Donnell's mother?"

Laurel nodded. "Cancer."

Sandra thought of Jenny, the shy girl in her first-period class, and felt her heart sink. The last thing such a fragile flower needed was to lose her mother. "That's terrible news!"

Mathilde slumped in her chair across from Sandra and rubbed her slender hands in worry. She had a delicate, diminutive frame, which she easily squeezed into a VW Beetle—Sandra had seen her pull into the teachers' parking lot on the first day of school. "It explains why she's been so quiet this first week back."

"So she's not always so . . . awkward?" Sandra asked.

Mathilde twisted her lips into an anxious frown. "She's always been introverted. But not so sad."

"She's one of my best students," Laurel said. "I've had her two years running. Her watercolors and sketches are always so full of life. She broke into tears after class yesterday. She told me her mother was dying. She could hardly speak she was sobbing so hard. All I could do was rock her in my arms." She shook her head as she revisited the memory. "High school can be such a difficult time for our young charges. The transition from childhood to adulthood comes with so many emotional aches and pains. To add something like the loss of a parent—and to cancer, no less—it's just not fair."

"That poor young woman," Sandra said. "What can we do for her?"

Laurel absentmindedly fussed with her blond braid, which was long enough to hang loosely over the front of her plum-colored blouse. "Her mother's funeral is this Friday. We could attend together."

"Let's," Sandra replied. "And perhaps we could do something extra, just to let her know we're thinking of her."

"Something extra?" Mathilde asked.

"A gift, perhaps," Laurel suggested.

Sandra nodded. "Yes, a gift. When I see Jenny, I see more than an awkward girl. I see the beautiful woman forming within her. She's like a butterfly waiting to burst from its chrysalis. We should get her something to signify her metamorphosis, something to *empower* her."

"And we'll write her a note," Mathilde added, jutting her chin forward with conviction. "She needs to know that her mother is still with her. You compared Jenny to a butterfly. We can use that metaphor to describe her mother's soul."

"Which is on its way to heaven," Laurel said.

43

"Wonderful!" Sandra replied.

~~~

That evening, Sandra stepped inside an old jewelry shop on Essex Street in downtown Lawrence. The musky scent of the Merrimack River and its North Canal, just two blocks away, followed her inside.

The shop owner, a graying gentleman with a pocket watch dangling from his vest, looked on as she stared at several necklaces beneath the glass. "Anything in particular you're looking for?"

She looked up from the glass and tried not to notice the gap between his front teeth as he smiled. "I'll know it when I see it."

Collar necklaces, matinee necklaces, chokers—there were many designs to choose from. Some of the necklaces were ostentatious. Others looked like romantic gifts. Diamonds and sapphires twinkled under the lighted glass. Pearls gave off an unmistakable smooth sheen. But nothing felt quite right.

Then she saw it: a silver butterfly necklace. Each wing, bisected in two, contained a delicate spiraling pattern. The body looked solid and substantial, but not heavy. The antennae were fanciful without looking cartoonish. And the chain connected to the top outer tip of each wing. Simple. Elegant. It was perfect.

"This one." As she pointed at it, she accidentally smudged the glass. She drew back in embarrassment. "I'm sorry."

The owner chuckled gently. "Don't worry about it, miss. It happens all the time." He unlocked the glass counter, opened it from the rear, and carefully retrieved the necklace from its display case. "Would you like the box that comes with it?"

"Yes, please," Sandra said.

"Is this a gift?" the man asked as he placed the box in a small bag.

Sandra nodded. "It's for a very special young lady."

44

Chapter 9

"Saints of God, come to her aid." As he spoke, Peter felt his voice crack for the first time since beginning the funeral mass an hour earlier. It had been a long day—but was far from over. "Hasten to meet her, angels of the Lord."

The assembly, which had filled St. James's little chapel to capacity, replied in unison: "Receive her soul and present her to God most high."

Peter waited a moment, careful not to rush the liturgy. "May Christ, who called you, Evelyn O'Donnell, take you to himself. May angels lead you to the bosom of Abraham."

"Receive her soul and present her to God most high," came the response from the assembly.

Again, Peter allowed for the briefest of pauses, just enough to let the words bloom and the rhythm breathe. "Eternal rest, grant unto her O Lord, and let perpetual light shine upon her."

"Receive her soul and present her to God most high." Those on hand bowed their heads.

Peter read the final prayer, and with each word, searched for solace, for some kind of comfort he could impart to those gathered before him. Though custom dictated that they hold the funeral mass at the parish church across town, Jenny O'Donnell's father had insisted they host the ceremony here, at the school chapel, where Mrs. Donnell had prayed as a student more than two decades earlier. Peter had been happy to oblige the request, for it served as yet another reminder that St. James's past was intimately connected to its present. Generations had been educated at the institution, often by the same instructors. The spirit of St. James emanated outward from this small chapel, whose dust floated in the rays of light pouring through the narrow, stained glass windows.

"In peace let us take our sister Evelyn to her final rest," the assembly said as soon as Peter finished the prayer.

The pipe organ conveyed a somber postlude, and Peter signaled to the male ushers to roll the casket down the center aisle. At the front of the procession, Peter kept his gaze straight ahead, his chin elevated ever so slightly. As he swung the incense, the smoke from frankincense and myrrh engulfed him briefly, then trailed behind. When one of the greeters at the back opened the double doors to the outside, he felt a late-afternoon breeze on his face, a welcome respite from the warm and cozy confines of the packed chapel.

With Jenny, her father, and the extended O'Donnell family gathered around him near the parked hearse, Peter read from Revelation 21:4. "And God will wipe away every tear from their eyes. And death shall be no more. And neither mourning, nor crying aloud, nor grief shall be anymore. For the first things have passed away." He turned to Mr. O'Donnell, a tall man with slumped shoulders and a full head of red hair, and handed him the crucifix that had been atop Mrs. O'Donnell's coffin. "Peace be with you and your family."

"Thank you, Father," Mr. O'Donnell said hoarsely.

Peter turned to Jenny and wrapped an arm around her shoulder. "Your mother loved you dearly. Never forget that." He glanced upward. "She's with you even now. She'll always watch over you."

Wearing a black dress with a lacy collar and cuffs, Jenny nodded but remained stone-faced. She looked too numb to digest the ongoing rituals meant to ease her family's pain. Such ancient rites, Peter knew, often were aimed more at the survivors than the deceased, but in Jenny's case, he wondered if anything could soften the blow of losing her mother at such a young and vulnerable age.

The steps outside the church began to overflow with people, and as if on cue, Laurel Nord, Mathilde Weaver, and Sandra Alvarez approached Peter and the family. Sandra looked breathtaking in a black dress that fell well below her knees. She wore her luxurious dark hair down—it was the first time Peter had ever seen it unconfined—and an elegant pair of black pumps. A pearl necklace contrasted sharply against the black fabric of her dress.

At the sight of them, Jenny dropped her head and turned slightly, her lower lip trembling. Her teachers walked straight to her and embraced her in a group hug. When they pulled away, Sandra retrieved a small box from her dainty purse and handed it to Jenny.

Jenny wiped away a tear. "What's this?"

"Just something to let you know we're here for you, honey," Laurel said.

"Open it," Mathilde added.

As Jenny pried open the small box, Peter took a step closer and glanced over Mathilde's shoulder. The butterfly necklace gleamed on a plush bed of silk.

Jenny's eyes widened.

"Put it on," Sandra said with a smile.

While Laurel gently guided Jenny's auburn hair away from her neck and shoulders, Jenny lowered her head so that Sandra could connect the clasp behind her neck.

Jenny stared at the butterfly resting on her breastbone and then glanced up at her teachers. "It's beautiful."

Now all four were crying, and as Laurel, Mathilde, and Sandra embraced Jenny in another all-consuming hug, Peter stepped back and turned toward Jenny's father, who was smiling sadly.

Chapter 10

Two hours later, following a short graveside service for Mrs. O'Donnell, Peter rushed through the main entrance of the school auditorium. He spotted Bobby sitting on the edge of the stage in the empty, dimly lit space. Peter offered a wave and then hurried down the center aisle, his footfalls absorbed by the carpet and the acoustic panels.

Just before Peter reached Bobby, someone clicked on the overhead lights. Peter turned to see Jonathan standing beside the bank of light switches.

A moment later, the three men were talking at the front of the auditorium. Bobby had slid off his perch to greet them, and Peter was relieved to see he was clean-shaven, with the exception of his sideburns and handlebar mustache. He wore jeans and a clean work shirt, and looked ready for his audition for Greg Bergmann.

Peter glanced at his watch. It was ten minutes before six. "Ah, good. We can take a moment to catch up before Mr. Bergmann arrives."

Bobby tossed his head to the side to maneuver his hair out of his eyes. "You look nervous, Uncle Peter."

"Me?" Peter suddenly felt self-conscious. "Not at all. I've just had a busy day is all."

"Oh yeah? What did you do today?"

"We buried the mother of one of our students."

Bobby frowned. "Sorry to hear that."

"Evelyn O'Donnell?" Jonathan asked. "An awful shame. She was too young."

"Indeed," Peter said.

"You're never too young to die." Bobby's face darkened, but just like that, he shook it off and asked Jonathan if he'd gone fishing over the summer.

Soon the men were talking about the Cape and comparing fishing from the shore with chartering a boat, which method had the most advantages, and when was the best time to employ each. They talked about cod, haddock, and winter flounder, and all Peter could think about was how right Bobby was: he *was* nervous. It seemed absurd. *He* wasn't auditioning for Handel's classic piece. *Bobby* was. And Bobby, despite—or perhaps because of everything he'd been through in Vietnam—looked as placid as the Cape on a calm summer day. Maybe he needed this audition as much as Peter and Jonathan needed him to need it. Maybe it could serve as an escape from his personal torment, a turning point of sorts.

Since his sister's visit, Peter had spoken to Susan over the phone and learned more about Bobby's disenchantment and reclusiveness since returning from the war. Despite overtures from family, friends, and even fellow veterans, Bobby kept to himself, spending most of his time at his cycle shop. Susan had reiterated she was fairly certain Bobby wasn't drinking or doing drugs, which was a good sign, but Peter knew she fretted about her son daily. After World War II, Peter had come home from the Pacific to a hero's welcome. Nothing could soften what he'd experienced on Saipan, but at least he felt supported and appreciated. Now, though, times had changed. Young men were burning their draft cards, students were protesting the war, and the nightly news brought the fighting into America's living rooms. Despite assurances from politicians and military officials, the war looked unwinnable, especially since the previous year's Tet Offensive, and maybe even immoral.

Greg Bergmann strolled in at ten after six wearing dark slacks and a white dress shirt, sans tie. As he ambled down the center aisle, he looked just as Peter had remembered him—confident, exuberant, and larger than life. He wore his jet-black hair slicked back and sported a cleanly shaven face that complemented his chiseled jawline.

He took Bobby's hand and shook it vigorously. "Bobby Jones! Great to see you! Thank you for taking the time to meet me. I appreciate your willingness to audition for this part."

Bobby returned the handshake and looked the conductor straight in the eye. "Mr. Bergmann, it's a pleasure."

Peter tingled with pride. Yes, Bobby had become a bit of a recluse, but he was still handsome, still charismatic, still the same young man with so much potential. Standing next to someone like Mr. Bergmann, who possessed such gravitas, Bobby could hold his own. He, too, seemed built for the spotlight.

Mr. Bergmann turned to Jonathan. "I'd say we owe this audition to you, Jonathan. Thanks again for putting me in touch with this young man." Now Greg was smiling at Peter. "And thank you, Father, for providing us with a venue."

"It was the least I could do," Peter said, marveling at the elegant man's graciousness.

Mr. Bergmann, not wasting any time, effortlessly hoisted himself onto the stage and removed the dust cover from the grand piano at stage left. A moment later, he was seated on the bench and playing snippets of beautiful arias that featured a tenor voice.

Peter traded glances with Jonathan, and they retreated to a pair of seats about halfway up the aisle. Best not to distract Bobby or Mr. Bergmann with their presence, Peter thought.

Bobby was in good voice from the beginning, and Peter knew he'd taken the time to complete a proper warm-up beforehand. His beautiful tenor voice soon was floating above the piano like a bird over a rolling landscape. As the audition proceeded, Peter heard one of the doors open behind him, and he turned to see Sandra Alvarez and

Mathilde Weaver peeking through the half-open door, their heads almost bumping. They quietly entered the auditorium and sat in the back row.

Mr. Bergmann seemed captivated by Bobby's voice, and Peter swelled with pride. Bobby exuded confidence, and had all the skills to back it up: power, range, articulation, and an uncanny understanding of libretto that he could accurately convey to the audience—even this tiny one.

When the audition was finished, Mr. Bergmann was effusive. "The part is yours, Bobby, if you want it."

Peter couldn't contain his joy and let out a hoot. He turned back to gauge Sandra's and Mathilde's reactions but saw that they'd already left. No matter, Peter thought. They'd soon hear the news of his nephew's small victory.

Peter was only a step behind Jonathan as they rose from their seats and approached the stage to congratulate Bobby and thank Mr. Bergmann.

Bobby wore a stoic expression, but he had to be doing cartwheels inside, Peter thought.

"Thank you, Mr. Bergmann. Mr. Bloom. Uncle Peter. I appreciate the opportunity." Bobby wrote down his address and phone number and handed it to Mr. Bergmann. A contract, no doubt, would be in the mail shortly. Then he excused himself and exited the auditorium. As he left, Peter thought he detected something resembling a skip in his step.

After the door swung closed, Mr. Bergmann turned to Peter and Jonathan, and his smile faded. "The young man has a stunning instrument—I have no doubt of that. But I'll be frank: given everything you've said, Jonathan, I have some concerns that he might not show up to rehearsals and the performance."

Jonathan seemed to take Mr. Bergmann's worries in stride. He stepped closer, his lanky frame stooped slightly. "I can assure you Bobby will attend every rehearsal, and will be there when it counts. Just to be safe, I can accompany him to rehearsals."

Mr. Bergmann stroked his chin. "And what about the mustache and sideburns? Some in the audience might find that kind of look disrespectful."

Jonathan offered a reassuring nod. "As you saw for yourself, Bobby Jones is a handsome young man. I'll make sure he's acceptably coiffed and dressed. He'll fit right in with the esteemed Boston Symphony Orchestra."

Mr. Bergmann nodded and, apparently satisfied, started for the exit, having already replaced the dust cover on the grand piano and gathered his music. Jonathan Bloom's word, after all, was as good as gold. Everyone in the community trusted him—one of the many reasons Peter so admired his longtime friend.

As the conductor reached for the door handle, he stopped and turned, revealing a sly grin. "One more favor."

"Sure," Jonathan said. "You name it."

"Make sure he showers."

Peter smiled at the unexpectedly frank comment, and could see that Jonathan was amused as well. Perhaps it was the timing of Mr. Bergmann's remark. Or the flat delivery. Whatever the case, the humorous dig put Peter further at ease, for it seemed to have connected the three of them on a personal, almost boyish level. Bobby's future, meanwhile, looked bright.

Chapter 11

Peter didn't mind waiting for a haircut. Part of the appeal of going to Lee's Barbershop on a busy Saturday morning was absorbing the ongoing spectacle. Four barbers, each in his own embroidered black smock and stationed at his own booth, made quick work of the customers seated in the swiveling chrome-and-red-vinyl chairs while the rest of the patrons waited patiently along the back wall. Mischievous young boys sneaked peeks at the backroom, where Playboy pinups hung from the walls. Clumps of freshly cut hair fell to the black-and-white tiled floor, only to be swept into the jaws of waiting dustpans. A symphony of snipping scissors and buzzing trimmers droned above the chatter. All this went on in relative obscurity, for the barbershop was tucked away on a quiet back street, cut off from the strip mall around the corner.

Peter stared at the *Life* magazine in his hands without registering its contents, a freshly lit cigarette dangling from his lips.

"What's eating at you?"

Peter looked up from his magazine and turned toward Jonathan, who was seated beside him and staring at him with a wrinkled brow. "What do you mean?"

Jonathan, also partaking in a ritual smoke, tapped his cigarette over an ashtray on the small table between them. "I thought you'd be elated this morning, what with Bobby's audition last night. But something's clearly on your mind. Come on. Out with it."

One of the benefits of having a lifelong friend, Peter mused, was also a disadvantage: he couldn't hide anything from Jonathan.

"If I tell you," Peter finally began, "I'll need your discretion. This isn't something I'm ready to broadcast. Not yet, anyway."

Jonathan threw him an indignant look. "Of course."

"Well, as I'm sure you're aware, Mr. Arthur York died recently."

Jonathan nodded. "So I hear. What a tragedy, to go so young."

"Yes, it is."

Jonathan's eyes were still on Peter's. "And?"

Peter drew a breath. "Well, the York family has been St. James's primary benefactor for decades. Mrs. York is in the process of selling the companies and won't have the means to continue the generous contributions. The diocese cannot make up the shortfall. If we don't find a way to pay our way, St. James will be merged with Notre Dame High across town."

"Merged? As in . . . closed?"

"I'm afraid so. Normally, we'd find some generous patron to come to our rescue, but we're talking about a lot of money. Half a million, in fact, and so much largesse is hard to come by these days. No such white knight exists, I'm afraid."

Jonathan took a drag from his cigarette, his still-youthful face furrowed in thought. "Might I offer a suggestion?"

"I'm all ears."

"Don't get stuck thinking conventionally. You've always been open to change—even today, with all the upheaval going on all around us. And St. James isn't stuck in the past. It can change too."

Peter drew back and smiled. "I like that, Jonathan. And you're absolutely right. Today more than ever, we need to be willing to adapt, to challenge the status quo. Our young people are leading the way."

Indeed, the war in Vietnam had ignited something in society, especially among the youth. Over the last few years, the word *friction* had increasingly found its way into Peter's utterances, but he knew that the abrasive contact between the past and the future, between old ways and ways yet to be conceived, would inevitably lead to change. It already had.

Cloistered away from the rest of the country, St. James often felt sheltered from the ongoing ruptures in the social fabric. Martin Luther King Junior's assassination, Woodstock, the lunar landing—all occurred well beyond the walls of St. James, but the reverberations had no doubt been felt by the staff and especially the student body. Peter liked to think that the traditions of St. James, most of them rooted in American culture and the Catholic faith, would steady the school during such turbulent times, for something about the energy at St. James seemed to transcend the times. Instead of becoming cynical or distrusting, those who walked the school's halls projected a can-do spirit of optimism, kindness, and tenacity. The school's long history, far from making it inflexible or rigid, gave it a kind of suppleness that buoyed Peter. Could he tap that energy and redirect it toward the school's survival?

Jonathan pointed with his eyes toward a boy who'd just sat down at the far booth. With tears in his eyes, he slumped into the barber's chair like a dental patient readying himself for a root canal, the red vinyl upholstery crumpling noisily with his every movement.

"Charles Major's boy," Jonathan said under his breath.

"Ah," Peter said with a knowing nod as he spotted Charles hovering nearby.

Like Peter, Charles Major had served in the Pacific theater during World War II. His short-sleeved polo shirt exposed just enough of his left bicep to highlight the USN eagle tattoo commemorating his service. Hardnosed, bright, and inquisitive, Charles was a European immigrant who had grown up during the Great Depression. His resume included a chemical engineering degree from Purdue and time as a naval officer. He was the consummate alpha male—disciplined, firm-jawed, and uncompromising.

Peter had met the man a few times, although they'd never spoken more than a couple of words to one another. Nevertheless, he felt a powerful bond with him, considering their shared sacrifice to the meat grinder of the South Pacific. Few men inspired in Peter a fiercer loyalty. In fact, only his maimed and fallen comrades engendered more.

At the moment, Charles was standing firm on the necessity of a haircut for his son, who appeared to be around twelve. "You'll do it, and I don't want to hear another word."

The boy sniffed back a tear, but the waterworks started all over again as soon as his first tuft of golden brown hair hit the tile. He'd let his hair grow all the way to his ears—an affront that few fathers, especially those of Charles Major's ilk, were willing to abide.

The barber, an older gentleman with more hair sprouting from his ears than his head, appeared sympathetic to the boy's plight but dutifully continued with the haircut.

Peter, too, felt bad for the teary boy, who looked miserable under the weight of his father's yoke. But he also understood Charles's obdurate stance. For the generation that had fought in the war, long hair symbolized an outright rejection of their valor and sacrifice. Understood as such, it couldn't be tolerated.

When the haircut was finished, the boy stood up from the chair upset and bewildered. But Peter, despite commiserating with the young lad, had to admit the barber had done the boy a favor. Perhaps close-cropped hair wasn't popular with the kids, but the boy looked a sight better now that his eyes weren't hiding behind a mop of unruly hair. Peter offered the boy an encouraging smile. The boy stuffed his hands into the front pockets of his blue jeans and followed his father to the cash register and then out the door without a word.

The barber turned to Peter. "You're up, Father."

Chapter 12

At the Monday morning faculty meeting, Peter assembled everyone in the lounge a half hour before school began. He knew he'd need more than a perfunctory meeting to deliver the bad news he'd been keeping to himself since the first day of school. He'd invited everyone on faculty, along with Maria Donatello, confident she'd keep him on task and tethered to the grim financial reality facing the school.

The lighting was dimmer than normal in the carpeted room, thanks to the overcast sky outside. No sunlight poured through the long bank of windows behind them. The familiar smoky haze gathered near the dingy white ceiling tiles.

Peter drew a breath and plunged ahead. "I know you're all pressed for time," he said. "I'll get straight to the point. Due to unexpected financial issues, St. James is in danger of being closed. Unless we can raise a huge sum of money by the end of this school year, the diocese will merge our student body with Notre Dame's across town. Most of us will likely be out of a job once the dust settles."

A collective gasp was followed by a question from the math teacher, Father Kovacs. "How *much* money?" he asked from the nearest couch.

Peter nodded to Maria, who was seated at a nearby table.

"Five hundred thousand dollars," she answered matter-of-factly.

Another gasp.

Peter, reticent to let the others ruminate over the problem, pushed the conversation toward more optimistic terrain. "I know this is a shock to all of you. It certainly was to me. But I'd like to use this time to focus on solutions. Until now, we've always been able to count on the financial support of certain well-to-do community members, but times are changing. Everyone has been affected by the recent downturn, including our wealthiest contributors. So we need to get creative. I'd like to open the floor to your ideas."

Coach Dean, seated beside Father Kovacs, shifted his portly frame. "We could get the booster club involved. Lord knows they could use something to do. Heck, I'd love to get 'em out of my hair. When they're not running the concessions stand at games, they're trying to run my team."

"All right," Peter said, resisting the urge to ask how, precisely, the booster club was trying to control the baseball team. "Any other suggestions?"

"Concessions . . ." Coach Kowalski rubbed his mostly bald head, which, from Peter's vantage, seemed to disappear straight into his barrel chest, with no neck between. "I've heard of football teams selling chocolate bars to earn money for equipment. I don't see why we couldn't do the same—with the money going toward the school's operating fund, of course."

"Excellent!" Peter chimed.

In fact, the idea amounted to a finger in the dyke that was the school's financial problems, but Peter found Coach Kowalski's optimism contagious. Getting the others involved, he suddenly realized, was a huge relief. Rather than concealing a problem from his staff, he was finally addressing it head-on, with the others at his side.

"What about a raffle?" asked Sandra Alvarez, seated toward the back of the room beside her sister. The two couldn't have formed a starker contrast: Sister Consuela Alvarez, dressed in her habit and exuding the solemn authority of the church, beside Sandra, who, despite wearing a conservative blouse and long skirt, radiated youthful beauty and could almost have passed for a student.

"We could host a fundraising dinner," Sister Consuela offered.

Now the ideas were flowing.

Maria raised her hand from her perch at the table that abutted the couches. She looked reluctant to speak but nevertheless duty-bound to contribute. "I should point out that the annual fundraising drive typically only raises a few thousand dollars. That kind of money won't even make a dent in the shortfall."

Peter saw the others' shoulders sag as the optimism faded. He couldn't let Maria's assessment, however grounded in reality, dampen the faculty's burgeoning enthusiasm.

"I think it's safe to say that no one solution will suffice," he said. "We're going to have to turn over every stone, and tap every source, if we want to save St. James." He directed his gaze toward the school's baseball coach. "Coach Dean, I like your idea of getting the booster club involved. Perhaps they could enlist volunteers to organize a bake sale and raffle. They could team with the PTA."

"What will they raffle?" Sister Consuela asked.

"Dinner and a movie with your sister," Coach Dean quipped.

The others groaned as Sandra's face flushed deep red.

Peter held up a hand, determined not to let Coach Dean's crass sense of humor derail their progress. He already had an idea, but had hoped not to share it until he'd gained approval from Jonathan. "A weekend at a beach house on the Cape."

Mathilde Weaver, seated beside Laurel Nord to Peter's right, spoke up for the first time. "That's a wonderful idea, Father."

Peter smiled nervously. He was confident Jonathan would be eager to help however he could, even if it meant offering a weekend stay at his family's vacation cottage as part of the raffle. But it was bad form to volunteer such a prize before confirming it with the owner.

"Ed," Peter said, addressing Coach Kowalski, "I also like your idea of selling chocolate bars. Do you think the football team will be amenable?"

Coach Kowalski shrugged. "Doesn't matter if they want to or not. They'll do it."

A smattering of laughter trickled across the room.

Peter turned toward Sandra in the back. "I can oversee the fundraiser dinner, Miss Alvarez, but I'll need your help."

"*Sandra*," she said, correcting him. "And I'd love to help however I can, Father."

"Splendid!" Peter said. "The price of admission will pay for the food and then some, but we can encourage attendees to donate more if they can afford it."

Maria raised her hand once again. Was it time for another splash of cold water?

Peter cringed. "Yes?"

"Maybe we can find a local company to make a matching donation," she offered. "And we'll want to make sure that all the bigwigs are there. Plus parents and alumni."

Peter could barely contain his enthusiasm. Even Maria seemed onboard. "Well done! Excellent ideas, one and all. We've got a lot of work to do, don't we?"

The others nodded.

"It will be a labor of love," Sandra said from her seat near the back windows.

Peter smiled. "It will indeed."

Chapter 13

Vice Principal JD Long hadn't spoken at the faculty meeting for the simple reason that he'd still been absorbing the news of the school's financial peril. But an hour later, as he left his office for another meeting, he acknowledged his pessimism about the proposed solutions.

The cloudy day had cast a gloom over the campus, a small collection of buildings clustered around a nicely landscaped courtyard. Most of the students were in class now, making JD's short walk to the athletic office a solitary one. He breathed in the mild air and sighed deeply. It wasn't his style to worry about what was beyond his control. In fact, he was more inclined to focus on the here and now—and the students.

He entered the lobby of the gymnasium and took an abrupt right-hand turn toward the athletic office, where Coach Dean was about to oversee a coaches' meeting, a weekly ritual that varied in attendance. JD spotted Coach Dean and the others through the large window beside the office door. They were seated around a circular table, sipping coffee and laughing about something. When JD ducked inside, lowering his head slightly to clear the lower-than-average door frame, they all looked up with smiles on their faces.

"What did I miss?" JD asked, closing the door behind him.

Coach Dean nodded to his assistant, Richie Sanders. Handsome and urbane, with a full head of blond hair, Coach Sanders was the consummate ladies' man. At just twenty-six years of age, he was at his physical peak, which, JD could tell, played on the insecurities of some of the older members of the staff.

"I was just telling them about the time Jan Slezak threw the discus into the woods," Sanders said.

JD laughed. He remembered the moment well. Slezak, a powerful, if a bit overweight, girl on the track and field team, had struggled to keep the discus inbounds at a home meet the previous spring. Each of her first two throws earned a dramatic "Foul!" from Coach Kowalski, who was officiating from a nearby folding chair. Her third throw ended up in the woods—one hundred and eighty degrees behind her. Kowalski had stood in frustration and cried, "Go find it, Slezak!" before walking away, shaking his head in disbelief.

"Not her best throw," JD said, still chuckling.

"What brings you to our humble office, Mr. Vice Principal?" Coach Dean asked. He was flanked by Sanders, who was still tittering from his story, and Coach Kowalski. On the other side of the table sat Sister Consuela, who oversaw the girls' athletics program and, like JD, occasionally sat in on the coaches' meetings.

JD smiled as he took a seat next to Sister Consuela. "I've been thinking about some of our—how should I put it?—less athletically gifted students."

Coach Dean leaned back from the table and let his hands rest on his ample belly, which was threatening to break free of the navy-blue sweatshirt stretched over it. A whistle dangled from the end of a string around his neck. "Don't see much of 'em around these parts, I'll admit. They seem to steer clear of team sports."

JD took a moment to formulate his thoughts. "I believe all students should be able to participate in some form of athletics or physical training. But because some aren't skilled at a particular sport, a divide develops between them and the more accomplished athletes. The non-athletes become isolated and frustrated. They don't feel they're of value and start to act out on their frustrations. They end up in my office. I'm tired of handing out detentions and suspensions. We need to get them involved in athletics somehow."

Coach Dean unwrapped a slender pink stick of Blammo and unceremoniously inserted the trendy new sugarless gum into his mouth. "Agreed. Not everybody can be a star pitcher. But athletes get all the recognition."

Sister Consuela frowned. "The *boy* athletes. They're popular with the girls. But the girl athletes don't earn the same level of recognition. But I see what you're saying, Mr. Vice Principal. These non-athletes—they become frustrated and end up wasting a lot of time on useless activities."

"That's right," JD said. Now they were getting somewhere. "Chronic frustration tends to drive a person away from proper time management. If you've already invested a lot of time into studies or sports and have failed, why would you invest *more* time into experiencing additional futility?"

"So let's alter the goal to include something that's achievable," Coach Dean said. "I've seen plenty of average high school students go on to become accomplished adults, although many remain frustrated and often become negative people. I'd say the difference is tenacity and work ethic."

Coach Kowalski rubbed his bald head. "I'd take someone with tenacity and work ethic over a talented player every time. Some of my more talented athletes have been told how gifted they are from childhood on. When real adversity strikes, they struggle with it."

JD, happy that everyone was contributing to the topic at hand, nevertheless felt like the conversation was moving in several different directions. It was time to focus the group. "We need to apply some analytics. Our overall objective is to reduce the frustration level of our average students and replace frustration with the kinds of things that lead to success—a good work ethic, proper motivation, and confidence. Do we agree?"

Everyone concurred.

"Allow me." Coach Dean stood, approached the blackboard behind him, and grabbed a piece of chalk. He then wrote the word *objectives* on the blackboard and jotted down a few notes. "Sometimes it helps to diagram the discussion."

It wasn't a diagram as much as a jumble of words, but as soon as everything was laid out on the blackboard, Sanders appeared to have an epiphany.

"How 'bout we start an off-season weight training and conditioning program that non-athletes can participate in?" the young assistant coach asked. "We can tailor the program to each individual. We'll typically see rapid results early, which will encourage the students, since they'll see the results of implementing a work ethic. The more they invest, the better the results. We could give 'em extra credit for participation."

Coach Dean, who was in the middle of blowing a pink bubble, popped it. "I think I see where you're going with this, Richie. During the off-season, the varsity athletes can serve as trainers for the non-athletes."

"Exactly," Sanders said.

"Richie, could you do the evaluations after receiving the non-athletes' physicals?"

"No problem, Coach. I can do the evaluations and set up a program for each non-athlete. The athletes will already have their conditioning assignments."

JD smiled at Sanders and then Coach Dean. "This sounds like a winner to me, gentlemen. But I'll need your athletes to encourage my students until they're comfortable. My guess is that some great relationships will develop, and everyone should benefit." He turned to Sister Consuela, who was bright-eyed and nodding. "What do you think, Sister?"

Sister Consuela folded her hands on the table. JD knew her to be as dedicated to the physical and intellectual development of her students as anyone. She always spoke plainly and without pretense—a trait that helped put her male colleagues at ease. "I think I'm glad you paid us a visit this morning, Mr. Vice Principal."

Chapter 14

Later that evening, Peter was walking through the school courtyard when his path intersected with Charles Major's. It was parent/teacher night, an annual gathering to connect students' parents with the school faculty. Charles was sharing a subdued laugh with another man Peter recognized as Wes Fredericks, a master plumber Peter had hired on more than one occasion for work at the school. Peter had learned from conversations over the years that Wes also was a battle-hardened veteran of the war in the Pacific, where he'd served in the Marines. He had done tours in Guadalcanal, Peleliu, and Okinawa, and had therefore seen some of the most savage fighting. His graying hair, trimmed short like Charles's, marked him as a Marine for life. But tonight, on a mild evening in mid-September, Wes appeared calm and content in the company of his comrade in arms. The fading sun cast shadows that obscured the lines on his face, and his gruff voice, the gravelly badge of a lifelong smoker, sounded almost soothing in the still air.

"Good evening, gentlemen," Peter said as he came to a stop a few feet from them.

"Hello, Father," Wes offered.

"Father," Charles said with a nod.

They continued on together and then stopped again a few feet down the path, this time in front of Hideki Fuchida, the school's forty-eight-year-old gardener. Mr. Fuchida was standing beside a graceful Japanese maple and appeared to be showing Mark Olivetti, a student, how to prune such a masterpiece. Peter greatly admired Mr. Fuchida, who wielded pruners like a painter played with a brush. He was a true landscape artist. More impressive still, he was a fine mentor to the students that the vice principal sent his way. Given a choice between sitting in a quiet room and helping Mr. Fuchida, students who earned detention often picked the latter. Mr. Fuchida, a true student of human nature, expertly guided his charges toward taking responsibility for whole swaths of the landscaped grounds. Few students failed to respond to his encouragement, and thus the school teemed with ornate paths, exquisitely shaped bushes and trees, and the occasional stone marker or garden ornament.

"Hideki Fuchida," Peter said, not bothering to hide the veneration in his voice, "I'd like to introduce you to Charles Major and Wes Fredericks, each the father of a student here."

Mr. Fuchida, whose slight frame and graying hair did nothing to diminish his energetic personality, bowed slightly to both men. "It's an honor," he said with no trace of an accent.

Peter turned to the other men and said in a respectful tone, "Mr. Fuchida is a Nisei."

Born in the US to Japanese immigrants, Mr. Fuchida had served alongside the other three men.

"Four Hundred and Forty-Second Infantry?" Charles inquired with an arched eyebrow.

Mr. Fuchida nodded. The 442nd Infantry had been comprised almost solely of second-generation Americans with Japanese roots, and had done most of its fighting in World War II's European theater.

"Impressive," Wes said as he shook Mr. Fuchida's hand.

"Just like your handiwork here," Charles added and motioned to the rich tableau of textures and colors around them. "I like how you've layered so many different kinds of plants. Nothing sticks out. Everything serves the whole."

Hardy azaleas, shapely English boxwood, and autumn-blooming chrysanthemums formed a bountiful understory beneath slender maples, redbuds, and Japanese snowbell trees.

Mr. Fuchida's face lit up. "You sound like someone familiar with landscaping technique."

"I am," Charles said. "But I'm an amateur by comparison. I just tend to a little rock garden at my home. I don't have much space to work with. The wife uses most of it for her vegetable garden."

"Have you ever given a thought to bonsai?" Mr. Fuchida asked.

"I haven't," Charles said. "But maybe someday."

Wes pointed to a small sprinkler head hiding at the foot of the lacy Japanese maple Mr. Fuchida had been pruning. "I've seen these all over campus. Are they all connected to the same system?"

Mr. Fuchida nodded proudly. "I even have them on a timer."

Wes's eyes widened. "Impressive!"

Charles elbowed him gently. "Figures the master plumber would be intrigued by the irrigation system."

The men chuckled, and as they continued to trade jokes, Peter noticed Mark, Mr. Fuchida's student protégé, standing awkwardly nearby.

Perhaps sensing the same thing, Mr. Fuchida invited the boy to join the conversation. "This is Mark Olivetti, one of my assistants. This section of the garden belongs to him."

Mark gave the men a bashful nod and took a hesitant step forward.

"Ah," Peter said, drawing the young man closer. "Then perhaps you can help me with something." He pointed to a hand-carved wood sign a few feet away that read *Debbie's Garden*. "Who's Debbie?"

The junior's olive-toned face reddened. "Debbie's my girl."

The comment drew smiles from the men.

"Tell them the story, Mark," Mr. Fuchida said. "Don't be shy."

Mark, a lean kid with long arms and oversized feet, leaned on his rake. "Well, I got in trouble for teasing Debbie Dante. She's only a sophomore. The thing is—I only did it because I was trying to get her attention."

"He got Vice Principal Long's attention instead," Mr. Fuchida quipped. "He ended up in detention. But it turned out for the best, didn't it, Mark?"

Mark offered a sheepish smile. "It sure did."

"Are you still in detention?" Charles asked.

"Nah," he said. "I just help Mr. Fuchida for fun now."

Charles gave the young man a knowing look. "Debbie must be a special young woman to have such a beautiful garden named in her honor. You've done a commendable job here."

Wes threw Mark a sideways glance. "You know, kid, if you ever want to play a good prank on someone, I can show you how to turn on the irrigation system remotely. All you have to do is step on one of these valves." He motioned to a galvanized valve near his feet. "You can soak unsuspecting students . . . and teachers."

Peter laughed and shook his head. "Don't give the boy any ideas!"

The conversation continued on in jovial fashion, but Peter couldn't help noticing that something was bothering Mark. Was he embarrassed about Debbie? Perhaps he was worried a fellow student would walk by and didn't want to be seen being so chummy with the adults.

Peter finally took the young man aside and, once out of earshot of the others, gently prodded him. "Is there something troubling you, son?"

Mark looked away, then finally met Peter's gaze. "It's something those two said."

"Mr. Major and Mr. Fredericks?"

Mark nodded. He was staring at his feet. "Just before you showed up, I overheard them talking after they saw Mr. Fuchida. Mr. Major said to Mr. Fredericks, 'Hey, Wes. Looks like we missed one.'"

Peter drew back. "Oh." He struggled for an appropriate response. "I can see why that would upset you."

"It's not just that," Mark said, shaking his head in confusion. "It's what Mr. Fuchida said. He heard them, too, but when I told him I was sorry about their mean comment, he said he took no offense. He said they're 'good men with deeply injured hearts,' or something like that. I don't understand. Shouldn't he be angry at them? Then to see all of you laughing together—I don't know what to think."

Peter wrapped an arm around Mark's shoulder. "I understand, son. But Mr. Fuchida's right. The war we fought in—it wounded all of us, even those of us who came home without a scratch. It's hard for Charles and Wes to look at a man of Japanese ancestry and not remember all the awful things they experienced during the war. But you saw what happened when they learned he was a fellow American. Their prejudices melted away. They realized they were talking to a brother."

Mark nodded, but still looked troubled. "Is it the same for you?"

Peter smiled grimly. He had to admit that he hardly understood the dynamic himself. Men like him, whose identities and outlooks had been forged in the crucible of war, had forever been scarred, but the very nightmares that haunted them were the glue that bonded them. There was a strange ecstasy in the pain. Only those who had been touched by it knew what it meant to carry such a burden.

70

Chapter 15

Danny Corvino stood erect in front of the class, dark slacks pressed clean, short blond hair meticulously shaped by more than a dab of Brylcreem. The smirk on his boyish face suggested he was toying with his audience. "Roses are red," he recited with melodramatic flair. "Violets are blue. Onions stink." He paused to deliver the punchline: "And so do you."

The performance earned a smattering of groans and boos, but Sandra Alvarez, watching from her desk a few feet away, smiled. She was willing to cut Danny a bit of slack. Like the other students, he'd warmed to her revamped lesson plan, which was luring them toward uncharted waters. Along with flexing their skills in creative writing, vocabulary, and grammar, they were learning to reveal themselves before their peers, trading their fear of vulnerability for a playful pursuit of exuberance and, better still, authenticity. Danny was entitled to a joke, Sandra mused, especially since she knew he was merely warming up his audience, softening them for what was to come.

With his joke out of the way, he proceeded to his real material. "If I told you what's in my heart, would you think less of me? If I told you what I dreamt last night, would you believe in serendipity? With each passing day, the sky turns a deeper hue. And every color makes me think of you."

This time, Danny's classmates responded with polite clapping. The girls, Sandra noticed, appeared especially receptive to the poem. Judging by their dreamy-eyed response, some even appeared ready to swoon.

"Very good," Sandra said as Danny returned to his seat in the front row. "But don't forget about the power of rhythm and word choice, especially where verbs are concerned. If we look at the last stanza, perhaps we could make a few subtle changes to affect the flow of the poem. 'With each passing day, the sky *reveals* a deeper hue. And every color *reminds me* of you.'"

Danny, having already established his receptiveness to constructive criticism and even the occasional playful jab, nodded thoughtfully.

Students continued with their readings, some stiff and wooden, others more relaxed and confident. Some asked Sandra to read their poems for them. She was surprised at the cleverness and humor in many of them. The atmosphere turned particularly electric when students were daring enough to deliver their poems with passion and poise. Such audacity seemed to inspire the same in others.

But some, Sandra noticed, appeared intimidated by their fellow students' success. Whether they lacked good material or the nerve to deliver it, they needed more encouragement to come forward. They needed *nurturing*.

She wrote the word on the blackboard and then turned to face the class. "Nurturing. Creativity can't exist without it. But what does it mean to nurture something or someone?"

The question was rhetorical, but to Sandra's surprise, Jenny O'Donnell, seated against the back wall as usual, raised her hand. She did so timidly, with her shoulders frozen in a shrug and her lips turned up in an uneasy smile, but it was clear she wanted to respond.

Sandra wasn't about to let the young woman second-guess her impulse. "Jenny?"

Jenny cleared her throat awkwardly. "When my mom got sick, I started taking care of her houseplants. It's a big collection: African violets, spider plants, Boston ferns, philodendrons. I kind of felt like it was an obligation at first, but then I started noticing how each plant was different, you know? Like how some were vines and others were little bushes or whatever. You can't treat them the same. Some like bright light, but others hate it. Same with water. Some like a lot. Some get all yellow if you water 'em too often. The soil makes a difference too. My mom put so much into them. I guess I wanted to keep them alive. Now that she's gone, my dad said we could get rid of 'em. But I told him I didn't want to. Taking care of them makes me feel calm and peaceful. It makes me happy."

Sandra realized that, like many of the students who had turned to listen, she was staring at Jenny with her lips parted in disbelief. There were so many layers to what Jenny had just said that it was difficult to know where to start. Finally Sandra managed a response, although it felt clumsy. "That's truly beautiful, Jenny. And creative! I know you're an artist, and your thinking is in line with your talent."

A hush fell over the classroom. Did the students understand the anguish Jenny was experiencing upon the loss of her mother? Could they, like Sandra, imagine Jenny at home tending to her plants, nurturing them as she worked through her grief?

Then it hit Sandra. "Nurturing doesn't just give the nurtured person joy," she told the class. "It gives the *nurturer* joy. We need the people or things we nurture as much as they need us." She thought a moment. "Tomorrow I'd like everyone to bring in a houseplant to nurture and care for. You can keep it on your desk. Or . . ." She glanced around her room. There were plenty of spaces to host plants. "Or on *my* desk."

The students laughed.

Sandra pointed to the old metal-framed windows that ran the length of the west side of the classroom. "Or on the windowsills. Find out what your plant needs. Bright sunlight? Dim light? Then put it where it's most likely to thrive."

~~~

It was almost five o'clock that evening when Peter pulled to a stop outside the small, red-brick building that housed Bobby's cycle shop. He turned the key counterclockwise, and the Comet's engine rattled once and then fell silent. The still air hugged Peter's ears as he walked from the car to the dilapidated building's entrance.

He'd traveled alone to see his nephew this time, but it was Jonathan who'd sparked the idea for the visit. More precisely, it was Jonathan, his wife Rachael, and Mathilde Weaver, St. James's music teacher, who'd hatched the idea. Jonathan and Rachael were friends with Mathilde and her husband and had learned during dinner one evening that Mathilde was struggling to develop the male singers at St. James. Perhaps, went the thinking, Bobby could help.

The chemical odor of spray paint hit Peter's nose as soon as he entered the building. He heard the familiar hum of the air compressor and followed it down a long corridor to the same dusty room where he and Jonathan had found Bobby during their last visit.

Once again, a bare-chested Bobby was hunched over one of his creations, meticulously applying an airbrush to it, but today Peter didn't frown at the sight of his nephew lost in his work. The image provoked in Peter a different emotion this time, something more akin to wonder. He admired his nephew's singlemindedness, his dedication to his craft. And he realized he was less worried about the state of Bobby's soul now that he knew the young man was once again involved in the music community.

Bobby, perhaps sensing his presence, turned a moment after Peter entered the cavernous space, which was lit only by the early-evening light pouring through the broken windows. He was wearing safety goggles and a paper air mask to block the fumes—two safeguards he hadn't employed before. "Hello, Uncle Peter."

Peter waited for him to stand and remove the mask, and then

shook his hand. "Good to see you, Bobby. What are you working on today?"

Bobby looked down at the pair of motorcycle fenders at his feet, each radiating a shiny new coat of metallic burgundy. "Nothing much. Just a repaint. Customer wants a purple-silver fade with flames, so this is just the base coat."

Peter nodded appreciatively. "They already look quite nice."

"Thanks." Bobby pushed up the safety goggles and propped them on his head. "Hey, I want to thank you again for putting me in touch with Mr. Bergmann. We start rehearsing in a couple of weeks. I'm really looking forward to it."

"Wonderful!" Peter said. "I'm actually hoping I can enlist you in something else."

"Another audition?"

"Not quite. This would be a volunteer position as a vocal coach."

Bobby looked surprised. "Teaching?"

Peter nodded eagerly. "For the high school. Mrs. Weaver needs some help with the male singers at St. James. I thought maybe . . . if you have the time . . . you might—"

Bobby cut him off with a brisk shake of his head. "I'm no teacher, Uncle Peter."

"You don't need teaching experience for this. We already have a teacher. What we need is someone with real experience—"

"No thanks."

Peter frowned. "You don't want to give it some thought?"

"What's there to think about? The last thing I want to do is be around a bunch of teenagers that are probably about as interested in singing as I am in juggling bowling pins."

Peter tried to ignore the callous dismissiveness in Bobby's response. "How do you know that? They need someone who can *create* that interest, someone who knows proper vocal technique. Someone like you."

Bobby shook his head again. "Not interested."

"Not interested?" Peter felt his blood pressure rising. "Look, Bobby, I understand if you're too busy, but to reject the idea out of hand—that seems rash, especially after what Jonathan just did to help you get the role in *Messiah*."

Bobby's eyes narrowed. "Is that what this is? Some kind of quid pro quo? You scratch my back and I scratch yours?"

"No, not at all. Besides your vocal gifts, I think you'd make for a great role model for these boys—"

"Role model?" Bobby issued a harsh bark of laughter. "I'm no hero, Uncle Peter. I'm just a guy trying to get on with my life." He pulled down the safety goggles. "So if you'll excuse me—"

"What's eating at you, Bobby?" Peter searched his eyes until the young man returned his gaze. "The war?"

"You can't change the past," Bobby said and looked away. "It is what it is. All any of us can hope to do is live with it."

Peter crossed over to the air compressor. Its noisy sputtering had begun to grate on his nerves, and he fumbled for the power switch. "How do you turn this thing off?"

Bobby moved him aside—a little too roughly, Peter thought—and flipped a switch. The room fell silent. Bobby's face, bathed in the golden light of the early evening, looked angelic as he turned back, but Peter knew his nephew felt anything but peaceful inside.

"Thank you." Peter stood silently a moment to compose his thoughts. "Son, what happened over there? What happened to you?"

Bobby offered a sour frown. "Nothing. I came home without a scratch."

Like Saul on the road to Damascus, Peter felt the scales fall from his eyes. So *that* was it! The boy felt guilty. All those names tattooed on his back . . .

"Any other questions?" Bobby asked, still staring through the goggles at Peter.

"No." In fact, Peter had dozens, but they'd have to wait for another time. He turned to leave. "You *are* a hero, Bobby Jones, whether you know it or not."

But the air compressor had already started sputtering and rattling, and Peter doubted his nephew had heard the words.

Chapter 16

He'd returned here hundreds of times, and vaguely sensed he was dreaming, but the nightmare was real enough to hold Peter in its grasp. Everywhere he looked, he saw wounded Marines writhing in pain. Their cries echoed in the landing ship tank's cavernous bowels, which only a few hours earlier had been bulging with landing vehicles and supplies. Those contents had been offloaded on the beach while under direct enemy fire, and now the LST's long metal coffin was overrun by wounded and dead Marines, its space having been hurriedly refitted to support the navy's triage team, of which Peter was a member.

After graduating high school in 1942, Peter enlisted in the navy and trained at the Great Lakes Naval Station. He'd vowed to contribute to the war effort, and two years later, here he was in the waters off Saipan, inside an LST that was still taking sniper fire, artillery thundering outside, the war a shrill cacophony of men and machines locked in a death grip.

Physicians, technicians, and medics labored ceaselessly in the sweaty steel tomb, but the wounded and dying kept coming. Marines, their bodies maimed by Japanese artillery and machine guns, thrashed on gurneys and begged for morphine. If the morphine didn't come quickly enough, a man called for his mother. And for the Marine whose suffering ceased, the drama played out the same each time: his lips stilled, his body fell silent, and death, a vulture ever hovering nearby, claimed him.

Peter stared at the wedding band on a young Marine officer who had given up the fight. The golden band was stout and handsome, just like its wearer. Someone, Peter thought, would have to deliver the news to his wife. Did they have children? There was no time to dwell on such morbid thoughts, for the triage process was like a river without end. The patients changed, but the flow never slowed.

Another artillery round exploded somewhere nearby, rocking the ship, and Peter's mind raced to the fuel-oil tanks in the hold just beneath them. All it would take was one direct hit, and everyone aboard this makeshift floating hospital would be incinerated.

As Peter hurried from one wounded man to the next, gracefully sidestepping a medic carrying a precious bottle of plasma, he realized he was dancing once again, just as he had back at Oahu while waiting to be shipped out. The jitterbug. The Lindy Hop. Peter's innate rhythm and athleticism had borne fruit on the dance floor, where he'd found his core—a strange, eerily silent center that moved with the music as easily as his lungs drew air. Dance competitions were more than just days on the calendar; they marked the passage from one world to the next, from an idyllic childhood to the gruesome carnage of war. They were pure fantasy, pure escape, and Peter lost himself in the sensuous pulse that propelled jive and swing. Inflamed with the passion of the music, he entertained countless dalliances with beautiful, patriotic nurses and administrative assistants, their affairs carried out on the dance floor while horn sections blared and jungle-like drums thundered. Every dance competition, Peter knew, might be his last, and so the celebration grew more passionate, each heady moment lived at one hundred and fifty beats per minute or faster.

While grim news of the fighting poured in from the Pacific theater, Peter danced. *Rock step, left, right, left, right, left, right. Underarm turn. Another triple step. Inside turn.* He could feel her soft hand in his—warm, pulsing with energy. He could see the smile on her face—bewitching, like a long summer day on the Cape. He knew the moment was fleeting, to be long forgotten in the coming days, yet

79

the longer it stretched outward, the deeper he lost himself in it. If the rest of the world had gone mad, he would remain here, in the space between downbeats, in the defiant melody of a clarinet, in the overheated air of a dance hall in Kaneohe Bay. The more he lost himself in the music, the more tightly he gripped her hand. He pulled her closer—close enough to smell the spearmint on her lips—and he thought he heard her say something. She mouthed the word again, but it was lost beneath a crescendo of piano and upright bass.

Finally, a voice broke through. "Help."

The word sounded strange in his ears. Out of place. Alien.

"Help."

Horns gave way to an aerial barrage. The hardwood dancefloor turned to steel lurching beneath his feet. A Marine, his face green-gray in the dim light, whispered the word again, and as he spoke, Peter felt his grip loosen. A bloody stump, dressed in soaked-through bandages, was all that remained of the young man's right leg. Another bandage had been taped over a sucking chest wound. Blood trickled from flecks of shrapnel pockmarking his face. His eyes remained open, but Peter knew in that instant that the Marine was gone.

The music was over. And the wounded kept coming.

Peter woke with a lurch, his body drenched in sweat. Alone in his upstairs bedroom in St. James's rectory, he felt at once relieved and exhausted, a man unable to outrun his past. It would be with him, he feared, for as long as he lived.

He turned toward the alarm clock on his nightstand and, finally comprehending its glowing face, decided to get out of bed. Dawn would arrive soon enough. A new day beckoned.

~~~

The houseplants arrived one at a time that morning, each in the arms of a young caretaker. A stubby African violet. A slender orchid. A bushy, rubber-leaved plant Sandra couldn't identify. By the time the

80

last student had taken his seat, Sandra was staring at a veritable plant nursery.

She paced the front of the room and stopped in front of Danny Corvino's desk. He'd brought a Christmas cactus, already setting pink-orange buds, and was holding it proudly atop his desk.

Sandra eyed the note affixed to it.

"It's from my mom," Danny explained. "Says I'm supposed to water it once every two weeks and add a drop of fertilizer to the water after it blooms." He held up a small yellow plastic pitcher with a long snout. "She gave me this to water it with."

"Does the note say anything about sunlight?" Sandra asked.

"Yeah," Danny answered, squinting at it. "Something about 'indirect' light."

Sandra judged the distance between his desk and the windows on the west wall. "Wonderful. It should do just fine where it is."

"Right on," Danny said and leaned back nonchalantly.

As she surveyed the rest of the houseplants, Sandra noticed others had arrived with notes as well—but only those in the care of boys. The mothers of the girls, it appeared, presumed their daughters already knew how to take care of the plants.

Thus, Sandra had the next assignment already in mind. "Class, I'd like to take a moment to direct your attention to an interesting phenomenon. It seems only the boys in our class have been given instructions on how to care for their plants."

The girls giggled, a few exchanging knowing glances.

"Why do you think that is?"

Molly Hansen, a diminutive blond with braces and a clear complexion, raised her hand in the front row. "Because girls are better caretakers."

Sandra cocked her head to the side. "By nature? Or is this a cultural construct?"

Molly shrugged her tiny shoulders. "Both?"

"Tonight, I want everyone to write a one-page paper on your thoughts on the matter," Sandra announced to a chorus of groans. "Why are women better suited to act as caregivers?"

Jenny O'Donnell, seated against the back wall, was already writing feverishly on a piece of paper beside her houseplant, a robust-looking English ivy specimen that was tumbling from its clay pot down the side of her desk.

Sandra caught her eye. "Anything you'd like to share with the class, Miss O'Donnell?"

Jenny's face reddened. "It's just a poem."

"*Just* a poem?" Sandra asked. "I'd love to hear it."

Jenny drew back, but offered a tentative smile. "It's not finished. But maybe when it's done."

Chapter 17

By the time Friday evening rolled around, Peter found himself inside the familiar confines of the confessional booth of St. James's chapel. Incense wafted from the chancel, and light from the evening sun poured in through the stained-glass windows and penetrated the tiny cross-shaped holes in the darkly stained oak booth. Sin, Peter had learned over the years, could be described in many ways and attributed to many factors, both within an individual's control and beyond it. But at the end of the day, he found it boring. He'd heard enough confessions to know that a person's will was entwined in a daily struggle with pride, laziness, fear, and lust, among other human foibles. Upbringing. Personality. Biology. Bad luck. Nobody was immune. And the battle never ended. For some, it came down to habit. Bit by bit, people made small concessions to selfish or unwise behavior until, lost and befuddled, they suddenly found themselves in need of counsel.

Tonight's parishioners, like so many others before them, revealed personal details both tiresome and tawdry—details that, depending on their delivery, invoked in Peter boredom, despair, or even a wry smile, which he dutifully hid. It wasn't until he heard Charles Major's commanding voice on the other side of the screen that his ears perked up and his back straightened.

"Hello, Father," Charles said after kneeling.

"Good evening," Peter replied.

Charles paused a moment before delivering a familiar refrain that, uttered by someone so authoritative, carried with it a sense of gravitas. "Bless me, Father, for I have sinned. It's been eight months since my last confession."

"May God the Father of all mercies help you make a good confession."

"Thank you, Father." Charles cleared his throat awkwardly. "Lately, I've been thinking a lot about the war."

Peter felt a familiar sensation in his chest, a strange combination of excitement and dread. "Go on."

"No matter how hard I try, I can't let go of what happened. I have these . . . memories. It's like it all happened yesterday. If I close my eyes, I can still see the cockpit of a PBY. We could barely see our instrument panels in the dark, but we had to fly at night. Otherwise we were an easy target for the Zeros. We went on some pretty hair-raising patrols. Also flew rescue missions and supplied the Marines. I loved my naval brothers, but the Marines—they made dreadful sacrifices. And the Japanese made their lives hell. I know I'm supposed to forgive my enemies, Father, but I just can't do it. No matter how hard I try, I can't. I haven't been able to say the Lord's Prayer for years. How can I ask God to 'forgive us our trespasses' when I can't forgive those who trespassed against me?"

Peter sighed heavily. So many people who came through the confessional booth struggled with life's inanities, but here was an individual who'd come face to face with death and was still grappling with the encounter. He'd faced the worst of humanity and was obviously horrified by its reflection in his own soul.

"I think about the day when the Lord will come for me," Charles added, "and I wonder if he'll be able to forgive me when I can't forgive the Japs."

Peter paused before delivering his answer in a somber voice. "You'll never be able to let go of your hatred. Not on your own. You'll require the assistance of the Holy Spirit. You must pray every day. Pray for a release from your hatred. Pray for your enemies. And be patient and gentle with yourself. You didn't bring this upon yourself. Evil on a titanic scale was thrust upon you." Such an assessment, Peter knew all too well, applied to himself as much as it did to Charles.

"Father Ryan," Charles said, not hiding the fact that he recognized Peter through the screen that separated them, "I can't forgive these people, and you want me to *pray* for them? Do *you* pray for them?"

Peter smiled sadly. It was a fair question, one that went to the heart of his own internal war. "I have mouthed the words," he finally said, "but have not yet done so in my heart."

The booth fell silent. Was Charles shocked that Peter struggled with the same injury to his heart? Disappointed that a priest, too, could not overcome events more than two decades in the past?

The answer came in Charles's tone, which exuded gratefulness and relief. "I appreciate your honesty, Father. I admit I feel better knowing I'm not alone."

"Far from it," Peter said. "Countless men walk in your shoes—and not just on our side. I like to remind myself that the men I'm struggling to forgive also are trying to move on with *their* lives. They need my forgiveness as much as I need theirs."

"Do you think it will ever get any easier?" Charles asked.

Peter shook his head. "Who can say? All I know is that a man in the grip of his past is incapable of living in the present, much less embracing the future. I want the same thing for you as I do myself: a healed heart."

"Thanks, Father." Charles chuckled softly. "It's not like I planned to become a naval aviator. When I graduated from Purdue in forty-two, I had a degree in chemical engineering, and all kinds of plans."

"But the war found you," Peter said, "like it did the rest of us."

"Right you are. As soon as I completed OCS, the navy sent me packing. Sailed right under the Golden Gate Bridge on our way to doing combat with The Empire of Japan. Everything I believed in—the Golden Rule, the Beatitudes, turn the other cheek—all that turned to vapor as soon as I witnessed the horrors of combat. As an officer, I felt a duty to protect my men, and as someone being shot at . . . well, let's just say my instincts kicked in." Charles's voice softened. "I think of my boy and the war going on over there in Vietnam, and I pray he never has to see what I saw, which, as far as I'm concerned, was the epitome of idiocy."

Peter thought for a moment. "What of your faith?"

"Still intact," Charles answered gruffly. "A life without God would be an exercise in futility. When I look at the world, I try to find evidence of the mind of God, if that makes sense. I figure all of this is God's creation. So the more we study it, the more we'll understand God."

"Are you much of a reader?"

"I am. For the last couple of years, I've been working my way through *A Study of History*."

"Ah," Peter said. "Arnold Toynbee, if I'm not mistaken. Not exactly light reading."

"No, it's not. I don't know anybody who'll discuss it with me."

"Well," Peter ventured, "maybe sometime you'll loan me your copy. I'd be glad to discuss the book."

"Books," Charles said, correcting him.

"Books?"

"It's twelve volumes."

Peter laughed. "Maybe *Reader's Digest* has a condensed version."

When Charles was ready to leave, Peter made the sign of the cross. "God the Father of mercies, through the death and resurrection of His son, has reconciled the world to Himself and sent the Holy Spirit among us for the forgiveness of sins. Through the ministry of the Church may God give you pardon and peace. I absolve you from your sins, in the name of the Father, and of the Son, and of the Holy Spirit."

"Amen," Charles said and stood.

Peter smiled sadly, satisfied with his response to Charles's confession yet unsure of his effectiveness, hopeful of a brighter future but all too aware of the thread that connected him to an unchanging, unforgiving past. "May God bless you."

~~~

After hearing the last confession an hour later, Peter stood and exited the booth. His knees felt stiff and his back a little sore, but his soul felt worse. It always did after hearing so many confessions. There was catharsis there somewhere—there had to be, Peter thought, for the ritual to be worth anything. But any feeling of satisfaction always sat side-by-side with others that were less pleasant to experience: inadequacy, sorrow, the fear of failure. He could only pray that God's grace began where his capacity to help ended.

Peter blew out the flickering candles at the altar, tidied a few pews where a hymnal or Bible had been left askew, and then strode down the center aisle to the front entrance. Once outside, he locked both doors and then turned to inhale the mild evening air.

"Hi, Uncle Peter."

Peter startled but quickly recovered. "Bobby! You surprised me. Did you want to say a quick prayer? I can let you in for a moment."

Bobby Jones, dressed in faded jeans and a matching jean jacket over a black T-shirt, shook his head. He stood at the bottom of the steps and, from Peter's vantage, looked strangely small. "Actually, I was hoping to talk to you."

Peter lowered himself to the cement stoop and motioned for Bobby to join him at the top of the stairs. "What's on your mind?"

Bobby deliberated a moment, as though waging some kind of

internal debate. Then he climbed the stairs and took up a position a couple of feet from Peter.

Not wanting to push him, Peter stared out at the small campus. The canopy of old hickories blocked out the stars, but beneath them, in the leafy understory, a handful of old-fashioned lanterns lit the brick pathway in front of them.

Bobby drew a deep breath, released it slowly. "I want to apologize for the other day."

"There's no need," Peter said. "I know things are hard right now."

Bobby took a moment to absorb this, then asked, "Were they the same for you? After the war, I mean?"

Peter chuckled softly. "Certainly. But the times were different back then. Nobody questioned the war, much less our part in it. Hitler had to be stopped. Afterward, all that was left to do was sort through our own experiences and do our best to forget them."

"How do you do that?"

Peter thought a moment. It was clear Bobby had come to confess, as it were, to lay bare his soul. But Peter knew he could help the young man only if he, too, was willing to lower his defenses. "It's a work in progress, I'm afraid. Sometimes, when I least expect it, I catch a whiff of it."

"Of what?"

"Death. I know it's not real, but for a split second, I can smell it in my nostrils, like it never left. It's been decades, but I can still smell the blood on my hands, my uniform, and my shoes. It didn't matter how often I scrubbed up. It was always there, always on me. Chest wounds. Head wounds. Amputations. The blood gets to you after a while, but you can't stop working because the men who are bleeding are also screaming for help. They need you."

"Is that why you became a priest?"

Peter lowered his gaze and stared down at the cement steps. "I suppose it could have played a role. I always thought of my choice to join the priesthood as a positive one. I was running toward God. But perhaps I was running away from something too." He paused a moment. "What about you, Bobby? Did the war change you? Did it leave a scar? For you, it's only been a couple of years."

Bobby shrugged but said nothing.

"It helps sometimes to talk about it. The alternative is to bottle it up. Think of it as an infection that needs draining. The wound will fester unless you puncture it."

"Seems like an accurate metaphor," Bobby said and sniffed at the air. "I smell it, too—the blood. But it's other things that get to me: mud, smoke, the smell of fresh rain. Seemed like it was always raining in the jungle. One downpour would start just as another was finishing. I got so tired of being wet."

He stopped talking, and Peter waited through a long silence. Then, without further prompting, Bobby began to let go the pain he'd been holding on to so doggedly.

"It's strange, though. On the night when everything went to hell, we never reached for our ponchos. Shoot, I don't think it rained a drop that night. Our assignment was to gather intelligence and to engage in close combat. We were supposed to draw blood—lots of it. I got my platoon combat-ready. We had four squads, nine men each. Sergeant 1st Class Lamar Jackson was my eyes and ears. Knew the lay of the land. Knew the enemy. I counted on him for everything.

"It was October 7, 1967. We were in the bush, near Khe Sanh, maybe ten klicks from the Laotian border. This was months before the big fight. I was getting bored. I *wanted* contact with the enemy. I wanted to test myself. Up until that point, all I'd seen was a few minor skirmishes. We'd taken a few prisoners. Ambushed a small patrol. Jackson said I was ready, said I knew everything I needed to know but still needed an education in 'real fighting.'" He shook his head and chuckled sadly. "Said there was nothing like a good old-fashioned firefight—when the rounds are coming in hot and heavy."

Peter shuddered. He'd seen "real fighting" first-hand—the noise, the chaos, the paralyzing fear—but he knew such experiences were far from desirable. They were to be avoided at all costs and, if survived, to be forgotten as soon as possible, even if such a thing was ultimately impossible.

"I got what I wanted," Bobby mused. "But it didn't turn out so good. I led my men straight into an ambush. We lost eight men in one night. Another nine from other squads were wounded. Sergeant Jackson—he was from Macon, Georgia—went home to his wife and kids in a body bag. But me? Like I said, I made it through without a scratch. Went home a year later. Untouched." Bobby's voice had grown distant, but he spat out the next few words like they were an obscenity. "I was *lucky*."

Peter swallowed but said nothing. Bobby was still at war, if only with his own heart.

"I appreciate what you and Jonathan did for me, getting me that audition," Bobby said after another long pause. "I'll help out with the St. James choir. It's the least I can do."

Peter glanced over at his nephew. "Are you sure? I don't want you to feel that it's an obligation of some kind."

"I'm sure that I want to give it a try," Bobby said. "I'm not at all sure that I can do a good job, though. I'm worried that you're giving me too much credit. Just because I can sing doesn't mean I'll make a good vocal coach. But I'll try."

"Thank you, Bobby. That's all any of us can do." Peter wanted to say more, but something seemed to have caught in his throat. He was suddenly unsure of his voice. Probably just as well. This was one of those times when more words weren't needed. He knew enough about combat's lingering destruction to know that no one could save a soldier who didn't want to be saved. Ultimately, it would be up to Bobby. But this felt like a promising first step.

Chapter 18

The following Monday afternoon, Sandra Alvarez had just returned to her classroom to lock up for the day when she spotted a young man in the back. Dressed in blue jeans and a white T-shirt, he stood with his back to her and was staring intently at something on Jenny O'Donnell's desk.

The man turned around as soon as she approached, and she recognized him instantly as Bobby Jones, Father Ryan's nephew with the golden voice. She'd watched part of his audition in the auditorium ten days earlier. His face turned red, and his eyes widened in embarrassment.

"Mr. Jones," Sandra said awkwardly as she stepped closer. "Can I help you with something?"

Bobby glanced at his shoes briefly and wiped something from his eye. Had he been crying? He looked away. "Just killing time. I'm volunteering with the choir. Got here a bit early and was just wandering the halls. Saw all the plants in here and was curious."

"Ah, yes," Sandra said. Now *she* was suddenly feeling self-conscious. There was something in Bobby's deep brown eyes—a wounded vulnerability—that drew her to him. "I heard you're assisting Mathilde with the tenors. That's wonderful." She waved a hand at the plants. "As for all this, just a little school project. The students are learning about nurturing. A bit unconventional for an English class, I'll admit, but I think today's youth—" She stopped talking when she noticed the small piece of paper in Bobby's right hand.

Bobby fumbled with the paper in an attempt to return it to the plant on Jenny's desk. Eventually, he gave up and set it down beside the plant. His face was burning red again. "Sorry to disturb you. I'll be going now."

Sandra stood only a few feet from him by then. Before she understood what she was doing, she reached out and placed her hand over his. It was obvious he was alone in his grief—a grief as dark as anything she'd ever encountered. But far from being frightened by it, she felt compelled to touch it, to soothe whatever was causing it.

For a brief moment their eyes locked, his bloodshot and welling with tears, hers searching for clues. She knew for certain that she wasn't misreading the situation.

"Sorry," he said and brushed past her on the way to the door. How had he escaped so easily? A second later, he was gone.

Sandra pursed her lips and stepped closer to Jenny's desk. She picked up the paper with the intention of returning it to its envelope and its home amongst the jumble of English ivy. Instead, she found herself staring at the paper, upon which had been written a poem in beautiful handwritten script. Several colorful monarch butterflies decorated the edges. And just like that, Sandra was reading the same poem that had brought tears to Bobby's eyes.

Mommy,
This plant reminds me of you.
It's beautiful.
Its delicate leaves are like your gentle touch.
There's something inviting and welcoming.
When I look closely, there are lovely surprises to see and explore.
I sense strength, warmth, and love.
There is new growth—bright green and waxy.

It seems to climb toward the sun.
I remember your final tear.
It flowed down your cheek as your soul rose toward heaven.
When I water this lovely plant, it reminds me of that tear that bonds our hearts forever.
You were such a wonderful mother.
I miss you.
I will be with you again when I return to the one who sent us.
Love,
Jenny

Sandra looked from the poem to the empty doorway. The sun's afternoon rays had given the classroom walls a fiery hue. Through an open window, Coach Kowalski's voice could be heard carrying from the football field. Autumn, the loveliest of New England's four seasons, was almost upon them.

Chapter 19

Maria Donatello burst into Peter's office the next morning, for once arriving ahead of her overpowering perfume. "He's here," she said through a tight-lipped frown.

"Ah," Peter answered. "Please, show him in."

A moment later, Brian Kelleher's tall and lanky frame appeared in the doorway. A graduate of St. James, Brian, now twenty-one, stood six feet, three inches and couldn't have weighed more than one hundred and fifty pounds. His curly brown hair fell just shy of his shoulders, and his already animated face brightened considerably when he locked eyes with Peter.

For his part, Peter could barely remember the young man, who had been a senior when Peter had arrived at St. James. As a student, Brian had been rather unremarkable. Beyond his activities with the yearbook, he largely kept to himself. Peter remembered him as quiet and introspective—and not nearly so tall. It was clear he'd gone through a physical and emotional transformation in the intervening years.

For the last hour, Brian had been leading a peace rally in the park bordering St. James. Maria had been the first to grumble, which was no surprise, given that her son was an artillery officer in Vietnam, and Brian had already used his bullhorn this morning to call American troops "baby killers" while leading a chant to bring them home. Maria, known throughout the office as someone who valued accountability, discipline, productivity, and competence, found the "new movement" among the country's youth objectionable. Peter had heard her disparage the movement's "sloppiness" in speech, dress, thinking, and morals on more than one occasion.

But the rally outside had become combustible when Coach Kowalski, in typical blunt fashion, had marched across the street to tell Brian and his fellow protestors what he thought of their protest. Coach Dean had joined the fracas moments later, and Peter had watched from his office window as tempers had flared on both sides and a physical confrontation had appeared imminent. When word had arrived that Brian wanted a face-to-face meeting with Peter, Peter had welcomed the tête-à-tête, and Peter had sent Father Kovacs, known for his razor-sharp intellect and aloof demeanor, to broker the meeting.

Now here was Brian with a small entourage in tow: Father Kovacs, a local newspaper reporter named William Brennan, and of course Maria, whom Peter had invited to sit in on the meeting.

"Come on in," Peter said. He had only two visitors' chairs, and both were currently covered in books, notes, and various clutter. He made quick work of the debris and then motioned for Brian and Maria to have a seat. "Sorry for the mess." He offered an apologetic smile to Father Kovacs and William Brennan. "Do you mind standing?"

"Not at all," Father Kovacs said.

Brennan, already scribbling in his reporter's notebook, shook his head without looking up. He wore dark-framed glasses that matched his short dark hair, and seemed intent on capturing the drama as it unfolded.

Peter returned his attention to Brian. "It's good to see you again, Mr. Kelleher. Have you continued your studies since leaving St. James?"

Brian nodded. "I'm studying political science and psychology at Northeastern University." He glanced at the reporter. "I thought about journalism for a while, but I'm more interested in politics and the study of human behavior."

Peter smiled. "Well, it appears you have a gift for leadership and public speaking."

"It might appear that way," Brian said, leaning forward in his seat, "but what you hear is the passion that I have for the new revolution."

"I see." Peter thought a moment. "Perhaps you could share your thinking regarding the protest and the movement that you so strongly believe in."

"There's a new way of thinking that's in the process of replacing the aging, defective systems that have brought warfare and misery to mankind," Brian explained. "Religion, capitalism, and colonialism are the primary drivers of hatred and war. Just look at the crusades. Heck, just look at what's going on today in Northern Ireland, where people are killing each other in the name of God."

"How does Vietnam tie into all of this?" Peter asked.

"The abuse of workers through a capitalistic economic model, along with colonialism, is the foundation of that conflict."

Peter stole a quick glance at Maria, expecting to see an indignant look on her face, but she appeared surprised by Brian's eloquence. The young man cut a striking figure, despite his Bohemian appearance.

"How do you envision replacing that existing order?" Peter asked, returning to the topic at hand.

"We need to move away from the Christian models—specifically Roman Catholicism but also the Protestant denominations—and replace them with agnosticism, science, reason, and Eastern philosophies. Compassionate government would become socialized with a gradual phasing out of private enterprise. Church properties would eventually become health care facilities. Philosophy and psychology would replace the great religions of the past."

These were radical ideas, Peter thought, but Brian was somehow managing to propose them in a reasonable way. It was clear he was frustrated with the horrors of the war in Vietnam, but he also was frustrated about social intolerance.

Brian shifted gears to the topics of slavery and racism, and then posed an interesting question. "Why does society show so much anger toward the length of someone's hair?" He tugged at his brown curls. "It's such a small, petty thing. If we're intolerant of long hair or beards, what does that say about us? Doesn't it indicate greater intolerances lurking within us?" He leaned back and eyed Peter across the messy desk. "Show me where I'm wrong."

Peter whistled under his breath. "I'm afraid that my areas of expertise are limited to the teachings of the Roman Catholic Church."

"Okay," Brian said in a tone that was less challenging but hinted at sarcasm. "I no longer believe in God or, for that matter, Christ. I *do* have an open mind. Again, please show me where I'm wrong."

Peter had encountered such skepticism before, and always found it helpful to maintain a respectful dialogue. He took a deep breath. "Thank you, Brian, for having the courage to articulate your thinking. Perhaps we can agree that man is an imperfect creature. Our vernacular would describe this as a 'fallen nature' or 'original sin.' You might believe that man still has vestiges of 'primal instincts,' which lead to anger and violence."

Brian nodded. "Yes, Father, we agree on that."

Peter pushed ahead. "Therefore, we need to address the issue of 'primal instincts' or 'original sin' before we can solve the more complex societal issues that we are facing today."

"Agreed," Brian said as his lips turned upward in a subtle grin. "But as society becomes more educated, many of these problems will be solved. Compassionate government will address and eventually correct most of these issues."

Peter tried to find common ground. "You have a point regarding education. Civilization has paid a terrible price for ignorance. But consider this: two highly educated societies, Germany and Japan, recently made choices that resulted in a world war. Perhaps we're missing a piece of the puzzle."

Brian's angular face, thus far projecting confidence and passionate conviction, softened. He was intelligent—anyone could see that, Peter thought. And his compassion moved him to protest the war and to seek out new ways to address age-old problems. But he was overcompensating. His solutions had been tried in Russia, China, and elsewhere—with deeply destructive results. The conversation needed to turn toward what mattered most: sacrificial love. The magnitude of Christ's love was difficult for most people to comprehend, Peter knew, but it was worth sharing, even if introducing such a concept merely sowed the seeds of future understanding.

"Brian, you grew up in the parochial school, K through twelve, correct?"

The young man nodded.

"And you completed the catechism, participated in Bible study, and heard the missal at Mass."

A grin appeared on Brian's face. "Yes, I did, Father."

"You're familiar with Genesis, Moses and the Ten Commandments, the Psalms, David, and some of the prophets?"

"Sure."

"And you're familiar with the Synoptic Gospels, the Sermon on the Mount, the disciples, and the Letters of the Apostle Paul?"

Brian nodded as a look of impatience crept across his face. "I'm familiar with all of this, Father."

Peter tried to maintain a calm voice. He was almost there. "You're therefore aware that Christ, the disciples, and the Apostle Paul paid with their lives for their faith."

"Of course!" Now Brian was sounding annoyed.

Peter smiled at the young man. He couldn't help but admire his earnestness, his passion, his determination to make the world a better place. "If you're unwilling to accept their words—men who were tortured and murdered for their faith and their desire to share their love of God with the world—why would you consider taking *my* words to heart?"

The room fell silent. Even William Brennan, who until then had been feverishly jotting down every word, paused and looked up from his notebook, his brow knotted in concentration.

For the first time since he'd sat down, Brian appeared to be at a loss for words. Slack-jawed and slumped in his chair, he sat silently across from Peter, clearly still struggling to craft a response.

"Brian, it's my hope that you find your life to be meaningful and satisfying," Peter said. "I'll pray that you ultimately possess the hope and peace you seek."

"Thank you, Father," Brian said softly.

Peter stood and offered a hand, and Brian shook it as their gazes met. In Brian's brown eyes, Peter saw confusion, hurt, even a touch of fear. But he also saw a determination to continue asking questions, to confront accepted wisdom.

The meeting dissolved in silence as, one by one, everyone departed deep in their own thoughts. Whatever enmity that had existed between the parties beforehand had, in Peter's estimation, vanished. They'd offered diametrically opposed ideas, but had done so in a mutually respectful manner. That kind of civility, Peter knew, was a rare and precious thing.

William Brennan, the last to leave, lingered in the doorway. He glanced at Peter and adjusted his thick black glasses, as if mentally preparing a follow-up question in his head, but then turned and left. What had begun as a potentially heated confrontation had ended with an invocation to peace and reconciliation—not exactly the kind of ideas that sold newspapers, Peter thought. He couldn't help but wonder what kind of article Brennan would write.

Chapter 20

The answer was waiting for Peter when he entered his office the next morning. A copy of the morning newspaper was already laid out on his desk. The peace rally had made the front page, and a photo above the fold highlighted the heated exchange between Coach Dean, Coach Kowalski, and Brian Kelleher. Coach Dean was glaring at Brian in contempt and disgust. Next to him stood Coach Kowalski, who looked like a middle linebacker zeroing in on the quarterback, ready to tear off his head. Brian wore a confident yet sardonic look on his face that seemed to mock the establishment and any proponents of the status quo.

"Oh dear," Peter said and sat down to read the article.

He'd barely made it past the lede when he caught a whiff of Maria's perfume. He looked up to see her smiling at him from the doorway.

"Did you read it?" she asked excitedly.

He set the paper on his messy desk and leaned back. "I just started to. But perhaps you can give me a recap."

"No," she said with a mischievous smile. "You should read it for yourself. I'll be back in a minute."

Peter watched her leave and then returned his attention to the article. To his astonishment, the story was neither inflammatory nor sensationalized. William Brennan had rendered a bare, accurate recounting of the day's events, beginning with the confrontation outside on the adjacent park's grounds and ending with the rapprochement inside Peter's office. No editorializing. No biased interpretation. Just the facts. He'd quoted Brian and Peter verbatim, and the piece that emerged portrayed a civil exchange between two men, one old enough to be the other's father, both articulate in the presentation of their beliefs. To Peter's delight, the article closed with his words about sacrificial love.

"Well, I'll be," Peter whispered in a hushed, almost reverent voice. He looked up just in time to see Maria return.

"Can you believe it?" She was clearly as astonished as he was.

Peter shook his head. "It's certainly not what I expected. Mr. Brennan is quite a journalist, isn't he?"

Maria nodded. "The next Walter Cronkite, perhaps." She sighed, and the smile slowly faded from her face.

"What is it?" Peter asked.

Maria absentmindedly patted at a gray streak in her long brunette hair, which she'd pulled back into a bun, as usual. "My mind keeps wandering these days."

"You're worried about how we're going to raise a half million dollars," Peter said.

"I am." She frowned and paced to the window, pausing to stare outside. "I don't want you to get too optimistic, Father."

Peter chuckled softly. He shared her dedication to reality, however grim it might be at times, but where they differed was in their response to it. "It's okay to be hopeful, Maria."

"But what if—"

He raised a hand. "And where hope ends, faith begins."

~~~

Later that day at lunch, Sandra sat across from Laurel Nord and Mathilde Weaver in the smoky faculty lounge. Sister Consuela joined them just in time to say grace, sack lunch and thermos in hand.

"You look frustrated," Sandra said, observing the worry lines on

102

her sister's forehead.

Consuela frowned. "It's these girls. Too many of them are in awful shape. They don't play sports. They don't participate in conditioning."

Laurel looked up from a steaming cup of soup. "Maybe that's a good thing. They'll be too weak to chase after boys."

Sandra laughed with the others. Promiscuity was always a danger among high school students, even at a Catholic school, but most of the girls at St. James struck her as the studious type. She glanced at her sister and could see the wheels turning in her mind. She'd witnessed the same look on numerous occasions dating back to their childhood.

Consuela turned to face Sandra. "What do you think," she began, "about teaching the girls the art of dance? You could do it after school as a PE elective."

Sandra smiled back at her sister, who knew her all too well. Consuela had left for college while Sandra had still been in junior high—long before Sandra had minored in dance at Boston College—but even then she'd already been exploring ballet, tap, jazz, and ballroom dancing. The art of dance was, in many ways, her first love. And now Consuela was inquiring if she'd like to teach it at St. James.

"Do you even need to ask? Of course I'd love to! But what about the logistics?"

Consuela fussed with her coif, the snug white cap that held her black headdress in place. It revealed only a tiny hint of the dark hair at her temples. "Let's take a walk as soon as we're finished."

The two sisters wolfed down their lunches, said goodbye to Laurel and Mathilde, and walked to the gym.

After they passed a male teacher in the courtyard, Consuela waited until they were out of earshot to ask, "Does it grow tiresome having men so obviously ogle you?"

Sandra blushed and grabbed her sister's hand, which felt warm and soft in hers. "I try not to notice." Indeed, seconds earlier, she'd consciously avoided making eye contact with the male teacher—a technique she'd honed over the years.

"Well," Consuela whispered, "you have to have noticed that the assistant baseball coach can't take his eyes off you."

Sandra shrugged. Not much had changed since she'd blossomed—an occurrence that had coincided with Consuela taking her religious vows as a nun. Consuela had never seemed jealous of all the attention Sandra received from men. More like concerned. Perhaps a little amused. In any case, Sandra respected her older sister too much to dwell on the physical differences between them. If others considered Consuela plain, Sandra saw the beauty that radiated from within her. She'd pledged her soul to God, and that kind of light-filled love was a sight to behold. Consuela's dedication, too, was worthy of admiration. She took great satisfaction in helping her students grow, which was why she could be impatient at times. That was clearly the case now. Consuela preached freedom through discipline and seemed shocked whenever her students were unable to grasp such an obvious truth. She often quoted Matthew 7:14, which was also a favorite of Sandra's: "But small is the gate and narrow the road that leads to life, and only a few find it."

After they entered the gym, Sandra paused to take in the drafty space. The hardwood floors, recently waxed, shone beneath the bright lights that hung from the rafters high above.

"The gym is almost always in use," Consuela said, her voice sounding small in the cavernous space, "but we only require a portion of the whole." She pointed to a section of the wooden bleachers. "They can be moved so we can install mirrors."

"Good idea," Sandra said. "What do we do with the mirrors when they're not in use?"

"Keep them in place. The bleachers will be returned and will protect them."

Sandra spotted a balance beam in the corner. "We can use that as a barre for stretching and exercise."

"That's the spirit!" Consuela said with a sunny grin. "What we need is a portable dance studio—something that can be quickly set up and broken down without too much trouble. Now . . ." She clasped her hands together and smiled with her eyes. "Let's see how many female athletes we can sign up for dance class."

Chapter 21

Peter was on his way to the faculty lounge the next morning when Eddie Romano, a burly tight end on the football team, stopped him in the hallway. Eddie, a man among boys, stood a good six inches taller than most of his classmates and typically sported a five o'clock shadow by second period. An oversized pair of ears framed his rugged face, which, like his body, looked like it belonged to a grown man, not a high school senior.

"Hi, Father," he said in a beefy voice. "You wanna buy some chocolate?"

Peter shifted his gaze from Eddie's smiling mug to the box of Nestlé $100,000 Bars he was holding in his right hand. He was the third football-player-turned-candy-bar-salesman to approach Peter. Apparently, Coach Kowalski had a friend at the Nestlé factory in Worchester and, using his own money, had managed to buy a trunk full of candy bars at less than wholesale. Coach Kowalski had called the investment "my humble contribution to the cause" and had insisted he was not to be reimbursed. Every penny made would go toward "keeping St. James on the map."

"Sure," Peter said and reached for his billfold.

"They're a buck apiece, Father," Eddie offered with a sheepish grin.

"I know," Peter said, having already forked over the money for an even dozen. A dollar was a hefty price for a candy bar that could be purchased at any grocery store for a nickel, but it was, after all, a fundraiser for a good cause. Peter didn't have a sweet-tooth, per se, which meant once again that he'd be distributing his bounty among the faculty and the office ladies, most of whom were already flush with candy bars. "I'll take five."

Eddie accepted the five-dollar bill and handed Peter five $100,000 Bars, each housed in the familiar red wrapping with yellow trim and decorated with a white $100,000 logo. Beneath the logo were the words *chocolate, chewy caramel, and crispies*. Peter wondered how many football players were eating more bars than they were selling. Hopefully they were good for it.

"Thank you very much, young man," Peter said. "So how's practice going? Getting ready for the next big game?"

Eddie shrugged his hulking shoulders. "Coach is working us hard. Says we're ready to turn a corner."

"Well, I don't doubt that for a minute, Eddie. Good luck Friday!"

"Thanks, Father."

"You're welcome, son."

Peter watched as Eddie lumbered down the hallway, never quite disappearing in the sea of students, his head remaining above the others' like a plastic fishing bob floating against the current on a slow-moving river.

~~~

Sandra barely noticed the arrival of autumn. The after-school dance class, which had been conceived on such a hopeful note, weighed heavily on her mind. Attendance was strong, and initially the girls had been eager to learn.

But after a week or so it became obvious that a plateau had already been reached and many of the girls appeared to be losing interest. What came naturally to her, Sandra had begun to realize, wasn't so easy for others. Worse, it was clear the students found the barre and floor exercises monotonous.

The program, still in its infancy, reached its nadir on a mild day in early October. As Sandra led the girls through another round of exercises on the makeshift barre, the baseball team began to assemble in the nearby bleachers, players eager to get started with their fall conditioning workout. Coach Dean's team used the gym every day immediately following the conclusion of dance class.

"Okay, ladies," Sandra said, eyeing the huge clock on the near wall, "last exercise of the day—grand battements."

The announcement was met with a chorus of groans, but the girls, most of whom were outfitted in matching loose-fitting royal-blue jumpers, dutifully took up their positions at the balance beam. One girl in particular, Greta Gronkowski, was slow to take her place and became even more reticent to begin the exercise when the boys began to whisper and point at her from the bleachers. Greta, although an accomplished student and a plucky member of the school debate team, was on the heavy side and struggled to do the exercises that required more than a modicum of flexibility. In this case, she was having difficulty opening up her hips enough to extend her right leg horizontally from the barre.

Before Sandra could regret her decision to save the ballet exercises for last, Mike Zuk, the baseball team's centerfielder and top prankster, shouted from the bleachers, "Hey, Gronkowski, how 'bout a few more salads?"

The players doubled over in laughter, and the bleachers shook with their hysterics.

Even Coach Dean, seated next to his assistant coach at the bottom of the bleachers, let go a short guffaw before comporting himself and turning around to scowl at his mouthy player. "You just bought yourself a week with Mr. Fuchida, Zuk."

Mike Zuk's face reddened, and he hung his head in shame, but the damage was done.

Sandra tried to maintain a positive tone with her girls, even going so far as to give Greta an encouraging nod after class, but in the days that followed, attendance began to drop, and enthusiasm waned.

By the middle of the next week, Sandra was at her wits' end as she related her troubles to Laurel and Mathilde in the faculty lounge during lunch.

"Mind if I offer a solution?" Father Kovacs smiled meekly at Sandra. He'd been eating a sandwich at the adjacent table.

Sandra, surprised that he'd overheard their conversation and even more astounded that the normally introspective teacher was offering his input, almost choked on her answer. "Please do, Father."

He left his half-eaten sandwich at his table and joined the women at theirs, bringing with him the faint aroma of paprika. "You have many pots without lids," he said as he lowered himself into a chair beside Sandra. "Why not invite boys to participate along with the girls?"

Sandra thought a moment. "I'm not sure I follow your thinking, Father."

"In Hungary, where I was born, everyone loves to dance. Why not invite the boys? And change the focus. Ballet is too hard. These kids want to dance! Teach them ballroom and swing dancing."

Sandra felt her lower jaw drop in amazement. It was so obvious. Why hadn't she thought of it? She'd turned a potentially fun activity into a grueling exercise routine.

Mathilde lowered her coffee mug. "How would we get the boys to participate?"

Father Kovacs shrugged. "Girls like to dance, and boys like to be with girls. Perhaps a demonstration could motivate the boys to participate."

Laurel was leaning forward, elbows on the table, and her chin on her fists. She asked the question now forming in Sandra's mind: "Who would demonstrate?"

"Father Ryan's nephew was on a ballroom dance team in

109

college," Father Kovacs answered nonchalantly.

Sandra exchanged glances with Mathilde. "Bobby Jones? He's already helping with the tenors in the choir."

"Then he's already on campus every afternoon," Father Kovacs said. "It's a *fait accompli*."

Perhaps, Sandra thought as she eyed her friends across the table. But approaching Bobby would take a certain degree of sensitivity. She'd heard the stories about his tour in Vietnam. She'd seen his pain first-hand in her own classroom. Bobby Jones seemed to live most of his life behind a protective wall. She could tell by the looks on Mathilde's and Laurel's faces—eyebrows raised, eyes locked on her—that the job was hers.

"Okay," she said with a sigh, breaking the silence. "I'll ask him."

Chapter 22

Sandra waited until the last tenor had exited the choir room that evening before stepping inside. She found Bobby peering out a window at the gloomy twilight.

He turned suddenly, startled, and then, with an embarrassed expression, stared down at his feet. "Miss Alvarez."

"*Sandra*," she said, correcting him. She felt clumsy as she searched for something to say. She hated small talk. "The days are growing shorter. I'm never quite ready for summer to end. But fall has its own beauty, don't you think?"

He nodded but remained silent.

She decided on the direct approach. "Rumor has it you have some experience in ballroom dance."

Bobby's eyes widened briefly in surprise, but just as quickly he frowned, as though even the slightest expression of enthusiasm pained him. "I danced with the Boston College Dance Club."

Sandra, in contrast, couldn't hide her delight. "So did I! We must have just missed each other. I joined when I was a sophomore."

"Small world," he said with a nonchalant shrug. "What did you major in?"

"English. How 'bout you?"

"International studies. I minored in music."

"I minored in dance! I didn't realize we had so much in common."

Bobby's shoulders dropped noticeably. Was he relaxing? "I took a couple of dance classes from Professor Vanderhoff. Remember that

111

old rascal?"

Sandra laughed. Professor Vanderhoff was a living legend at Boston College. He was a wizard on the dance floor, but awkward everywhere else. "How could I forget that awful comb-over?"

"Or his musty old tweed jacket?"

"You could smell him coming a mile away!" For the first time since meeting him, Sandra was beginning to feel at ease in Bobby's presence. She was determined not to waste the opportunity. "We have a little dance club here at St. James."

"Yeah?" Bobby leaned in closer.

"It's been a challenge. Every day we have to move some of the bleachers in the gym, and we use a balance beam for a barre. But the real struggle has been to keep the girls interested."

"It's girls only?"

"Well, hopefully not for long. We want to get the boys involved and change the program from performance dance to ballroom dance."

"Seems smart. Music and dance styles change over time, but classic ballroom dancing never changes." Bobby, normally so reserved, became more animated with every word on the subject. "For me, the beauty of dance can be found in the nuances. Every individual is unique. That's because we process music through the mind first. Then we turn it into physical art through the medium of dance. When we watch someone dance, we're watching their mind at work."

As Bobby continued to expound on the subject, Sandra found herself so enthralled she almost forgot why she'd visited him in the music room. She waited until he finished before segueing to the more mundane task at hand. "I was wondering if you'd be willing to help us."

Bobby lifted an eyebrow. "How so?"

"Well, we need to get the boys interested in the program. We have the gym right before the baseball team, and they typically start arriving toward the tail end of our session. They sit in the bleachers and watch, and, well, you know how boys are."

"They like to tease," Bobby said.

Sandra nodded and offered an exasperated sigh. "The girls are discouraged, and attendance is down. I feel like if we could somehow get the boys involved, then maybe the girls would—"

"We should demonstrate a foxtrot while the baseball team is watching from the bleachers," Bobby said. "Then you can invite them to dance."

Sandra drew back in surprise. It was a clever—if unexpected—idea. "Do you think anyone would have the courage to join us?"

"Yes, I do."

Bobby answered so confidently that Sandra was more than happy to take him at his word. "Would you be able to demonstrate, say, this Friday afternoon?"

"I'm finishing a big project at the shop, so we better make it next week. But it would be my pleasure. How does 'Just the Way You Look Tonight' by Sinatra sound?"

Sandra, unable to hide the growing affection in her voice, smiled as she spoke. "Bobby Jones, you're becoming pretty indispensable around here. First you volunteer to help with the choir, and now this. St. James owes you a debt of gratitude."

~~~

At lunch the next day in the faculty lounge, Sandra continued to replay in her mind her conversation with Bobby. His depth of understanding had both surprised and gratified her. It seemed that beneath his mysterious persona lurked a passionate, if complicated, soul. To the casual observer, he probably appeared shy, introverted, withdrawn—even a little disheveled, what with his long hair and sideburns. But she'd seen him lower the protective wall he used to shield himself from others. He was warm and engaging, and his

113

confidence was impressive. Indeed, he struck her as the kind of man others would follow into battle.

"You there, little sister?" Consuela asked.

Sandra blinked and looked across the table at her sister, who, along with Laurel and Mathilde, was staring at her with concern. They'd been carrying on an animated conversation, and Sandra hadn't heard a word of it.

"Sorry," she finally said. "I'm just a little distracted."

Laurel lowered her voice to just shy of a whisper. "Was it that bad?"

"What?"

"Your conversation with Bobby!" the three women exclaimed in unison.

Sandra held out as long as she could and then cracked a smile. "Actually, we had a very pleasant conversation. He's coming to dance class next week. We're going to demonstrate a foxtrot."

~~~

After a quick breakfast Saturday morning, Peter drove with Jonathan to a familiar vacation spot: the Bloom family beach house on Cape Cod. Jonathan said he'd gotten permission from Rachael to have a "guys' overnight" on the Cape, which meant it would be just the two of them for the weekend. By five o'clock that evening, the two were reclining in a pair of Adirondack chairs on the deck, watching the Atlantic Ocean change hues in the fading sunlight. The tourists were long gone.

Peter smiled wistfully as the last of the sun's rays warmed the side of his face. "I hope you don't mind, but I volunteered a weekend here for the school raffle."

Jonathan, whose rangy frame barely fit in the weathered cedar reclining chair, chuckled. "Thanks for asking."

"It was the least I could do."

114

"I haven't seen your mug in the paper since the demonstration next door to the school. What gives?"

Peter feigned a frown. "I guess what we do at St. James just isn't newsworthy." His thoughts turned to Brian Kelleher and the meeting. "He made a few good points, didn't he?"

"Who?"

"Brian Kelleher. The young man with the bullhorn."

Jonathan rubbed his prominent jaw. "There's no denying the excesses of capitalism or the downside of colonialism. And God knows the Catholic Church has made its share of mistakes. Same for any creed. But why abandon religion and all the good the faithful do? Society finds compassion and greatness in the spirit of God. Why toss it out in exchange for oblivion? And why toss out capitalism and all the blessings it provides in exchange for socialist mediocrity?"

Peter couldn't argue with Jonathan's logic, but there was more to it than just taking sides in a philosophical argument. "I was amazed at the young man's poise and leadership capabilities. He had the courage of his convictions, but at the same time, he expressed a willingness to engage in peaceful discussion of ideas and ideology."

Jonathan visibly stiffened in his chair. "We've seen what happens when ideology goes awry. Nazi Germany. The Soviet Union. The result is always genocide and war. Bad ideology, whether from the left or the right, manifests itself in the same destructive manner." He fell silent for a moment. "Do you ever wonder why the first two of the Ten Commandments have to do with idolatry?"

Peter, curious, turned toward Jonathan. "I'm not sure where you're headed with this."

"'Thou shalt have no other Gods before me, and thou shalt not make unto thee any graven image.'" Jonathan stared at the ocean, one side of his face lit by sunlight, the other in shadow. "If there's no God, there's no need for faith or love of God. But we still need an ideology for guidance. That ideology becomes the idol, and we become shackled to it. Brian's ideology is similar to the Soviet model. Why would anyone, especially a young person who's accustomed to freedom, want that? Brian's ideas make me shudder. They lead to tyranny."

Peter nodded and leaned back in his chair. "I understand. I share your concerns. I think Brian and young people like him are blissfully ignorant and are overcompensating for the ills of our society. As you said, why throw the baby out with the bathwater? But I think he'll find his way back to his roots in Christianity. With his leadership skills, he may bring a few people back with him!" He sighed heavily. "I don't think his youthful excesses are that unusual. As a society, we often overreact when trying to correct our worst problems."

"That's exactly right!" Jonathan's tone was one of epiphany and relief. "It seems like we overbake every—" He sat up rigidly, wide-eyed with panic, as if he'd been stung by a hornet. "Shit on a shingle! We forgot about the roast!"

Peter raced inside, a second after Jonathan, and arrived in time to see smoke billowing from the oven.

Jonathan jerked open the oven, grabbed a pair of oven mittens from the counter, and liberated the roast from the smoldering inferno. Engulfed by smoke, he set the roast on a burner and gingerly lifted the lid, a grimace on his face.

Peter, peering over his shoulder, was afraid to look. What he saw left him crestfallen. Their beef tenderloin and roasted potatoes and carrots was blackened beyond recognition. He turned and winced at the bottle of pinot noir from the Côte de Nuits that he'd opened earlier and left to breathe on the kitchen counter.

Jonathan had already produced his car keys. "I'll drive into town and get us dinner." He motioned with his eyes to the pinot noir. "Better put a cork in that. How does pepperoni pizza and Ballantine beer sound instead?"

Chapter 23

Dance class began at the usual time the following Tuesday. Sandra led the girls through a handful of light stretches, careful not to rush them, and then guided them through a series of more active maneuvers: spine roll-downs, the Charleston step, and arm and leg swings. While the girls warmed up, Sandra spied Laurel and Mathilde sitting beside Father Kovacs in the bleachers, the latter holding a thick textbook under his arm.

One by one, members of the baseball team strolled through the entrance to the gym and noisily assembled in the bleachers. They gaped at the girls with their usual opportunistic grins, some fixated on the young beauties, others waiting for Greta Gronkowski and others to flounder.

Sandra ignored them and tried to focus on the task at hand. But ten minutes into the warm-up it suddenly hit her: *He's not coming.* Bobby Jones, the mercurial young man with the vulnerable gaze and the dark charisma, wasn't going to show. She was on her own.

As she stared at the entrance to the gym, waiting in vain for Bobby's arrival, a flurry of emotions hit her in quick succession. Panic. Disappointment. Then, finally, resolve. She would go on with the lesson just as she always did. And she wasn't alone.

She turned and addressed her class. "Stretching, exercises, drills—these repetitions are designed to give you a command of the language of dance. It might seem tedious, but it's all part of the fun. Because once you've mastered the fundamentals . . ." She gave Father Kovacs an imploring grin. ". . . You can start dancing!"

Father Kovac's face registered alarm, but he quickly seemed to grasp the situation. A moment later, the middle-aged mathematician with Hungarian roots stood up, set down his textbook, and ambled toward her with an air of confidence and a smile on his wizened face.

"How does a waltz sound, Father?" Sandra asked.

Father Kovac's eyes were already dancing. "Perfect."

Sandra motioned to her sister to start the record player perched on a nearby table and waited for Father Kovacs to take the lead. And that he did. He was rusty at first—and not nearly as fluid or nimble as someone who'd been practicing—but Father Kovacs took to the hardwoods with aplomb.

Sister Consuela, meanwhile, had read the situation perfectly and had chosen Johann Straus's "The Blue Danube," a classic that surely Father Kovacs knew by heart. Such a dance was more advanced than the American slow waltz Sandra had taught the students—and not well-suited to beginners—but Father Kovacs's Hungarian roots ensured he'd know the Viennese waltz step for step.

As she glided across the court, Sandra felt all eyes on her and Father Kovacs. It wasn't the galvanizing moment she'd hoped for—an electrifying demonstration that would entice some of the boys to join the class—but it had to have found a mark with some of the girls. Perhaps they sensed for the first time that the dull exercises could lead somewhere fruitful, that a world both exciting and romantic awaited them on the other side.

Such a possibility was all that kept Sandra, now flushed, from giving in to the mortifying disappointment haunting her every step.

~~~

Peter searched his desk for a pen or pencil. "Come on," he muttered in frustration. "Anything will do."

He'd scheduled a meeting with Sister Consuela, and although he'd managed to find a blank notebook among the rubble, his search

118

still failed to yield any writing utensil. The drawers were stuffed with ancient clutter he'd removed from his desk, and his desk, in turn, was buried beneath the usual mountain of letters, paperwork, and "junk," as Maria Donatello liked to call the keepsakes and other memorabilia he couldn't bear to throw away.

He looked up as soon as his nose detected her peony-scented perfume.

Maria stood in the open doorway, a sly smirk on her face. She waved a blue ballpoint pen in the air. "Looking for one of these?"

Peter didn't have time to grovel. "Yes!" he exclaimed and liberated it from her grasp as soon as he met her in the doorway. "You're a godsend, Mrs. Donatello."

She might have blushed, but he didn't have time to notice. He was already on his way out of the office. A few minutes later, he was standing outside the classroom where Sister Consuela taught health. He felt sheepish and more than a little reticent—like he was about to be served a generous slice of humble pie—but the meeting had been his idea.

Lately, Peter had noticed a recurrent theme in the confessional when counseling the female students at St. James: vanity. It seemed to be the driving force behind many of their actions, not to mention the cause of much anxiety. Yet he sensed something more was at work, which was why he'd arranged to speak with Sister Consuela.

Peter took a deep breath and slowly opened the door.

Sister Consuela was seated at her desk and appeared to be in deep thought while reviewing some handwritten notes. Her tunic, as always, was perfectly pressed, its dark fabric contrasting sharply with the pink glow of her hands and face. She was a plain woman and not nearly the breathtaking beauty that her younger sister was, but she radiated something that Peter found just as striking. She was wise, the owner of a fierce intellect, and as earnest as anyone he'd ever met. As far as he could tell, she'd dedicated every aspect of her life to God—and was filled with joy and serenity because of that single-minded focus.

"Sister Consuela," he said, unable to hide the warm affection in his voice, "thank you for seeing me."

She looked up from her work and smiled. "It's my pleasure, Father. I want to compliment you on your willingness to seek a deeper understanding of the issues our female students face. You'll be an even greater help to the girls than you already are if we can arm you with more knowledge. Please take a seat."

Peter returned her smile and lowered himself into one of the desks in the front row, notebook and pen at the ready. "As I told you earlier, I feel like vanity is a problem among our female students, but I can't help wondering if it's merely the symptom of a different kind of ailment."

Sister Consuela nodded. "I think you're on the right track. If you're going to understand the mindset of the typical female student at St. James, however, you need to see the world as she does. Girls today face enormous pressures in society to be 'attractive,' not just to please the opposite sex but to compete with one another."

"Why?"

"Movies. Television. Magazines. Billboards and commercials. Everywhere a young girl looks these days, she's being told to stoke her vanity." Sister Consuela frowned. "Sex appeal sells advertising and brings the masses into theaters. And where there's a profit to be made, corporations rush to fill the void. They sell products that glorify sexuality and cater to a woman's vanity."

Peter set down his pen. "I see what you're saying, Sister. It's all around us. But I'll admit, as a middle-aged man who couldn't care less about his appearance, I don't feel the same pressure to conform or impress others. My concern, like yours, is with the beauty of the soul. We need look no further than the Virgin Mary, who is the perfect example of femininity. But I'm afraid after two thousand years of being a revered figure, Mary might not speak to modern women, who are being told to admire something else entirely."

"Look at Hollywood," Sister Consuela said, her voice rising, her forehead displaying a sea of worry lines. "Movies today portray beautiful women who are angry at society. The leading lady always takes up with an attractive, like-minded man. They rush into a sexual relationship despite knowing little about each other. It looks romantic on the big screen, but in real life it usually ends in broken relationships and broken hearts. The spirit becomes calloused. If the process repeats enough times, real emotional damage can occur."

"Well," Peter said, "I guess I'd fall back to our religious studies program, which provides the foundation that supports everything we do."

"Ah, the keel metaphor," Sister Consuela said with a chuckle.

Peter chuckled with her. "Yes, the keel metaphor."

Since coming to St. James, Peter had shared his favorite metaphor on more occasions than he could count. Religious studies were the keel of a person's ship, he liked to say, and he was confident the metaphor hit home with families who spent endless summer days at the Cape. Sheltered from the high seas of the open ocean, Cape Cod Bay was the ideal place to learn how to sail, to master the skills of seamanship. As for the keel, thanks to its shape and height, it helped prevent drift and provided stability, just like religious studies. Each student was the captain of his own ship, Peter counseled, and responsible for his own voyage. Wind, current, waves—all mirrored the vicissitudes of life.

"It's a wonderful metaphor," Sister Consuela said, "but . . ." She let the sentence drift as her eyes pointed heavenward. Was she searching her memory or formulating her thoughts? She finally continued. "Acceptable social mores for women are being challenged.

Women are entering the marketplace and beginning careers that traditionally belonged to males. We're still teaching home economics. How does that address today's problems? As society and the demands of the marketplace change, antiquated social models change with them. We've witnessed tremendous change: Woodstock, free love, the antiwar movement. Many young people today reject the precepts of our faith."

Peter, suddenly feeling overwhelmed, held up his hands like a traffic cop directing a driver to stop. "You're giving me a lot to think about. Social pressures, economic pressures. But I think this might be too much for me to digest in one serving!"

Sister Consuela laughed. "Apologies, Father. My passion sometimes gets the better of me." She stood, revealing her tall frame, and walked to the blackboard behind her. "Grab that pen of yours, and we'll go through it point by point."

~~~

Peter returned to his office, his thoughts still cluttered with the subject of vanity and the myriad pressures young women faced on a daily basis. He began to gather his things. It had been a long but productive day, punctuated by his wonderfully instructive meeting with Sister Consuela, and he was ready to retreat to the rectory, where he could ruminate in silence and relative anonymity. With coat and briefcase in hand, he turned to leave, but stopped when he saw Sandra Alvarez standing in the doorway.

"Pardon me, Father," she said. "Do you have a moment?"

"Of course," he said and, setting down his coat and briefcase and returning to his desk. "Come in."

Sandra entered his office and closed the door behind her. With drooping shoulders and downcast face, she looked like a child who'd just learned Christmas had been cancelled.

"My word," Peter said in a hushed voice. "You look positively crestfallen. What happened?"

The first part of her response was unintelligible—a mix of broken syllables and choked-back sobs. But eventually her story came into focus. Bobby had promised to join her in a demonstration for her dance students but had failed to show. With Father Kovacs's help, she'd made the best of it. But the experience had left her feeling embarrassed and chagrined.

"I told everyone he was coming," she said and brushed away a tear. "Well, not the students. It was going to be a surprise for them. But Laurel and Mathilde and Father Kovacs—they were all there to watch. Father Kovacs stepped in for Bobby on the spot and was amazing. It if hadn't been for him, it would have been a total disaster. I feel like a fool."

Peter sensed there was more to Sandra's disappointment than mere public humiliation, horrifying as it might have been, but he knew enough not to push the matter. Instead, he tried to offer Sandra some solace. "You did nothing wrong. In fact, you made a wonderful gesture to include Bobby in your class."

Sandra shook her head. "That's just it. It was *his* idea. I mean, I came to him to ask for his help. But *he* had the idea for the demonstration. He seemed so excited. It was the happiest I've seen him."

And there it was, Peter thought. Sandra was developing feelings for Bobby. His no-show wasn't just disappointing on a professional level; she felt it in a personal way.

"He's your nephew," Sandra said. "I guess I was hoping you could give me some insight. Is it the war? Did he experience some kind of trauma over there?"

Peter leaned back and sighed. He didn't feel at liberty to tell Sandra what Bobby had confided in him, but it was clear she needed something definitive to help her make sense of Bobby's unpredictable behavior. "A soldier's burden is a heavy one. To see war first-hand is to witness unspeakable horrors, butchery on a scale unimaginable. You think you're strong enough to withstand it and move on with your life. But to carry that burden is to live with a kind of corrosive pain that never goes away. It's a wound that never fully heals. The nightmares—"

Sandra stared back at him, her deep blue eyes wide. "Go on."

Peter waved away the request. "I fear I'm no longer talking about Bobby."

"Did you serve in the military, Father?"

"World War Two," he said with a nod. "It was a long time ago, but I think I know a bit about what Bobby's going through."

Sandra looked ready to ask another question but bit her lower lip. Perhaps she understood Peter's reticence to dive too deeply into such dark waters.

Peter thought a moment. "Miss Alvarez, I want to ask you to do something for me."

"Sandra," she said with an affectionate smile.

He chuckled. "Sandra, I need you to do one thing for me."

"What's that?"

"Be patient."

She pulled back slightly, a frown forming on her lips. "Patient?"

"Think of Bobby as a work in progress. He's a fine young man, and he needs people like you in his corner. He will no doubt disappoint us from time to time." Peter thought of Bobby's audition and his upcoming role with the Boston Symphony Orchestra. Would he let down Mr. Bergmann, Jonathan, and everyone now counting on him? The question couldn't be answered. The problem was still in motion, the outcome still a mystery. "All we can do is be patient. Don't give up on him, Sandra. He might surprise us still."

124

Chapter 24

Vice Principal JD Long was among the first to arrive at the weight room the next morning. He'd been keeping track of Richie Sanders's conditioning class, which, according to the assistant baseball coach, had been successful in its core mission: giving non-athletes a chance to excel at a physical activity. That said, Sanders was purportedly having trouble with the cool kids, a small group of boys who deemed it cool to exert minimal effort in everything they did. Such an attitude was clearly a mask, a way to avoid the risk of failure. These were boys who had felt the keen disappointment of underachieving in other areas of their lives, whether academic or social, and were no longer willing to expose themselves to further peril. For them, it was better to assume the guise of indifference, lest they be found unworthy by their peers.

JD took up a position along the back wall in the windowless outbuilding that constituted the school's weight room. It sat next to the athletic fields, a stone's throw from the main campus. Cool-to-the-touch cinderblocks in various shades of gray played backdrop to a jumble of posters, articles, and Xeroxed copies of workouts that had been taped to the walls. Dumbbells, weight benches, and various contraptions competed for space with glossy red mats on the cement floor.

Coach Sanders, wearing a baseball hat and a sleek track suit, entered a moment later and approached JD with his patented dashing smile. "Thanks for stopping in on us, Mr. Vice Principal."

JD shook his hand and found the assistant coach's grip reasonably strong—for someone who was about eight inches shorter and probably one hundred pounds lighter. Not that JD was counting. "Thanks for inviting me."

The students were just beginning to wander into the bunker-shaped building, their faces flushed from the exertion of the brisk walk from the main campus. Some went straight to various machines and began their workouts like seasoned experts. Others loitered about, waiting for friends, perhaps, or some kind of instruction.

"So what's this I hear about a secret weapon?" JD whispered as the last of the students wandered in from the blustery outdoors. He could smell freshly clipped grass on the soles of their shoes.

"You'll see," Coach Sanders said, his eyebrows dancing. He turned to the students. "All right, everybody. Gather 'round."

Those who had already begun their workouts seemed reluctant to interrupt their progress, but they still arrived before the loiterers, who, JD was beginning to sense, were the cool kids Coach Sanders had warned him about.

Once the students had gathered around him, the coach motioned for one of them to join him in the center of the semicircle. "All right, class. Most of you know Sarah Conway. She's volunteered to be my new assistant."

Standing a petite five feet, three inches, if that, and weighing no more than one hundred and twenty pounds, Sarah took a step forward and grinned, revealing a perfectly straight set of teeth and a winning smile. JD, like probably everyone there, instantly recognized the star sprinter from the girls' track team. Sarah, one of the most popular students at St. James, was impossible not to admire. Along with being an extremely gifted athlete, she was a bright-eyed beauty whose optimism and confidence were contagious. A champion of the meek and the downtrodden, she made everybody around her feel better about

126

themselves. Now here she was, clad in her track warm-ups, ready to demonstrate for the class.

"Brilliant!" JD whispered under his breath.

"Sarah here is going to walk us through a handful of exercises and show us proper form," Coach Sanders said of the spunky blonde.

What followed was a master demonstration in proper technique. Posture. Form. Breathing. Sarah attacked each exercise with determination and enthusiasm, and while she exhibited the finer points of hand placement and spinal alignment, the too-cool-for-exercise boys watched in muted wonder. Coach Sanders had just instituted a clever policy of subtle intimidation, and Sarah was his finely honed instrument of delivery. Along with capturing their attention, she was no doubt appealing to their collective male ego, which, no matter how diffident, could not be bested by a girl, even if that girl happened to be one of the fastest sprinters in the state of Massachusetts. If she could lift more than her body weight while completing ten reps on the leg-press machine, surely they could too.

After the show was over, Coach Sanders took aside the cool boys, draping his arm over the shoulders of two of them as he spoke. "All right, boys. Sarah is going to be your personal trainer. She's going to pace you through your workouts, help each of you establish a baseline, and oversee your progress. She's in charge, so whatever she says goes, all right?"

The boys nodded, clearly too intimidated to do anything but agree.

"Great," Coach Sanders said. "Get to it!" He left the boys to Sarah's care and then turned to JD with a look of mischief playing on his grinning lips. "What do you think?"

JD could only shake his head in amazement. "I think those kids are going to whip themselves into shape—or die trying."

~~~

Halloween fell on a Friday that year. Peter passed a pirate, a clown, and a ghoul on his way to Sister Consuela's classroom that afternoon. Two days had passed since their meeting, and since then he'd spent much of his time deliberating and praying. He'd been given an important opportunity and was determined to do right by his audience.

Sister Consuela introduced him to her eighth-period health class, which was comprised entirely of eleventh-grade girls.

"Father Ryan and I engaged in a rather interesting conversation the other day," she began. "We spoke about the daily pressures young women face. Along with trying to excel in the classroom, in athletics, and in other extracurricular activities, many of you are under great strain to meet the expectations of modern society." Sister Consuela pressed an invisible wrinkle from her habit. "And those expectations are changing. A woman's role has never been more challenging. The world of my youth is long gone. Your challenges are far different. I invited Father Ryan to speak to you today in the hopes that he might help you navigate this new world."

The girls clapped politely, and Peter, who had been standing off to the side near the doorway, took his place at the front of the brightly lit classroom. He smiled at Greta Gronkowski, who stared back at him expectantly, and then Jenny O'Donnell, who, to his immense satisfaction, met his gaze with confidence in her eyes. The formerly shy student seemed to be coming out of her shell, despite—or perhaps because of—all that she'd been through in the past few months. Sarah Conway, bright-eyed and smiling broadly, sat in the front row alongside Carol Major, Charles's precocious daughter.

"I want to begin by pointing out the obvious," he said. "I'm a man—and a priest to boot!"

A few of the girls giggled.

"What that means is that I can only empathize with the

challenges you face; I can never walk in your shoes. Be that as it may, please know that I *do* empathize." He glanced at Sister Consuela, who had swapped places with him and was standing near the door, now closed, with her hands together in front of her, a warm smile on her face. "Sister Consuela and I spoke at length about the pressures you face. Your parents say you should act one way. Hollywood says you should act another. Everywhere you go, you received mixed messages: from your peers, from the billboards you pass on the side of the highway, from the glitzy ads in your favorite magazine. These mixed messages produce stress and anxiety. Should I do this or that? Act this way or that way?

"If it's any consolation, please know that you're not alone. And your situation is not unique. Every generation is challenged with determining its own role in the arc of history. And every individual is challenged with determining his or her own response to the forces of change. Will you bend with the wind or stand tall in your faith? If you're feeling confused, that's okay. So are your friends. So are your parents. So am I, frankly."

The girls laughed again, this time a little more heartily.

"This just adds to the anxiety, doesn't it? If everyone's struggling to keep up with the times, who can we look to for wise counsel? Who can we emulate?"

As he spoke, Peter thought he saw recognition on some of the girls' faces. Were they seeing themselves in the challenges he was discussing? Were they finding comfort in the universality of their plight? He had a hunch he was articulating forces and emotions that they'd thus far been unable to put to words. Perhaps it was frowned upon by tradition, but he preferred to speak to the girls as equals—or at least as aspiring equals. He wanted them to know that he respected them, not just to boost their confidence but to give them ownership in their growth and maturation. Ultimately each student would be responsible for the path she took. He could only offer a bit of wisdom and the occasional gentle course correction.

"I saw an ad the other day," he continued. "It was for a cigarette manufacturer. It showed an attractive woman in a rather lurid pose and read, 'Cigarettes are like women. The best ones are thin and rich.' Another ad—I think it was for Tipalet cigarettes—showed a man blowing smoke into a beautiful woman's face. It said something about her being willing to follow him anywhere." Peter shook his head. "Because the man blew smoke in her face!"

The girls were no longer laughing. Concern appeared to be tugging at the corners of their mouths, which were slowly bending into frowns.

"Or how about this one?" Peter asked. "I saw it in *Life* magazine. It showed a woman in what appeared to be a space suit. She had long eyelashes and pouty lips like Raquel Welch or some other Hollywood star. She was holding a bottle of Lestoil cleaner. The ad read, 'Women of the future will make the Moon a cleaner place to live.'" Peter had been pacing as he spoke, and stopped in front of Sarah Conway's desk. "Sarah, what does this ad say to you?"

Sarah, who always projected a cheerful countenance, looked confused, her smile long having faded. "Well, I guess it's telling me I should be beautiful."

"What else?" Peter asked.

Sarah shrugged and looked away. "That it's my job to clean up after people."

The other girls were nodding, some grumbling, all sober-faced.

"We hear a lot these days about 'free love' and 'women's lib,'" Peter said. "But this woman doesn't sound very free or liberated, does she?"

Peter spent the next several minutes reviewing the contents of Sister Consuela's bulletin points—peer pressure, fashion, movies, female role models. As he neared the end of class, he opened the floor for questions. An eye-opening discussion ensued, with the girls venting about various pressures they faced and Peter doing his best not to interrupt the flow of ideas and anecdotes.

When they were nearly out of time, Greta Gronkowski raised her hand and spoke. "No one has ever discussed these things with us before, Father. I don't think my parents understand this."

Peter wasn't sure whether to feel dismayed or relieved. On the one hand, Greta had confirmed what he feared most: these girls were alone with their problems. On the other hand, she'd also just implied that his lecture had given the girls a much-needed forum.

The chimes rang out, bringing class to an end, and Sister Consuela was quick to assume the reins. "How 'bout we invite Father Ryan back on Monday to lead another class?"

The girls, who were busily packing up their books and belongings, stopped to cheer.

Chapter 25

Peter spent the whole weekend preparing, making notes, reading scripture, and digging for relevant information. By the time Monday afternoon rolled around and he was again standing in front of Sister Consuela's class, he was ready to rally the girls once more.

But then a funny thing happened. Just a few paragraphs into his finely honed lecture, he realized he was no longer connecting with his audience. He glanced at the girls in the front row. Sarah Conway was doodling on the back of her notebook. Carol Major was fighting off a yawn. No one appeared to appreciate his eagerness to review last week's discussion points before plunging into a wide-ranging discussion of female role models.

He looked at his index cards, studying the next one in line, and then stopped. For a brief moment, a wave of terror washed over him— the kind that only someone groping for a way forward in front of a critical audience can fully grasp. But a second later, he found comfort in a distant memory, and just like that, he was ready to lead again, although not in the way he'd planned.

"I remember one time," he said, wiping away the beads of sweat that had begun to form on his forehead, "I was sitting in the parlor with my mother and my older sister, Susan. I was a young boy. Maybe eight years old. Mother was teaching Susan about needlepoint. While they talked, I spotted a basket full of needlepoint projects my mother had already completed. I reached into the basket and pulled one out to examine her artwork, and suddenly it hit me: needlepoint was a manifestation of my mother's love. It was as if I were holding her

132

loving heart in my hands. I turned over the project repeatedly, studying every aspect of her work. It was a thing of beauty, created by my mother's hands."

Once again the girls were with him—eyes up, chins forward.

He plunged ahead, not willing to waste the moment. "Who here has seen needlepoint art being created?"

Jenny, seated in the back, raised her hand. "My mom loved needlepoint. So did my grandmother."

"Did they portray particular images or patterns?" Peter asked.

"Mostly images. Home, family, pets, flowers—that kind of thing. I often watched my mother as she worked. She had really slender hands. *Graceful.*" Jenny looked momentarily lost in the memory, her eyes cast to the side as if searching the past. Then she continued. "They were beautiful. My grandmother's, on the other hand—they looked worn and weathered, which always made me think of all the years she'd been creating art."

Peter was almost afraid to interrupt. "Did you ever flip over their needlepoint and look at the back?"

"Yes," Jenny said with an impish smile. "It looked like a mess!"

Her classmates laughed, and Peter joined them.

"Indeed, it always does," he said. "Both Mom and Grandma had a picture in mind before starting their projects, correct?"

Jenny nodded.

"Did they modify their project as the work continued?"

"Sure," Jenny said.

Peter took a deep breath. He didn't want to rush to the main point, but he could hardly contain himself. Would they make the connection? Finally, he spoke. "Our lives are very much like needlepoint art. First, we conceptualize what our life will look like, and make the necessary decisions for the beautiful picture to become a reality. If we make a mistake, we correct it. Some mistakes require more time to correct, but they can still be corrected—and we learn not to make the same mistake again. Our skill and speed increase as the work progresses. It may look a bit messy on a day-to-day basis, and we may experience some frustration, but eventually the beauty of our art becomes a reality."

Jenny was nodding and smiling, and soon the other students appeared to have internalized the story. Greta cocked her head to the side. Sarah leaned back in her seat, her gaze unfocused as she seemed to grapple with the metaphor.

"If we honor our vision," Peter said, "we can make something beautiful."

~~~

Peter returned to his office to find Ed Kowalski seated across from his cluttered desk.

The stout football coach stood to greet him. "Hello, Father. Just wanted to drop this off with you before I head out to practice." He handed Peter a $100,000 Bar. "It's the last one, and it's on me."

Peter couldn't hold back an amazed smile as he accepted the gift. "Your team sold all those bars?"

"Every last one," Coach Kowalski said. "The boys did good."

"Congratulations, Coach."

Coach Kowalski rubbed his mostly bald head. "All told, we sold four thousand bars. Forty-four kids on the team, so that's almost one hundred bars per player, although some did better than others. As you know, I gave all the proceeds to the school. This here's an investment in our future."

Peter rested a hand on Coach Kowalski's shoulder. "That's awfully generous of you, Ed. Everyone at St. James thanks you."

Coach Kowalski's sunburned face turned a deeper shade of red. "I'll admit, my motives are selfish. Our kids are all grown and moved out, but we've still got a mortgage to pay, my wife and I. Can't do that without a job. Coaching football and teaching PE keeps a roof over our heads."

Peter realized that he hadn't thought nearly enough about what a school closure would mean for the staff at St. James. He'd been so caught up in the students, the school's long history, and its connection to the community, that he'd all but forgotten the economic plight of its teachers, coaches, and administrative workers.

"Well, I've got a bunch of rambunctious teenagers waiting for someone to tell them what to do," Coach Kowalski said, turning to leave.

Peter's mind raced. He wanted to reassure the man, to somehow lighten his burden, but he could only nod apologetically.

The coach had hardly disappeared when Peter's nose detected a familiar scent. Maria Donatello entered a moment later and sat in the now-vacant chair.

"Did you hear any of that?" Peter asked.

Maria nodded. "Impressive feat—selling all those chocolate bars."

Peter paced to his window and gazed outside at the sugar maples, which were turning iridescent red. "It makes you want to extend yourself further, doesn't it? Turn over every rock. Chase down every available penny."

Maria offered a stoic frown. "Pennies won't save this school."

"Perhaps not."

Peter felt a strange sense of calm overtaking him as he sat behind his desk. He hadn't thought much about the school's financial problems lately, mostly because he'd been caught up in doing what he was there to do: administrate, facilitate, educate. But he found Ed Kowalski's dogged efforts, though insufficient by themselves, somehow reassuring. Countless people had a stake in St. James, and not just those on the school's payroll. St. James was a treasure to the whole community, and Peter had faith that its value would ultimately prevail.

He looked up at Maria and offered a hopeful smile. "Don't count us out just yet."

~~~

Sandra put the girls—and two boys, thanks to Father Kovacs's heroic performance—through the usual paces that afternoon at dance class. With the weather growing chillier, the gym felt draftier every day. Sandra used each warm-up session to put her thoughts in order. She'd hoped to jumpstart the class with Bobby's help, but it was almost better this way. Attendance had stabilized, allowing her to focus on the task at hand: winning one convert at a time. The girls were no longer a regular target of the baseball players, most of whom seemed better behaved now as they waited in the bleachers. And interest and support from others on the faculty remained strong. Today, Father Kovacs once again sat in the front row, a book under his arm.

Sandra was about to introduce the students to their first Latin beat when she heard it: a buzz in the bleachers not unlike the hum coming from an electrical appliance. She turned and saw Bobby Jones standing in the double doorway. Everything about him—his long hair and sideburns, his handlebar mustache, his swagger—set him apart from the boys in the bleachers. Garbed in blue jeans, a black T-shirt, and a pair of black, leather-soled shoes, he didn't have to abide by the school's dress code. His reputation as a grizzled, if troubled, veteran of the war in Vietnam was currency among the baseball team, many of whom would enter the draft after graduation. He was, in the lingo of the students, a "bad-ass," and Sandra had to work hard to hide the grin forming on her lips.

He sauntered her way and then, stopping directly in front of her, spoke just loud enough for her to hear. "I owe you an apology."

She felt her face burn with embarrassment. Although tempted to ask why he'd been a no-show three weeks earlier, she simply

136

whispered, "Better late than never."

Indeed, with the others watching her every move, she thought it best to focus on the here and now. As it was, she'd never been one to hold a grudge.

"You still want to show these kids how to dance?"

She nodded and threw a glance to her sister. Sandra hoped she remembered which song to play. To her relief, Sister Consuela was already taking the record from its sleeve.

Sandra turned to her students. "Class, today we have a very special guest. Bobby Jones is here to help demonstrate the foxtrot."

The sound of static as the needle hit vinyl was followed by the first horn stabs of Frank Sinatra's "The Way You Look Tonight."

Sandra, no longer able to suppress her smile, gracefully extended her left hand to Bobby. "Shall we demonstrate?"

Bobby looked like cool personified as he took her hand, and a moment later the two were gliding across the hardwoods together, moving as one. As Sinatra's smooth-as-pudding voice echoed off the rafters, Sandra focused on each move. She spun away from Bobby and then rejoined him, and with her hands entwined in his, stole the occasional glance at their audience. The girls looked starry-eyed, and the boys stared with mouths agape.

The song lasted all of three minutes and twenty seconds, after which the gymnasium fell silent. Before doubt could creep into Sandra's mind, the baseball players jumped to their feet for a standing ovation, shaking the bleachers in the process. The girls, too, were cheering—so loudly that Sandra could only laugh in delight and astonishment.

She waited for the excitement to subside and then addressed the baseball team. "Are there any young men who would like to learn what Mr. Jones just demonstrated?"

The boys, exuberant before, sank to the bleachers and traded blank stares, each no doubt hoping someone else would volunteer.

That someone was the prankster himself, Mike Zuk. The center fielder took his feet, trotted noisily down the bleachers, and joined Sandra and Bobby on the floor. "I'm game."

"Great!" Sandra said. "Would you like to choose a partner?"

With his chin up and eyes showing something akin to chivalry, Mike looked in the direction of Greta, who was leaning against the balance beam like someone too afraid to believe she was worthy. "Greta Gronkowski."

Greta's eyes widened in disbelief, but once she'd absorbed the shock, she straightened and hurried to join them on the dance floor. Just like that, the bleachers emptied, and the boys began finding partners.

It was around the time Coach Dean normally began gathering his team for warmups, but when Sandra turned toward him, he waved her off. The coach and his assistant, Richie Sanders, looked eager to see what might happen. Baseball, after all, required a similar skillset as dancing—agility, grace, and quick feet.

Thus, the dance club, though still in its infancy, was reborn at St. James High.

Sandra grabbed Bobby's hand. "We did it!" she exclaimed, marveling at what they'd accomplished.

He squeezed her hand in return. "We sure did."

Out of the corner of her eye, Sandra spotted Father Kovacs, still seated in the bleachers, the thick textbook he'd brought with him resting beside him now. Their eyes met, and she felt a pang of guilt. Did he feel jilted or disappointed that his efforts had been eclipsed by a younger, flashier volunteer?

Her fears vanished when a broad smile appeared on his face and he gave her a thumbs-up.

Chapter 26

Two weeks before Thanksgiving, on a Wednesday evening in the school cafeteria, Peter was elbows deep in sudsy dishwater at the stainless steel industrial-sized sink. He glanced over his shoulder at the enormous clock on the far wall and saw that it was almost ten o'clock. Thirty minutes had passed since the raffle and bake sale had come to an end and the final guests had departed. One of the student volunteers cleaning the cafeteria had turned on a radio, and Peter could hear the final stanza of The Archies' "Sugar, Sugar" coming through the crack in the kitchen door. He wasn't a fan of rock and roll but nevertheless found himself tapping his foot in time with the bouncy song.

The student volunteers, meanwhile, sang along, their voices rising above the music.

The boys sang the main part: "Oh, sugar! Pour a little sugar on it, honey! Pour a little sugar on it, baby!"

Then the girls came in for the soprano line: "I'm gonna make your life so sweet!"

The kids erupted in laughter as they sang the final lines in unison: "Yeah, yeah, yeah! Pour a little sugar on it, honey!"

Was he feeling optimistic? Peter thought so. They'd raffled off several items, including movie tickets, gift certificates, and the beach house weekend getaway, and had sold, among other baked goods, two dozen Bundt cakes, fourteen fudge cakes, six banana cream pies, and more cookies and cupcakes than he could count. In the process, they'd made a mountain of dirty cups and saucers, courtesy of the coffee and

139

tea provided by the Booster Club. Judging by the size of the enormous punch bowl, which had arrived at the sink with nary a drop left in it, the night had been a success.

"We did well," Maria Donatello said over his shoulder, startling him.

"Really?" Peter threw a disbelieving glance at her. She was standing just inside the doorway, hands on her hips, hair pulled back in a bun, a smile on her lips.

"Well, technically, we didn't do as well as the football team with their candy bars," she said. "But if your friend Mr. Bloom hadn't offered a weekend on the Cape, I doubt we would have had so many people enter the raffle."

Peter chuckled. "Yes, that was awfully generous of him." He thought a moment. "I'll admit I'm surprised to hear you singing such a happy tune."

Maria offered a barely perceptible grin and shrugged. "It must be the kids. They're so full of energy. It's contagious."

"If they only knew what was at stake," Peter mused. "Do you think they can sense the precariousness of our situation?"

"I bet they can. Besides, word travels fast around here. You know that. They probably know all about our 'situation.'"

Peter marveled at the thought. "And yet here they are, dancing and singing as they work."

"Give 'em another decade. Once they have careers and children of their own, they'll be just as tired as the rest of us."

Peter laughed. St. James was in a constant state of renewal. After each class of seniors graduated and ventured forth to make its mark on the world, a new crop of freshman arrived to begin the cycle all over again. Whenever he despaired at the state of the world or at the contents of his own heart, he remembered the inexhaustible supply of hope that was the St. James student body.

Eddie Romano, the football team's hulking tight end, appeared behind Maria in the doorway. He was holding a pile of bunting, neatly stacked in his burly arms. "What do you want me to do with this?"

With his hands already spoken for, Peter nodded toward the nearby counter. "You can just set it there. Someone from the Booster Club will be by to pick it up."

"Sure thing, Father."

Eddie unburdened himself and disappeared from the kitchen a moment later. Maria soon followed.

Alone again, with only the dishes and the music to keep him company, Peter whistled along to Marvin Gaye's soulful version of "I Heard It Through the Grapevine."

~~~

"He'll be with you in a moment," Gayle Fallows said from the doorway.

"Thank you," Peter said and watched her turn and leave.

As Peter sat down in Bishop Woodbury's luxurious office, he could almost feel himself shrinking in the plush chair he'd been offered. Leather-bound books stood side by side on mahogany shelves. Sacred artwork hung from the walls. A pair of wall sconces glowed warmly, the net effect being one of refinement and repose. If Peter's office was a disaster zone, the bishop's was a monument to high-brow organization. A tornado had blown through the former, a compulsive maid the latter.

Peter stood when the bishop entered. "Bishop Woodbury. How are you?"

Bishop Walt Woodbury, a tall, angular man with just enough charisma to make up for his oft brusque demeanor, smiled down at Peter, who suddenly felt conscious of the height disparity between them. The lanky bishop stood a good four inches taller. "Just fine, Father. It's good to see you."

141

After offering a perfunctory handshake, Bishop Woodbury took a seat behind his enormous, clutter-free desk. The ocean of mahogany between them gleamed in the late-morning light that poured through three tall windows.

Peter lowered himself once more to his seat and steadied himself with a deep breath. "So . . . you wanted to see me?"

"Yes, I was hoping to hear how you're fundraising is coming along at St. James. I recognize that it's only November, but it seems you've had enough time to settle on an approach of some sort, if not an outright plan."

Peter wasn't surprised at the inquiry, just the timing. He'd expected the demand for answers to come earlier. But perhaps the bishop had decided to give him some time to work on a solution.

"I guess you could say we're leaving no stone unturned," Peter finally answered. "Kind of an all-hands-on-deck approach."

Bishop Woodbury frowned, his graying eyebrows meeting below his mostly bald head. "Well, you've certainly got your clichés in order."

It was the first dig of their meeting. Would there be more? Peter tried to ignore it. "We just had a bake sale and raffle last night. My good friend Jonathan Bloom was generous enough to donate a weekend at his family's beach house. And Coach Kowalski—I'm sure you've met him—did quite a job with his football team. They sold chocolate bars and raised more than—"

Bishop Woodbury held up a hand to silence him. "Are you telling me your plan to raise five hundred thousand dollars is to sell chocolate bars and weekend getaways?"

"No, of course not. But every little bit helps. It's beautiful to see everyone contributing, and as far as I can tell, it's doing wonders for school morale."

The bishop looked bored. "Please tell me you have something

more that I can take to the archbishop. Otherwise, we might as well start planning the merger now."

Peter forced a smile. He didn't want to sound desperate—or ruffled by the bishop's dismissive tone. "We still have a fundraising dinner in the works for early next year. We're planning on inviting alumni from all over the community. And I'm personally going to find a company to act as a matching donor. Whatever we raise will therefore be doubled."

The bishop remained straight-faced, so Peter pushed on with his best sales pitch.

"And of course, we're still holding out hope that we can find a new backer, someone with deep pockets who can make up the shortfall."

"I see," the bishop replied with skepticism. "And who might that be?"

"Antonio Federici."

The bishop raised an eyebrow. "Well, that would certainly be a coup for you. Is he willing?"

Peter sank deeper into his seat. He wasn't in the habit of attributing negative thoughts to others, but it seemed clear Bishop Woodbury wasn't just holding Peter's feet to the fire. The man wanted St. James to fail. Indeed, it seemed he was *planning* on it.

"We haven't spoken with him yet."

"And why not?"

"He's out of the country at the moment. But we plan to meet with him as soon as he returns."

The bishop nodded. More skepticism. More boredom. He glanced at the ceiling a moment, as though gathering his thoughts, then leveled his gaze at Peter. "The archbishop is still giving you until the end of June to make up the shortfall at St. James—that's not much more than seven months from now. Frankly, I doubt such a feat is possible, but it's obvious the archbishop wasn't put off by my lobbying on your behalf. That, or he has a soft spot for your little school. Either way, Father, I suggest you keep knocking on doors. Perhaps one will open to you."

Chapter 27

Peter sat in an aisle seat in the middle of the half-full auditorium, the lights still on, his thoughts unfocused. Thanksgiving had come and gone, and one of his favorite holiday rituals, the annual Christmas concert at St. James, was scheduled to begin in less than an hour, leaving him in a giddy state of restlessness. The choir and orchestra had prepared selections from Handel's *Messiah*, no doubt a challenging piece for the young singers and musicians. Peter viewed the exquisite choral work as a window into scripture, its libretto evoking the most sublime imagery. For Peter, the libretto —in this case scripture—*was* medicine for the soul, and magnificent music was the vehicle to most effectively deliver the medicine. Exposure to scripture and classical music was never time wasted, for it seeded hearts and minds with transcendent truths that would flower unexpectedly in the future. Families, friends, students, faculty—all would be exposed to Handel's masterpiece tonight, some perhaps for the first time.

But Peter had barely gotten comfortable in his seat when he spotted Mathilde Weaver scurrying toward him, panic written all over the music teacher's face.

"We have a problem," she said in a hushed voice as soon as she reached his aisle.

Peter leaned forward. "What is it?"

"Erik can't make so much as a noise. He's lost his voice!"

"Laryngitis?"

The diminutive teacher nodded anxiously. "He says he was fine

145

just an hour ago."

Erik Twombly, along with playing second base on the baseball team, was the choir's star tenor. He was known for his quick reflexes, split-second-decision-making abilities, and melodious voice. Bobby had been helping him prepare for this performance. His presence in the choir, at least in Peter's estimation, lent a certain credibility to the enterprise due to his popularity among his classmates. Many people would be coming tonight just to hear him sing.

"Who will perform the opening movement?" Peter asked, trying in vain to sound calm.

Mathilde, perhaps anticipating the question, didn't pause to think it over. "I only know one person who could step in at this point."

Peter smiled in relief as soon as he realized where she was guiding him. "Bobby Jones! Vocal coach turned understudy. I think it's delightful."

Mathilde wrung her hands. "Do you think people will object?"

"There's only one way to find out," Peter said with a shrug of his shoulders.

Mathilde was already scurrying back the way she'd come, no doubt to ask Bobby if he'd consider stepping into the part he'd prepped Erik to sing. Peter was confident Bobby would agree. Otherwise, how could the concert go on? In the past few weeks, not only had Bobby warmed to his volunteer position at St. James, he had, according to Jonathan, thus far made good—and then some—on his contract with Mr. Bergmann and the Boston Symphony Orchestra. One-on-one, Bobby was still as evasive and enigmatic as ever, but on stage and in the choir room, he was quickly earning a reputation as a dependable professional.

Jonathan and his wife, Rachael, joined Peter, who had been holding seats for them. Peter filled them in on the news as the auditorium filled to capacity. A few minutes later, folding chairs were brought out to accommodate the overflow crowd, which was buzzing with anticipation. Peter searched the room and spotted Mathilde chatting with Sandra, Laurel, and Sister Consuela in the first row. The four women looked nervous but excited.

When the lights finally dimmed, Mathilde walked up the stairs and took center stage. "Thank you all for coming," she announced as soon as the crowd quieted. "We're sorry to inform you that Erik Twombly, the choir's lead tenor, has fallen ill with laryngitis and will be unable to perform." A smattering of groans greeted the announcement, but Mathilde pressed on. "Bobby Jones will be performing in his place."

The mood quickly changed to curiosity, even intrigue. Many in the crowd knew Bobby personally, or at least knew *of* him. They knew his story, which meant they knew of his service in Vietnam. They also knew he'd kept to himself since returning home. He was a mystery of sorts, and this last-minute development no doubt added to his mystique. Peter wondered how many in the crowded auditorium had heard Bobby sing. Probably precious few.

Concert master Andy Marecek stepped onto the stage, and the audience applauded. After the orchestra tuned its instruments, Mathilde and Bobby took center stage to an enthusiastic welcome. Bobby, dressed in black slacks, a white dress shirt, and a black jacket, looked calm and confident. Handsome, if a bit rough-edged, he exuded the perfect blend of eagerness and humility. His stage presence was undeniable.

The orchestra intoned the first notes of the *Messiah's* overture, ornate and rhythmic, setting the stage for the remarkable spiritual journey ahead. Then Bobby stepped forward and delivered the opening lines:

Comfort ye, comfort ye my people, saith your God.

Speak ye comfortably to Jerusalem,
and cry unto her, that her warfare is accomplished,
that her iniquity is pardoned.

The voice of him that crieth in the wilderness;
prepare ye the way of the Lord; make straight in the desert a
highway for our God.

The libretto came to life, and as Peter looked on, he felt as if the
Holy Spirit were pouring forth from Bobby's injured soul, bringing
peace and solace to him and the audience. With each note, he appeared
to let go of the hurt, anger, and despair that had shackled him since
returning from the war.

The tenor aria immediately followed:

Every valley shall be exalted,
and every mountain and hill made low;
the crooked straight and the rough places plain.

Ebullient. Virtuosic. The aria imparted hopeful anticipation of
Christ's birth and God's entrance into human history, which marked
the dawn of a new era and a new understanding of love that surpassed
what had come before it. Peter felt lost in Bobby's suffering, which,
laid bare for all to see, brought to life the true meaning of the text.

After the final note had been delivered, Bobby quietly walked
down the steps in the dim auditorium and took a seat in the front row
beside Sandra. As was tradition with sacred compositions, applause
would be held until the end. But the crowd's stark silence told Peter
that he wasn't the only one almost afraid to exhale. Bobby's
performance had been riveting.

Bobby nodded to the orchestra and conductor, conveying

something akin to gratitude, and the orchestra and choir followed the aria with an uplifting chorus punctuated with joy:

And the Glory of the Lord shall be revealed,
and all flesh shall see it together:
for the mouth of the Lord hath spoken it.

Mrs. Reid's elementary school chorus joined the high school choir and sang "Silent Night" for the closing piece. The fourth and final stanza ended with a soprano descant that stunned Peter. The children joined the sopranos, and together they produced a fragile, ethereal effect that left a tear in Peter's eye, for he felt blessed, surrounded by love, and acutely aware of the transitory reality of life.

~~~

A week later, Peter sat in an easy chair across from Jonathan in the Blooms' cozy living room, the heat from the fire warming his face. They'd just enjoyed a sumptuous dinner of chicken paprikash paired with Grüner Veltliner, an Austrian white wine, followed by Viennese pastries and Turkish coffee. Now Rachael, their erstwhile cook, was joining them by the fire.

"Wasn't that a wonderful performance by Bobby at the Christmas concert?" Jonathan asked, his eyes seemingly held fast by the flames in the fireplace.

"I recognized several lines from the book of Isaiah," Rachael said. "Do you think Bobby found them cathartic?"

Peter nodded along with Jonathan, who stood and walked to the liquor cabinet.

Rachael aimed her next question at Peter. "Who was that stunning brunette Bobby sat next to after his performance? She's absolutely lovely. Do you think Bobby noticed her?"

Peter exchanged grins with Jonathan, who was already returning

149

from the liquor cabinet with a bottle of armagnac in his right hand and three glasses in his left.

"You two are being naughty," Rachael said, twisting her lips into a mock frown. Dressed in navy-blue slacks and an ivory silk blouse, she'd pulled her long blonde hair back but had long since discarded her apron. "Who is this beauty, Peter?"

"She's extraordinary, isn't she? Her name is Sandra Alvarez. We're privileged to have her as our new English teacher."

"Do you think there's a chance of getting her and Bobby together?"

Jonathan had just finished filling all three glasses and, grinning, handed the first one to Rachael. "That might knock Bobby out of his funk."

Rachael rolled her eyes. "You're being bad, Jonathan."

The three sat silently for a while as the shrunken oak logs, now not much more than glowing embers, hissed softly in the fireplace, occasionally launching a spark with a perfunctory pop.

Peter could hear the wind rattling the windowpane behind him and dreaded the thought of ducking into a cold automobile for the ride home. He stared at the fire a moment and then glanced up at Rachael, who looked deep in thought. Rachael, never one to sit idly by when relationships could be kindled or repaired, was clearly ruminating over Bobby and Sandra. She loved Bobby as much as Jonathan and Peter and was no doubt hatching a plan of some kind that would bring her matchmaking skills to the fore.

Though it would have been bad form, Peter was tempted to tell Rachael what he suspected: Sandra already appeared interested in Bobby on more than a professional level.

Chapter 28

Christmas break ended January 5, 1970, the first Monday of the New Year. Peter entered the faculty lounge that morning and rubbed his hands together for warmth. Outside, the snow had stopped falling, the streets had been plowed, and the sun was shining weakly. Inside, the air was still chilly as the school's ancient radiators slowly came to life. A new decade was upon them, and Peter was eager to share a bit of good news.

"Good morning, everyone," he said as the others gathered round.

Someone had rearranged the sofas, which now formed a U in the center of the lounge. Several chairs were scattered behind them.

Peter stood in the front and smiled. "I wanted to let you know that I've found a matching giver for the dinner fundraiser: the Merrimac Paper Company."

Vice Principal JD Long nodded his approval as he lowered his enormous frame onto the couch to Peter's left. "Nice work, Father. Merrimac is a fitting sponsor. They've been around forever."

Indeed, the owner of several paper mills in the region had roots that ran deeper than St. James's. Peter had assumed he'd have his work cut out for him in approaching the storied company, but a visit to the mill on the other side of the Merrimac River had earned him an audience with the company's new public relations officer, a young man fresh out of college who had instantly warmed to the idea of participating in the fundraiser at St. James.

Peter blew on his hands, which he was still rubbing together.

"We owe a debt of gratitude to Coach Kowalski and the football team. Between their efforts and the raffle, we've already earned over six thousand dollars."

Coach Kowalski, wedged between Coach Dean and the vice principal, waved off the acknowledgment, his freshly shaved face turning a shade of pink.

"The dinner fundraiser," Peter continued, "is only five weeks away. I'm open to any and all ideas on how we can best prepare."

Sister Consuela and Mathilde Weaver spoke one after another, each offering ideas on how to make the most of the opportunity, but Peter found himself distracted by Sandra Alvarez, who was seated directly across from where he stood. Rachael's suggestion—that the dark-haired beauty might be able to soothe Bobby's pain—had stuck with him since his dinner with the Blooms. Peter was no matchmaker and had little knowledge of romantic relationships, but he'd sensed the same potential between his troubled nephew and the young English teacher. In fact, unless Peter had read things incorrectly, Sandra's visit to his office a month earlier had suggested that she felt something for Bobby. At present, Sandra was giving Mathilde an earnest listen, her face showing a depth of concentration that suggested she, too, was highly invested in the fundraiser's success. Her attentiveness was the mark of a serious person; Bobby would need just such a friend at his side if he were to have any hope of liberating his heart from the ghosts of war.

When the ideas slowed to a trickle and finally a stop, Peter glanced at his watch and saw that first period was about to begin. "I don't want to hold you any longer. I know you have places to be. Welcome back, everyone. May Christ be with you in this new year."

~~~

Dance class was almost finished Wednesday afternoon when Bobby Jones made another surprise appearance in the gymnasium.

Sandra did a double-take when she saw him in the doorway. He was wearing black slacks, not his usual blue jeans, and had shaved his mustache and cut his hair. Dressed in a maroon turtleneck and sporting black leather wingtips, he looked like he'd just stepped off the pages of *Gentleman's Quarterly*, or *GQ*, as the magazine had recently rebranded itself.

"Oh my," Sandra murmured.

Most of the students, busily pairing up for the day's last dance, didn't seem to notice his entrance.

Bobby sauntered toward Sandra and then, stopping a few feet short, made a half twirl and raised his palms. "What do you think?"

Sandra tried to act nonchalant, but the words that came out of her mouth told the truth. "I think you clean up nicely."

He offered a devilish smile. "Finished up early with the choir. Thought I'd drop in for a visit."

"As usual, Mr. Jones, you never fail to surprise me." She returned his smile. "Speaking of which, I loved your performance of Handel's *Messiah* with the Boston Symphony Orchestra."

He lifted an eyebrow. "You were there?"

"Yes. It was beautiful, and very inspiring. As you could tell, the audience loved it too. I imagine Mr. Bergman must be eager to have you back sometime."

Bobby shrugged modestly. "That's what he says. I have to admit that . . ." He paused. "Well, it was inspiring for me too. But no more than my work with the St. James choir. I have to say, I really like working with the kids."

Sandra gestured to the record player. "You're just in time. They're about to dance the foxtrot. Should we give them another demonstration?"

Bobby pumped his eyebrows. "What's playing?"

"Dean Martin," Sandra said. "'Ain't That a Kick in the Head?'"

Bobby nodded. "Sounds like a gas. I'm in."

Sandra walked over to the record player, which sat on a table near one of the few outlets in the gym, and turned to the students. "Everybody ready?"

The students appeared to have finally noticed Bobby and were wide-eyed and tittering with excitement. "Ready!" several called out.

"Okay," Sandra announced as she lowered the needle to the record player. "Here we go!"

Horns blared over a swing beat, and a moment later, Dean Martin's melodic baritone filled the cold gymnasium like warm water rising in a bath. Sandra closed her eyes. When she opened them, she was spinning in Bobby's arms. They skimmed the floor, feet moving in unison, every movement in tandem with the walking bass line and the dynamic snare drum, the latter chugging along in the background during the verses and popping as loud as the horns during the choruses.

My head keeps spinning.
I go to sleep and keep grinning.
If this is just the beginning,
My life is gonna be beautiful.

Heat rushed to her face. Was this a demonstration or something else? Were the students staring? She ignored the goosebumps forming on her skin and instead followed Bobby's lead. He seemed more confident, more engaged than he'd ever been, but behind those deep brown eyes she saw something rough that needed smoothing, something wild that needed taming. Was it pain? Fear? Both? Bobby Jones had cultivated an air of mystery about himself, but she knew it was purely a defensive maneuver, a way to keep prying types from getting too close. Whatever he'd hidden was encased in a hard, protective shell. Sandra thought of her father, a veteran of World War

154

II, and suddenly understood why she found Bobby so intriguing yet familiar. Like her father, he was a man of action: laconic, subdued, unwilling to display his emotions for others to see. And like her father, he was a gentle soul, someone who had been eager to fight for his country but was unsuited for the costs incurred.

> I've sunshine enough to spread
> It's just like the fella said
> Tell me quick
> Ain't love a kick in the head?

Flushed and out of breath, Sandra needed a moment to compose herself after the final refrain and the song's bombastic finish. "Very good, class. You all did wonderfully. We'll see you tomorrow."

The baseball players joined their teammates and coaches in the bleachers, and most of the other students wandered toward the exit. Coach Dean stood with a smile on his face. He looked proud of his players, who were learning new skills that could increase their dexterity on the field.

Sandra turned to Bobby, who was grinning ear to ear. "You're different."

"It's just a haircut and a shave," he said with a shrug.

Sandra gave him a knowing smile. "That's not all that's changed about you."

Chapter 29

It wasn't until his third lecture to Sister Consuela's health class that Peter finally got around to addressing the issue that had inspired the series of talks in the first place. By now, though, he realized that vanity was a symptom, not the cause, of many of the issues young women faced at St. James. Thus, he was able to approach it in a more nuanced way, with less riding on the subject than he'd originally thought.

On an icy Tuesday afternoon in late January, with temperatures just below freezing, Peter sat on the edge of a table in front of the eleventh-grade students and began his lecture.

"I'd like to introduce you to the ultimate beauty treatment," he announced.

Sarah Conway straightened in her seat, as did the rest of her classmates.

"The ultimate beauty treatment," Peter said, deliberately stretching out his words, "can be found . . . in the Eucharist."

He paused to gauge the girls' reactions. Greta Gronkowski, staring at him with a blank expression, looked confused. Jenny O'Donnell, seated in the back, narrowed her eyes in anticipation, clearly eager to hear more. Sister Consuela, occupying one of the empty seats in the front row, looked incredulous. No doubt she wondered where he'd take this.

"When we receive the host," Peter explained, "we receive the actual body and blood of Christ. It interacts with virtually every cell in

156

our body. If we allow this to fully manifest within us, we cannot help but glow with the beauty of the Holy Spirit." He raised his voice a notch. "What could be more beautiful? Each of you is unique. Therefore, the manifestation of the Holy Spirit reveals your unique beauty. The Eucharist, which provides us with so much, also can be thought of as a beauty treatment for the soul."

By the time Peter finished his lecture, Sister Consuela's face had relaxed, her incredulous gaze replaced by a look of contentment. The girls, meanwhile, seemed enthusiastic but also reassured somehow. Had he relieved them of their burden? They broke into a boisterous round of applause just as the chimes sounded.

While the students filed out, Sister Consuela rose from her seat, pausing to straighten her habit, and then approached Peter. "I can sense the affection the girls have for you, Father. I believe your lecture was a hit."

Peter felt light on his feet. "You think so?"

Sister Consuela nodded. "From now on when the girls receive communion, they'll think of it as their beauty treatment. It's a wonderful metaphor, Father, and one that I predict will stand the test of time at St. James."

"I don't know about that," Peter said, suddenly feeling sheepish.

But Sister Consuela appeared adamant in her enthusiasm. "Mark my words, Father. Years from now, students will refer to the Eucharist as Father Ryan's Beauty Treatment."

~~~

Peter pressed his face against his office window and searched the predawn landscape on the other side, using his hands to shield the reflection coming from his desk lamp. He squinted a moment, struggling to locate the light in the parking lot, and then frowned when he spotted its dim, downward-cast glow. The snow was still coming down as hard as ever.

Not that it mattered anymore. A Nor'easter had struck New England two days earlier and had dropped more than a foot and a half of snow in twenty-four hours, resulting in a rare school closure. Now, in the early-morning twilight of the first Friday of February, Peter knew he had no choice but to concede defeat. The fundraiser dinner was scheduled for the following evening, and he'd have to postpone it.

Maria Donatello, one of the few staff members to brave the conditions in order to work a brief shift at the office, appeared in the doorway. Still wrapped in a navy-blue wool coat and matching scarf, she stuffed her hands into her pockets and gave him a sad smile. "Forecast says blizzard conditions all weekend. Time to throw in the towel?"

Peter nodded. "I'll make the calls. Go home to your family."

She leaned her head against the door and frowned. "You sure?"

"I'm sure."

She nodded and turned to leave but then stopped and turned back. "You saw the letter, right?"

"What letter?" Peter already regretted his curt response, which was a reflection of his downtrodden spirit.

"From the bishop," Maria said. "I left it on your desk yesterday morning."

Peter glanced at the chaos covering his desk.

As if recognizing his increasing sense of hopelessness, Maria stepped forward and rummaged through the debris until she found the letter in question. She thrust it toward him.

"You mind reading it?" Peter asked. "I have a hunch I know what it says, and I'm not sure I can take any more bad news."

Maria slid a long fingernail underneath the flap and then read the letter to herself. As her lips silently mouthed the words and her eyes traveled across the page, Peter turned to look outside once more. The skies were beginning to lighten, the bare outlines of a winter wonderland slowly taking shape. At least he had nowhere to drive, he told himself, no obligations beyond keeping the rectory warm enough to prevent the pipes from freezing.

The sound of paper being folded told him Maria had finished reading the letter. He looked up in time to see her stuffing it back inside the envelope.

"Bad news?"

She offered a tight-lipped nod.

"How bad?"

"The bishop," she said with a sigh, "still wants to know what our plan is. He wants to know how we're going to raise five hundred thousand dollars. He didn't say it in so many words, but I think he thinks we're stalling. They're obviously eager to move ahead with the merger at the end of the academic year. Unless—"

"Unless we find the money." Peter steepled his hands. "We can't do this alone."

"No, we can't. We would need years to raise that kind of money."

Peter smiled wryly. "You've been awfully kind to indulge me. But I don't think St. James can survive my delusions for much longer."

She shook her head, and the sad smile returned to her face. "You had to try. I don't begrudge you that."

"So." Peter felt his voice catch in his throat. "When is Antonio Federici due back to the States?"

Maria gave Peter an affectionate smile. "This spring."

Peter glanced again out the window and tried to see past the brightening snowscape. "If the forecast holds, it'll be too dangerous to drive soon, too dangerous to simply take a walk in the neighborhood. Lawrence will disappear in a whiteout." He smiled defiantly. "But nothing lasts forever. Spring is just around the corner."

Chapter 30

A month and a half later, Peter climbed the weathered bleachers behind the visitors' dugout at a baseball stadium forty-five minutes southeast of Lawrence. With the sun warming his face, he could smell hyacinths in the breeze. In tandem with a multitude of crocuses, the hyacinths had been the first flowers to poke through the melting snow just a few weeks earlier. Now they were in full bloom, their sweet scent marinating in the mild spring air.

Baseball season in New England was a time of optimism and unfettered joy. Leather baseball gloves kept all winter in storage, each softened with oil and holding a baseball in its webbing, were eagerly unwrapped. Outfields were mowed and infields raked smooth. And Angela Finn, an institution in the St. James' bleachers, made her first game-day appearance of the spring. Angela, the mother of Kenny Finn, the team's right fielder, was a full-figured black woman who had grown up in Boston.

"Hello, Mrs. Finn," Peter said as he lowered himself to the bleachers beside her. "I see you brought your knitting with you today."

Angela chuckled. "I always do." With a knitting needle in each hand, she sat beside a basket of yarn in a riot of colors.

Children seemed to flock to Angela and were playing nearby, pausing occasionally to peer into the basket of yarn. Perhaps like Peter, they sensed her deep spirituality.

"What are you knitting today?" Peter asked.

"A sweater," Angela said, her voice tinged with pride.

160

At the moment, the jumble of yarn in her lap didn't look like much, but Peter had seen enough of Angela's creations to know that her loving hands only made works of art.

Today's preseason exhibition game wouldn't count in the standings, but it was nevertheless an important one for the players. College scouts were on hand, which meant potential scholarships were on the line. Exams Week, unfortunately, was scheduled to begin Monday, so Peter had suggested to Coach Dean that the players pack their textbooks for the road trip and study before the game.

As the team took the field for pre-game warmups, Peter marveled at the players' poise and confidence. Jacob Bloom, Jonathan's son, was the first on the field and took up his position at third base. As far as Peter understood it, Jonathan had enrolled Jacob at St. James to expose the boy to the school's excellent music and arts programs. But Jacob, the only Jewish student at St. James, had gravitated toward sports instead. He was an excellent fielder and had a cannon for an arm.

Danny Corvino stood next to him at shortstop and Erik Twombly at second base. Danny struck Peter as an optimistic kid with a kind spirit. He also was quite the looker, which explained why the girls seemed to be drawn to him. Like Jacob, he was an excellent fielder. Erik, meanwhile, was the smartest player on the team, always focused on the task at hand, never wavering.

In right field, Angela's son Kenny tossed a lazy rainbow to centerfielder Mike Zuk, who caught it, turned, and lofted the ball to leftfielder Aki Fuchida, Mr. Fuchida's nephew. Kenny, the team's only black player, posed a dual threat: speed on the bases and power at the plate. His soulful personality seemed to give the team hope, especially when all seemed lost on the field. Mike, meanwhile, was known for his humor and calm disposition. He never lost his cool. Like his uncle, Aki was quiet, witty, and disciplined. He had the fundamentals of the game down pat and was perhaps the team's most consistent player. Peter had never seen him display it—indeed, the young man appeared to pick his moments—but word had it that his "samurai face" never failed to elicit laughter from his teammates. Squinty eyes. Buck teeth. The whole routine.

Kevin McCelvey, the team batboy, was slow in speech and intellect, but he was a big-hearted kid with a perpetual smile and a dry sense of humor. Everyone loved Kevin, and Mike Zuk had appointed himself as Kevin's guardian and protector. Any would-be bullies had to come through Mike if they wanted to pick on Kevin.

The players looked upbeat, if a bit ragged. But every throw was a little sloppy, and every catch was punctuated not with the smack of a glove but with a dull thud or unintended bobble. It had been a long time since Peter had played catch, but as he watched the team warm up, he imagined the ball carried an extra bit of sting in the cool air.

"They sure look relaxed," Angela said.

Peter nodded. "Maybe *too* relaxed."

Coach Dean and Coach Sanders stood a few feet apart near the visitors' dugout, each with his arms crossed, each occasionally shifting left to right. Coach Dean seemed to do most of the talking. Was he thinking out loud? It seemed that way to Peter, who had watched the dynamic between the two for a few seasons now. Coach Dean was known for his dry observations. "We've got a Jew, a Jap, and a colored fella on the team," he'd say matter-of-factly. His assistant would just nod his head. Richie Sanders appeared to relish his role as the head coach's sounding board. Peter often watched the team practice, and the two coaches engaged in the same routine. The only time Sanders ever became talkative was when Sandra Alvarez was near. Once, when she'd stopped by to watch the team practice, Sanders tried to make small talk with her. Afterward, Peter overheard Coach Dean grumble, "Maybe you need to go sit on a block of ice, Richie."

When game-time drew near, the St. James Crusaders retreated to the dugout. While the other team warmed up in the field, Peter smiled to himself as a familiar phenomenon began to take shape in the bleachers: parents, friends, and fans of St. James crept closer to Angela, as though seeking her calm, gentle confidence. Usually such a migration took place after the game had begun, particularly after a turn for the worse. But there was something off about today. Peter could sense it, and it appeared the others on hand could as well. Coach Dean had dubbed Angela "The Great Spirit." Her tranquility was palpable, and everybody wanted a piece of it.

Mike Zuk led off for St. James at the plate. He looked sleepy, maybe even a little disinterested. But he swung at the first pitch and drove it over the centerfield wall.

Peter leapt to his feet and joined a chorus of cheers. "What a start!" he hollered, trading smiles with Angela.

Zuk, meanwhile, stood at home plate and watched the ball sail over the yellow-rimmed top of the centerfield fence.

"What are you gaping at?" Coach Dean hollered. "Move!"

Zuk almost missed second base as he loped around the bases. He was greeted in the dugout by his smiling teammates, who hooted and hollered and slapped him on the back.

But Zuk's shot soon proved an aberration. The next three batters for St. James struck out, and once they took the field, Coach Dean's boys more closely resembled a comedy troupe than a seasoned baseball team. Misjudged fly balls. Overthrows to first base. Pitches nowhere near the strike zone. The team's catcher, a scrappy kid named Jack Carafello, could barely maintain his catcher's stance without falling on his backside.

Peter turned to Angela. "Is he sick?"

She stared back at him in wide-eyed disbelief. "If he is, he's not the only one."

163

Parents, children, and other stunned onlookers drew closer to Angela, no doubt hoping to draw strength from her inspiring presence, but as the innings wore on, some drifted away. A game that had begun with so much promise degenerated into a blowout loss. The O'Malley brothers, usually reliable pitchers, were shelled, and everyone struggled at the plate. St. James's baseball team was an embarrassment, and, like the others in attendance, all Peter could do was watch in horror.

~~~

Peter was still trying to absorb the baseball team's abysmal performance when Maria Donatello appeared in his office doorway Monday morning, preceded as usual by her eye-watering perfume.

"Good morning, Father," she chimed in a singsong voice that suggested she was about to spring something on him.

Peter studied her face for a moment, searching it for clues. "Good morning to you, Mrs. Donatello. If I didn't know better, I'd say you have some good news for me."

Maria took a seat across from him, chin up, a smile playing on her coral-colored lips. The tiny crow's feet at the corners of her eyes betrayed her excitement. "The Federicis have returned from Italy."

Peter felt his heart skip a beat. "How do you like that? Wonderful news!" He noticed the impatient look on Maria's face and realized she wasn't finished. "There's more?"

She nodded eagerly. "They've agreed to meet with me. *Tonight.*"

Peter gulped. He wasn't sure whether he should be excited or terrified. "Tonight?" He stood up to pace. "Should we meet with the faculty? Discuss a strategy?"

Maria raised her right hand like a stop sign. "Father, please. Let me take care of this."

Peter dropped to his chair, suddenly feeling confused and, if he was being honest with himself, a little deflated. "Do you want me there?"

Maria smiled as she shook her head no.

"You don't want my help?"

"Not yet," she said. "For the moment, I think it's best if we keep the discussion based on financial reality."

The comment gave him pause, for it revealed something about himself that he knew to be true. He was, for better or worse, focused on matters of the soul, sometimes to the detriment of more practical matters. As a professor during his seminary years had once told him, there were two ways to tell time: Kronos and Kairos. Most people lived in the world of Kronos, which was a world of numbers, hard lines, and well-defined truths. It was a world of facts, a world that answered first and foremost to the economic imperative. Kairos, on the other hand, was all about inspiration and transcendence. It was a prayerful orientation that lent itself to art, music, and dance, a spontaneous, revelatory outlook that answered to inspiration first. That same professor had advised Peter that he would make an excellent priest—but a lousy accountant.

Peter smiled meekly at Maria. "Good luck, Mrs. Donatello."

Chapter 31

Peter made a beeline from the rectory to his office the next morning, pausing only briefly to admire the daffodils blooming along the path. He was fifteen minutes early and already regretted hurrying to work. It would have been better, he suddenly realized, to have arrived *after* Maria. Now all he could do was wait.

Fortunately, he didn't have to wait long. He heard her voice in the outer office as she greeted another employee, smelled her perfume as it rolled toward him like the tide, and saw her face a moment later. Her frown told him everything he needed to know.

"He said no."

She nodded. "I wish I would have waited. They've been back less than a week and were obviously in no mood to make such a major decision. I should have read the situation better."

Peter was almost afraid to know, but he had to ask. "Were they adamant?"

"What do you mean?" Maria asked as she slipped off her raincoat.

"I mean, did they dismiss the idea outright, or did they say they would think about it?"

"Well," Maria ventured, "Kathleen seemed amenable at first, but then Antonio started talking about the expense of their trip, all the time he'd lost that he should have been dedicating to his work, and so on. Before I knew it, he was telling me no."

"What was Kathleen's reaction?" Peter asked.

166

"She seemed apologetic, almost embarrassed." Maria cocked her head at Peter suspiciously. "What are you thinking?"

"I'm thinking you caught the man off guard. I'm also thinking his wife has been chewing his ear ever since you left. I think they just need a gentle push in the right direction."

Maria gave Peter a crooked smile. "Why, Father, I didn't realize you had the mind of a salesman."

Peter chuckled. "I wouldn't go that far. But I do consider myself a student of human nature. The Federicis value St. James. Their ongoing contributions show that. Antonio has lost his mother and closed out her estate. Part of him is no doubt downcast at such a turn of events. He's had to say goodbye to the woman who birthed him into this world and to the home that nurtured him as a boy. But I'm guessing he's ready—more ready than he thinks—to move forward with a new adventure. He'll need to pour himself into a worthwhile cause."

Maria was nodding slowly. "And St. James is that cause."

Peter reached for his phone, which, like a stubby lighthouse rising above the mists, poked through the cloud of debris that cluttered his desk. "I'm going to need Mr. Federici's phone number, if it's not too much trouble. We have important business to discuss."

~~~

"Are you ready, Father?"

Peter was already on his feet, butterflies flitting inside his stomach. "Is it time?"

Maria nodded from his office doorway.

Friday afternoon had arrived. It was time to make their pitch to Antonio Federici, who, after fielding Peter's call earlier in the week, had invited him over for dinner.

The two walked silently through the empty campus and stopped at Maria's Ford Fairlane in the otherwise deserted parking lot. From there, it was a short drive to the Bloom residence.

Lost in his own thoughts, Peter felt a sense of relief that the time had finally come. He also felt a surge of panic. What if he'd misjudged the situation? What if Mr. Federici said no? Peter hardly noticed the pink buds on the bare branches of the redbuds lining the streets.

They pulled into the Blooms' driveway and walked silently to the front door, where Rachael greeted them with a smile. Wearing an apron over her chocolate-brown turtleneck and matching slacks, she led them through the house and out the back door. "Jonathan's fussing with his trees."

Always ready to offer moral support, Jonathan had agreed to accompany them. They found him standing beside an older apple tree, which, like the others, had just begun to bud. Tufts of daffodils bloomed at the foot of the tree.

"Peter, Maria," Jonathan said as soon as he spotted them. "I'll be ready shortly. Just checking on this support." He gave a hearty tug on a cable that had been guyed to the tree's largest limb. "This one still has years of production left if I can keep it from snapping. Sometimes these older branches can't handle the weight of the apples."

Seemingly satisfied, Jonathan removed his gardening gloves and offered Peter a warm hand to shake. Peter and Maria followed him inside and waited for him to change out of his coveralls and into something more presentable.

A few minutes later, they were back on the road. Jonathan was unusually talkative during the final leg of the trip, and Peter had to stop himself from glaring over his shoulder at his chatty friend in the backseat.

"Come on, Peter," Jonathan said, clearly sensing Peter's irritation. "It feels like we're going to a wake."

Peter could barely manage a chuckle. "We have a lot riding on this, Jonathan. No Plan B, in case you forgot."

Maria turned down a long driveway and waited for an enormous black gate to open. "We're here," she said nervously.

Peter glanced at his watch and saw that it was five o'clock sharp. He was relieved to have arrived on time.

Once through the gate, they crested a short rise, after which a stunning French Provincial home came into view. With its granite exterior and slate roof, it blended seamlessly into its well-landscaped surroundings. Though a modern structure, it looked to Peter like it had been there for centuries.

Peter was the first out of his seat and waited in the early evening sunlight for Maria and Jonathan to emerge from the Fairlane before leading them to the front door. He pushed the doorbell and waited, all the while only vaguely aware that he was biting his lip.

The oversized oak door beneath the stone archway swung open, and there stood Kathleen Federici with a radiant smile. Though married to one of the richest men in the city, Kathleen was just as Maria had described her: sweet-natured and down-to-earth. She was dressed in a black skirt and a white blouse and wore her dark hair pulled back.

"Maria," she said as she enveloped Maria in a warm hug. "So good to see you again."

After Kathleen greeted Peter and Jonathan in turn, Peter felt his shoulders relax. Their hostess exuded a kindness that was impossible to miss. She had a clear zest for life, which was no doubt what had drawn Antonio to her.

As they stood in the sumptuous living room, Peter spied a Steinway grand piano in the adjacent room and nudged Jonathan.

Jonathan's eyes widened when he saw it. "What a gorgeous instrument!"

Kathleen smiled. "Antonio just had it rebuilt. It's his favorite new toy." The tone in her voice suggested amusement but also affection.

She led them down the hall, through a spacious and well-lit

kitchen, and out the back French doors. Peter gaped at the lawn, which looked as plush as any shag carpet and was surrounded by a well-tended flower garden and a thick grove of trees that made it feel like they'd entered a forest, not the backyard of someone's sprawling estate. Like some of the perennials at their feet, many of the trees were still dormant. Still-maturing tulips bulged beside a large pool and cabana, both of which were surrounded by granite boulders, more trees, and a smattering of annuals and primroses in full bloom.

Kathleen escorted them to the cabana and stopped at the bar, where Mr. Federici was seated on a stool and chatting with someone who appeared to be among the hired help. Was he exclusively a bartender, Peter wondered, or did he also serve as a butler, handyman, or groundskeeper?

"Antonio, sweetheart," Kathleen said, "this is Father Ryan from St. James."

Antonio, a bear of a man, slipped off his perch and took Peter's hand with gusto and then enveloped him in a suffocating hug. He pulled back and smiled at Peter as though they were old friends. "Pleased to meet you, Father," he said, revealing a heavy Italian accent and a full head of salt-and-pepper hair.

"It's my pleasure," Peter stuttered, overcome by the man's generous outpouring of affection. He motioned to Jonathan. "This is my longtime friend Jonathan Bloom. Jonathan is a pianist with the Boston Symphony Orchestra."

Antonio shook Jonathan's hand and then wrapped him in a hearty hug. "Impressive." He turned to the bartender behind the bar. "This is Patrick McNally. We fought against each other in the war. Now he's my right-hand man."

Patrick, a roguishly handsome man, sported a square jaw, a heavily muscled physique, and short-cropped red hair with a wisp of gray in it. "I was an NCO with the Eighth Army," he said with a British accent. He aimed a thumb at Antonio. "He surrendered to me when the Allies took a village near Pisa."

"We eventually fought on the same side," Antonio said, taking over the story, "after I was attached to the British and Americans. After the war, he followed me to America and went to work for me. The rest is history."

Patrick drummed the top of the bar. "Can I pour anyone an aperitif? Perhaps a glass of Gavi?"

"I'll take the Gavi," Peter said.

"Me too," Jonathan said.

"Excellent choice," Patrick said as he hoisted a bottle of the white wine and liberated the cork.

"Patrick is a knowledgeable sommelier," Antonio explained. "Not bad for a former rugby player from the mean streets of London, eh?"

Now the picture was complete, Peter thought. With his starched shirt and black tie and his knowledge of wines, Patrick could almost pass for a sophisticated English butler. But his athletic build and blue-collar cockney accent gave him away.

Patrick turned toward Maria. "And what will the lady be having?"

"Do you have any iced tea?" Maria asked sheepishly.

Patrick nodded. "Sweetened or unsweetened?"

"Unsweetened, please."

Peter didn't notice that Kathleen had disappeared until she returned from the kitchen with a tray of hors d'oeuvres, including fruit, chicken, and sharp cheeses.

"We thought we might eat outside," Kathleen said, "what with the lovely weather and all."

"It's not an Italian spring," Antonio grumbled, "but it will do."

The appetizers paired perfectly with the next bottle of wine that

171

Patrick opened: a Barbera grown in the Piedmont region of northern Italy. Peter mostly listened as Kathleen and Maria reminisced about humorous parent-teacher moments at St. James, and Jonathan and Antonio culled their memories for Boston Symphony Orchestra highlights.

Antonio turned to Peter. "So you say you and Jonathan here are old friends. When did you first meet?"

Lubricated by wine and appetizers, Peter opened up about his childhood, about meeting Jonathan for the first time, about their adventures in the Bloom family orchard and the high school halls. By the time he reached the topic of World War II, Kathleen was offering a tray of beef and lamb shish kabobs. Patrick, meanwhile, had already suggested another wine, this time a Nebbiolo in both the Barbaresco and Barolo appellations.

With twilight fast approaching and the air beginning to chill, Patrick flipped a switch behind the bar, and several old-fashioned lamps began to shine brightly.

Peter gazed at a marble statue and then another and quickly realized they were just two of several surrounding the pool. "Those statues," he said as he admired them in the warm glow from the poolside lamps, "they're quite remarkable."

"And authentic," Antonio said. "They're my pride and joy, Roman statues from antiquity. I've been collecting them for more than twenty years. The oldest dates back two centuries before Christ."

The closest appeared to be a carving of a leader of some sort, the folds of his robes taking on a life-like realism.

"That's Virgil," Antonio said.

"Ah," Peter said. "The poet."

"Indeed. Not all are in such good shape. Some are missing limbs, noses, and ears. But I'd sooner part with my life than any of them. They span three centuries."

Maria wrapped her arms together against the creeping night air, and Antonio was quick to notice.

"Shall we retire to the house?" he asked.

No one protested the idea, and Peter stood on wobbly legs to follow the others inside. As they entered through the French doors, he realized he'd had one too many glasses of wine. His head continued to swim when Antonio led them upstairs to his second-floor office. Floor-to-ceiling bookshelves were interrupted by another pair of French doors, which opened to a small balcony with a view of the lawn, the grove of trees, and a lake beyond them.

Peter blinked at the lake, unsure of what he was seeing among the dark silhouettes in the distance. "Is that an island?" On what looked like a tiny island, a cross rose from the tower of a small church. "And is that a chapel on it?"

Antonio nodded. "You can't make it out in the dark, but it has a lovely stone exterior and Celtic-cross stained-glass window. The chapel was a gift from the original landowner to his wife. She was Catholic, and there was no Catholic church in the area. The owner was Protestant, but he built the church for his wife and her Catholic neighbors."

"A true act of love," Peter mused, "and generosity."

Antonio's eyes darkened. "A group of teenagers vandalized it thirteen years ago, and it's been in a state of restoration ever since." He turned and led them back into his study, stopping at a round table across the room from his mahogany desk. "Shall we go over St. James's financials?"

Peter traded bewildered glances with Jonathan, who looked like Peter felt: tipsy. Even when sober, Peter didn't know the difference between a balance sheet and a cash flow statement. Neither did Jonathan—of that, Peter was certain. The two tentatively took seats at the table, and Peter turned to Maria, who, thank the heavens, was already producing a well-worn leather portfolio.

"I know you saw everything on Monday, Mr. Federici," Maria said, "but it can't hurt to take another look at the numbers."

Antonio donned a pair of reading glasses. "If the school's finances are in shambles, I won't perpetuate a hopeless situation." He read for a moment and then looked up from the documents. "Of course, someone like myself can discern a 'story' from financial statements. And the story that the St. James's financials tell me is one of great dreams and optimism—with a cash flow that has disappeared. Hindsight being what it is, the land and building initiatives were obviously overly optimistic." He fixed Peter's gaze. "Mrs. Donatello here has already made it clear to me that the school needs help. I need *you* to make a case for perpetuating St. James. Why not just merge it with the regional high school, as planned?"

Peter gulped, suddenly feeling put on the spot. But as he groped for an answer, he realized he didn't need to work out what he should say. The words were already written in his heart.

"Mr. Federici," he began, "I'd like to tell you about our faculty at St. James. We have a vice principal who looks like he could play for the Celtics—better yet, the Patriots—but has a heart as tender as a child's. He's in charge of enforcing discipline on campus, and he does so very effectively. But the students don't fear him as much as they love him. Because when a student struggles academically, our vice principal reorients him toward a class that better suits him. When a student misbehaves, our vice principal hands him over to our school gardener, a man of Japanese ancestry who fought for this country, a man who has managed to pass his love of horticulture on to our youth, one misbehaving student at a time. When our vice principal became concerned that not all of our students were capable of flourishing on the athletic field, he enlisted the help of coaches, who in turn got help from their athletes to introduce general conditioning to the student body.

"We have an English teacher who, in her first year at St. James, has already started a dance class that's popular with shy girls *and* cocky baseball players. She's taught her students how to write poetry in the classroom and dance the foxtrot in the gymnasium. When one of her students lost her mother last fall, she somehow found a way to bring that young lady out of her shell, to get her to see beauty in this fragile world."

Peter hardly paused to take a breath. There was so much he wanted to say.

"Many of our programs depend on the volunteer hours of skilled professionals, such as Bobby Jones, who has donated countless hours to the—"

"Bobby Jones?" Antonio asked. "I've heard of the young man. People say he's the most exciting young vocal talent to come out of Boston in years!"

"He's my nephew," Peter said, unable to hide the pride in his voice. "He tutors the young men in our school choir. He took the lead role at the Christmas concert when our star tenor fell ill." Peter motioned to Jonathan beside him. "Jonathan has coached him since his early youth."

"What a fantastic privilege for the high school choir!" Antonio exclaimed. "From what I understand, Bobby served in Vietnam. His story has inspired many in the community."

Peter, feeling like he was just getting warmed up, pushed ahead. "Mr. Federici, we have at our school a certain chemistry, a kind of synergy that is wholly unique. I fear that if we were to break up the faculty and disperse the students, the community would suffer a great loss."

Antonio frowned. "I detest the thought of a regional high school. Father, if I commit to funding the shortfall at St. James, how can I be assured that the school won't close anyway, and my funding absorbed by the regional high school?"

Maria reached into her portfolio and produced a short stack of papers. "I've already thought of that possibility. To guard against it, I've created documents that prohibit just such an outcome. The funding would be earmarked for St. James exclusively." She held up the papers. "This is a document of intent and would be formalized later by attorneys representing you and the diocese."

Peter could feel his heart in his throat. Maria, once again, had proven to be the consummate professional. But was it enough?

Antonio stood and walked to the French doors, pausing just beyond them to gaze out at the night sky. He turned to Peter and the others and spoke from the balcony. "Our lives are finite. We have limited opportunities to invest in noble endeavors." He stared outside once again, this time glancing down toward the direction of the pool and his beloved Roman statues. "You've made an excellent case for keeping St. James open, Father, and I want to help. The synergy you speak of, though unquantifiable, is invaluable to our community. I know that. I knew it before you came here this evening."

Peter felt his heartrate pick up. He'd come to the Federici home as more of a Hail Mary than anything else. But now it sounded as though Antonio was more than willing to help. Could it really be this easy?

Then Antonio spoke again. "The problem is the timing. Much of my wealth is tied up in hard assets. Due to my mother's passing, I'll be taking ownership of even more capital, a good deal of it liquid. But these things, as I'm sure you're aware, take time to sort themselves out. In fact, my mother's business and estate funds are frozen and will remain so until the legal restrictions are removed from the estate—a process that could take several years."

Peter, unable to mask his shock and disappointment after feeling success in his grasp, felt his jaw drop. Years? The future of St. James would be determined in a matter of a few short *months*.

Antonio rejoined them at the table. "I'm willing to give, Father. I can pledge you that the funds you need will materialize—eventually." He acknowledged the stricken look on Peter's face with a nod. "I know the situation is critical, and I know this isn't what you were hoping to hear. But for now, we must have faith that all will work out."

Peter slumped in his seat. He knew he should feel thankful to the man for his generosity, but it was all he could do to quell the frustration rising inside him. All the momentum was toward a merger, which was obviously what the powers-that-be wanted. Peter knew that a future pledge of funds wouldn't be enough. Without the necessary funds in hand, St. James would be closed by the end of June.

Peter glanced at Maria and saw the disappointment in her eyes. Jonathan, too, seemed to sense that they'd won an empty victory.

"Don't look so glum, Father," Antonio said and patted him on the back. "Faith can move mountains. I've seen it in my own life, and I'm sure you have as well."

It was an odd turn of events, Peter thought, to be lectured by a wealthy man on the power of faith. Was it not easier for a man of substantial means to put his faith in the future?

Patrick, who had been standing near the doorway, stayed true to form and maintained a stiff upper lip. "If I may, Father, I'd like to reiterate Mr. Federici's sentiments. A solution will present itself—of that you can be certain."

Peter was too overwhelmed to speak, for he suddenly saw in Patrick's grit and stoic faith the story of the centurion in the Gospels. The centurion's utter faith in the power of Jesus's word had astonished even Jesus. Of course, his faith had been answered in the very hour of his need.

Antonio smiled warmly. "Until that moment comes," he said in a deep baritone, "let us make merry. Jonathan, piano four-hands. What do you say?"

Still in a state of confusion, Peter accepted another glass of wine from Patrick and then tromped downstairs with the others. What followed was a tipsy celebration in the piano room, with Antonio and Jonathan plunking out several duets on the refurbished Steinway. While the piano reverberated with Shubert, Strauss, and then a selection of show tunes, Patrick plied them with the finest armagnac and cognac. Even Maria partook in a toast, clinking her champagne flute against the others'.

Soon, Peter was fighting for a place on the piano bench, although all he could contribute were enthusiastic, if out-of-key, vocals. He had given in to the moment, to the power of faith in things unseen.

"I think Father Ryan is clobbered."

"I think they're *all* clobbered!"

Peter wasn't sure who spoke first—Kathleen or Maria. Nor was he sure when they left, although he was pretty sure someone had said something about it being past midnight. After thanking Antonio and Kathleen profusely, he stumbled into the backseat of the Fairlane and closed his eyes for the drive home. At some point he realized the car was no longer moving, the engine having fallen silent. He heard Maria speaking to another woman—Rachael?—and felt someone take him by the arm and lead him up a short set of stairs.

"Perhaps Father Ryan should sit on the other side of the screen tomorrow morning during confession," one of the women said with a giggle.

Peter wanted to protest, but he could barely stand, much less speak intelligibly, and before he knew it, he was being lowered to a soft bed. He heard a door click closed, and the room briefly spun. Undeterred, he let his mind drift to happier, less woozy times, having accomplished far less this evening than what he'd set out to do.

Chapter 32

Peter awoke to the sound of someone knocking on a door. He sat up and stared at his surroundings in confusion. The room was dim, the furnishings and knickknacks unfamiliar. *Where am I?* He suddenly realized he was still dressed. Only his shoes had been removed.

Rachael's voice reached him from the other side of the door. "Time to wake up, Father. You have confessions this morning."

Then it hit him in quick succession: the wine, the appetizers, the next round of wine, then dinner, followed by a drunken celebration of the virtues of faith in Antonio Federici's piano room.

Faith alone couldn't save St. James, but it was the only thing sustaining Peter at the moment.

He reached for his forehead and winced. He felt like a vertigo patient aboard the *Titanic*, with a tongue made of sandpaper and a head full of icepicks. No matter which way he moved, he incurred the wrath of a thousand stabbing pains. He tried to remember the last time he'd overindulged but drew a blank. He'd probably been wearing a navy uniform.

"Just give me a moment," he said hoarsely.

Cool water from the bathroom faucet refreshed him, but only briefly. Rachael was waiting in the kitchen. She handed him a plate with two pieces of lightly buttered toast, but the smell of food made his stomach lurch. He had no choice but to push it away.

As if ready for just such a possibility, Rachael gave him a bag of ice and two aspirin. "Try these instead, Father."

After Rachael dropped him off at the rectory, Peter trudged to the bathroom and once again splashed cold water on his face. Then, after tucking the ice under his arm and donning a pair of sunglasses, he made the short plod to the chapel.

As he took his place inside the confessional booth, he smiled bitterly at the irony of a hungover priest hearing the sins of his flock. An effective confession led the confessor to a clear understanding of his sin, followed by an unequivocal articulation of that sin, which in turn was followed by a true sense of remorse. It sounded easy enough—almost freeing—but few things were more difficult than coming to grips with sin, for it required total honesty and a spirit of repentance.

The first person to enter the booth that morning was Coach Dean. "Bless me, Father, for I have sinned." His words, though delivered as softly as the coach's gruff voice would allow, sounded like a jackhammer in the claustrophobic confessional.

Peter hid his own discomfort and dove into the ritual, hoping at the very least to lose sight of his own pain while alleviating another man's suffering. What he found, instead, was something else entirely.

"Father," Coach Dean began, "you know I'm not one to mince words, so I'll get straight to it. As you know, the team played lousy on Saturday. I knew there had to be a reason, and I found out it was 'cause the boys were high. I've been wrestling with how to punish 'em. I've got no proof—nothing that could stand up in court, anyway—but I know what happened. There's no use dragging the school's reputation through the mud for something I can't prove. The team would be suspended for the season, and everyone would be all up in arms. But I feel like the players need to answer for what they did, and if I've got any integrity at all, so do I. Those boys are my responsibility, and I let them down."

Peter was confused. "How did you let them down?"

"Well, for starters, I should have left Sanders to supervise 'em in the bus while I went to scout the teams playing in the first round. Instead, I took Sanders with me. I figured the kids could handle themselves in the parking lot. Figured they'd be busy studying for Exams Week. But boys are easily distracted, as you know, Father."

Peter shook his head, engulfed in his own sense of shame. Who was he to admonish the coach or his team? He was still sweating out the alcohol he'd consumed the night before.

Mike Zuk, the team's centerfielder, was the first player to enter the confessional booth after Coach Dean. He didn't sound like he carried too much guilt about the incident. If anything, he seemed all too happy to recount the day's adventure.

"We were all studying—just like Coach Dean asked us to—when we heard a big commotion in the parking lot," he began. "Jack stuck his head out the window and gave us the play by play. He said a bunch of cops were chasing someone through the parking lot. Turns out they were chasing Rodriguez. Remember him, Father?"

Peter removed the cool ice from his forehead. "I do. He was quite a football player."

Frankie Rodriguez, a wiry split end with speed to burn, had graduated the previous spring, having set numerous school records while returning kickoffs and punts.

"He sure was! And what a trip, Father, watching a bunch of overweight cops try to chase him down! He was like a gazelle. Eventually, he tossed something through my window, and we all cheered him on as he gave the cops the slip and disappeared. The cops didn't notice the grocery bag he tossed into the bus, but *we* did. We opened it up and saw it was full of sandwich bags, rolling papers, lighter, a pipe—you name it. And every single one of those sandwich bags was stuffed with marijuana. Must have been ten pounds of Mary Jane in that bag! We argued a while about what to do with it. Should we hand it over to the police? Hide it?

"Finally, we agreed to smoke a toast to Rodriguez, and next thing you know, Kenny is rolling us a few bones. We figured we had at least a few hours before we were supposed to play. You should have seen it, Father. The parking lot is crawling with cops, and here we are, lighting up in the bus. We smoked so many joints you couldn't see past your hand. So someone says we should open all the windows and let the smoke out. Everybody but Kevin McCelvey was lit up like a Christmas tree. Kevin didn't smoke any."

Mike's voice dropped an octave, as though he realized his story was overflowing with braggadocio but lacking in remorse or shame. "Somebody got out an eight-track player, and we started listening to the Doors and Led Zeppelin. You ever heard of them? Oh, and Eric Clapton. Everybody was drumming along to Ginger Baker and strumming along to Clapton. We were singing along to the Grateful Dead's 'Truckin'' when someone said they had the munchies. So we sent Kevin with a pile of money to get us snacks from the concessions booth. You ever overindulged, Father?"

Peter reapplied the ice, this time to his neck. If only the boy knew. "No one is without sin, son."

"Well, the thing about marijuana is you feel euphoria at first. Everyone's having a great time. Then everyone starts laughing at everything. Seems like life is one big comedy. And then it's like someone hits a light switch and you start to mellow out. We put on an acoustic instrumental by Led Zeppelin, and everyone got lost in their own thoughts. The bus was pretty quiet by the time Kevin came back with the food—and Coach Sanders. Coach Sanders told us the schedule had changed and we were playing the next game. That scared me to death, 'cause I knew I was in no shape to do anything 'cept stuff my face and just, you know, relax."

A parade of players followed Mike Zuk one at a time into the confessional booth, and each told the same story. A few embellished it here and there while withholding various details. Unlike Mike, most seemed mortified to have to share any of it with a priest. Peter listened patiently, all the while silently praying to God for forgiveness of his own sins.

The last player to give his confession was Danny Corvino, who, more than any of the others, seemed to enter the booth burdened with shame. It wasn't long before Peter realized the boy's guilt had little to do with Saturday's debacle.

"Sometimes I use foul language," Danny said. "I drink alcohol at parties sometimes."

Both revelations struck Peter as trifling. There was something else eating at the boy.

"And?"

"I . . ." Danny's voice trailed off. "The guys on the team like to call me a lady's man and all that, but . . ." Once again, he stopped himself from going further.

"You don't feel good about your reputation," Peter said, "do you?"

"No."

"Why do you suppose that is?"

Danny was quiet a moment. "I guess because of the girls. They have feelings, you know?"

"They do indeed." Peter appreciated Danny's honesty. The boy seemed more sensitive than some. Still, he needed to be warned of the grave dangers that lay ahead. "They also have reputations, which every young man should endeavor to protect. Have you done something that you wish to confess?"

"Father, I've had inappropriate intimacy with Shannon McGuire. And Eileen McGill. And . . . Greta Gronkowski."

Peter heard a strange welling sound in the basement directly below them, like a storm surge being born, and then he recognized it:

the howling laughter of several teenage boys who had no doubt been listening in on Danny's confession and could no longer contain themselves. He knew who the voices belonged to and where they were hiding.

"Young man," Peter said in a stern tone, "it is wholly inappropriate to share the names of your conquests."

"I'm sorry, Father!" Danny blurted out. "I'm just so nervous."

Peter assigned an appropriate penance to the boy and then hurried to the tool storage closet in the basement. The dusty closet directly beneath the confessional booth was dark and empty by the time he reached it. He picked up a broom that had been knocked over. Half the baseball team probably had squeezed inside the closet to listen to Danny Corvino's confession, he thought, and now they knew the names of the three girls who had made the mistake of becoming intimate with the school's most popular playboy.

It seemed the baseball team's hijinks weren't finished, and more confessions would be needed. For the moment, Peter focused on what he could control: from then on, the basement would remain locked at all times.

Chapter 33

It didn't take long for things to settle back into a routine. The baseball team returned to its winning ways, its preseason fiasco at the out-of-town tournament all but forgotten. Whether he was behaving more gentlemanly or merely being more discrete, Danny Corvino seemed determined to keep a lower profile. And the rest of the student body began to show the sure signs of spring fever: restlessness, short attention spans, and a shared fondness for staring out the window. Faculty members, meanwhile, wore anxious frowns whenever the topic of the school's financial problems was raised. No solution appeared imminent.

Peter was determined to take each day as it came. It seemed only fitting that the question of St. James's future had become at its core a matter of faith, something he'd always tried to cultivate in others. At the moment, he'd just eased himself onto a stool at one of the labs in the biology class, where he planned to watch Father Kovacs step out of his specialties and act as a substitute teacher. Father Kovacs was a mathematician first and a chemistry instructor second, but today he had to fill in for the biology teacher, who had fallen ill.

Seated mere inches from a microscope and within arm's reach of a Bunsen burner, Peter felt sufficiently distracted from his troubles. While sideways rain from a blustery April shower tapped at the windows outside, students began to arrive and take their seats. This was just what was needed, Peter thought, a normal day at St. James.

Slight in stature, taciturn, and easily irritated, Father Kovacs was one of the last to enter the room. Judging by the grimace on his face, he wanted to be there even less than the students, who fell silent upon his arrival. Had he found any time to prepare for his lecture? Peter doubted it. That was the nature of substitute teaching.

"Good morning, class," Father Kovacs said without looking up from the lesson plan. "I'll be your teacher today. It appears we're studying dangerous bacteria and contagious—"

Two students—Terry Wisniewski and Sally Schneider—burst through the doorway while engaged in a heated debate. Terry, a big kid with an even bigger personality, was red-faced and angry.

Sally had a finger in his face and was all but reading him the riot act. "That's not what I said!" she hissed. "You're taking everything out of context!"

"Students, please!" Father Kovacs stood nearly a foot shorter than Terry but made up for the height disparity with his authoritative demeanor. "What in heaven's name is this all about?"

Both began talking at once.

Father Kovacs silenced them once more. "One at a time, please." He nodded to Sally. "You first."

Sally, whose lanky frame accentuated the fact that her navy-blue knee socks didn't quite reach her knees and that her plaid skirt was too short to make up the difference, turned her head to the side impatiently. "We're just talking about theology class is all. The Sacrament of Reconciliation."

"Ah," Father Kovacs said. "But why the argument?"

"She doesn't believe in original sin!" Terry yelled, his voice approaching a dog's bark in sheer volume and guttural tone. Terry was the school's heavyweight wrestler and didn't shy away from throwing his weight around. His father, an excavator and heavy equipment operator, was known for attending all the wrestling matches and unleashing his bullhorn of a voice while cheering on his son. Mr. Wisniewski also happened to be the Eucharistic minister at the St.

James parish. His massive frame and huge hands contrasted sharply with the stereotypical image of a Eucharistic minister delicately handling the host with the utmost reverence. He was rough-hewn, Peter thought, but a good man to the core of his being.

"Sally is entitled to her opinion," Father Kovacs replied calmly, "and her opinion should be respected."

"I don't get it," Terry said, shaking his head. "You're a priest!"

The class fell silent. Such an outburst was not tolerated at St. James, even from someone like Terry, who was known for being unable to filter his thoughts.

Peter had to admit that part of him was enjoying the spectacle, if only because he was curious how Father Kovacs would handle the situation.

The mathematician didn't disappoint. "Terry," he said in an even softer voice, "in order to have a civilized debate, there has to be a mutual clarity of understanding on the premise of the debate. Do you two have an understanding of the premise of the debate?"

"No," Terry said.

"Will there ever be one?"

Sally spoke up next. "No, Father."

"Fine," Father Kovacs said. "Let's move forward with today's lesson."

Peter smiled to himself, impressed. Father Kovacs had managed to defuse the situation without raising his voice. Moreover, he'd stopped a potentially misinformed debate dead in its tracks. No one would benefit from hearing two largely uninformed students using cherry-picked snippets of scripture in order to support their particular bias.

But while Sally found her seat, Terry remained where he stood. "Father, what is sin?"

"You can take your seat, young man. Then I'll explain." Father

Kovacs waited until Terry was seated to formulate a response. "Sin entered the world through Satan, whose goal was to destroy the beauty and perfection of creation. Satan succeeded. He infected creation with an always-fatal virus called sin. It first attacks the mind by disfiguring the image of our perfect creator, in whose image we were made. As a result, we become disfigured, though we remain unaware of it. The disfiguring process ultimately leads to our destruction and death.

"Our creator saved us by sending an antidote to this fatal virus. Unfortunately, the antidote resides only in the body of one perfect man, the creator's son. Perfection cannot coexist with sin. Therefore, the son was put to death by mankind. The son was resurrected by God and returned to God. The son is our only antidote, because we are all infected by the sin virus. Hence the Sacrament of Reconciliation. We love the son, and upon our sincere request, He offers forgiveness for our sin. We are therefore clear of the virus but must live amongst its deleterious effects until we pass to the next world, where sin is unable to exist."

"Okay," Sally said, "I guess that makes sense. But why would a loving God allow his son to be murdered? It's horrible."

Father Kovacs gave her a sad but tender smile. "What a lovely, compassionate heart you have, young lady. Do you remember the story of Abraham and his beloved son Isaac?"

Sally nodded. "God stopped Abraham from sacrificing his son."

"Correct," Father Kovacs said, "but sin returned without an antidote. God allowed His own son to be slain because He deemed us worthy of the sacrifice. His love for us is at a magnitude beyond our understanding. He obviously believes each of us is immensely valuable. We're loved with an intensity we cannot comprehend. He only wants to be loved in return."

Sally bent her head thoughtfully, then gazed up at her instructor. "That's beautiful, Father. It's also very disturbing."

"I agree," Father Kovacs replied. "Life can be unsettling and disturbing."

The class once again fell silent. But this time, Peter thought, the kids were searching their own thoughts, not merely waiting to see a conflict escalate.

"Please remember," Father Kovacs said, addressing the entire class, "that upon the death of Christ, the Holy Spirit, or counselor, is available to guide and encourage us. It's also here to comfort us in times of difficulty. The Holy Spirit lovingly beckons those in confusion and disbelief. There is a mysterious nature about the Holy Spirit that is far beyond our ability to comprehend."

Father Kovacs finally moved on to the lesson plan, but Peter, looking on as an observer and administrator, sensed a different sort of energy emanating from the students. Terry and Sally had been not only mollified, their dispute had been reconciled, their hostility disarmed. Whether the lesson would have lasting impact was anyone's guess, but for one fine hour, Peter thought, peace reigned in the biology classroom at St. James.

Chapter 34

The next morning, Vice Principal JD Long dropped in again on the conditioning class. By all accounts, the class had become immensely popular with students. Sometimes he worked out with the students, pretending not to notice their awed expressions as he moved mountains of weight. Other times he poured over their workout logs to track their progress.

But today's session was different. It was being held in the gymnasium, and JD quickly understood the reason why. Hanging from the ceiling near the far wall were two thick ropes, around which the students and Coach Sanders had gathered. Nobody would be lifting weights or riding a stationary bicycle today. Fastened to a beam on the ceiling, the ropes hung side by side and measured at least thirty feet each in length.

Coach Sanders, wearing a pair of cotton shorts and a windbreaker, nodded to JD and then addressed the students. "How many of you have climbed a rope before?"

Only a few students raised their hands, and those who did appeared reticent to do so, most of them glancing around in search of support.

"Good," Sanders said, seemingly determined to remain upbeat. "Looks like we've got some experienced climbers here. For those of you who've never done this, we've got a couple of volunteers to demonstrate."

Jacob Bloom and Aki Fuchida stepped forward, each dressed in the customary shorts and plain white T-shirt required of gym participants at St. James.

"Show 'em how it's done, boys," Sanders said.

Each took hold of one of the thick ropes, and soon the boys were gliding up, side by side. JD could only shake his head in admiration. The pair made it look effortless.

Fuchida touched the beam a split second before Bloom, and the two returned to the mat beneath them, neither displaying the least bit of fear or hesitation.

Sanders turned to the others. "Okay, pair up and get in line."

The kids murmured to one another as they found partners and then formed a haphazard line. Some, especially those drifting toward the back of the line, looked like they wanted to disappear into their sneakers. JD couldn't blame them. He doubted he could lug his heft up a rope even half as long as the two still swaying gently in front of them.

As the climbing began, it quickly became evident that not everyone had the same upper body strength. Some stopped halfway, whether out of exhaustion or fear of heights. Others hardly made it a few feet. The boys generally climbed higher than the girls, and small and spry climbers generally outpaced their heavier counterparts.

"All right," Coach Sanders said. "Last up!"

Phil Major and Mike Morgan had waited out the others, perhaps hoping to avoid the task altogether, but when they began their climb, a hush quickly fell over the gym. Mike, like many of the others, struggled, but Phil scurried up the rope like a spider monkey, all ropey legs and sinewy arms.

Dressed in the same dirty Chuck Taylors he wore around campus, Phil looked embarrassed as he shimmied back down. Mike, meanwhile, never made it to the top. Eventually, he gave up and eased his way back down to the mat.

Sanders stared at his stopwatch in disbelief. "Mr. Major, you just beat the all-time record, held by Fuchida here." He nodded at Aki, standing to his right. "Wanna go again?"

Phil shrugged. "Sure, I guess."

Sanders turned to Aki. "What about you? Ready for another go?"

Aki clapped his hands together. "You bet."

And just like that, a rivalry of sorts was born. JD, who'd been leaning against a wall as he watched the proceedings, stepped forward to get a closer look at the showdown. The non-athletes rallied around their new hero, chanting, "Phil! Phil! Phil!" The athletically inclined gathered around Aki, their cool-as-a-cucumber champion.

As the boys readied themselves at the ropes, each rope sporting a large knot at the base, someone shouted: "Come on, Aki. Smoke him!"

The last of the cheers echoed in the cavernous space, and Coach Sanders nodded to the two competitors. "Are you ready, gentlemen?"

Aki nodded with a cocky grin, and Phil, looking as though he wished he could hide behind his sandy brown bangs, gave a sheepish nod.

Sanders raised a hand. "Ready . . . Set . . . Go!" He brought down his hand, and the race was on.

JD found himself rooting for the underdog, and sure enough, Phil rocketed to the top and was the first to touch the beam, beating Aki by a good six feet. The students went wild.

Coach Sanders was the first to congratulate the young man after he returned to the floor. "Well done, son," he said and shook his hand while looking him in the eye.

Phil accepted the praise with an embarrassed shrug, his cheeks flushed from the exertion. His fellow students gathered round to deliver "attaboys" and pat him on the back.

JD caught himself smiling ear to ear but did nothing to hide his joy. He turned and left for his office, whistling with every step.

~~~

Peter was staring at a pile of mail on his desk later that afternoon when Father Kovacs stopped by for a visit.

Small of stature but nevertheless a force to be reckoned with, the bookish mathematician took a seat across from Peter and smiled wryly. "Sometimes I think my students have more to teach me than I them."

Peter chuckled. "I've often had the same thoughts about my staff and my parishioners—it never ceases to amaze me how much I can learn from those around me. So tell me: What did you learn today?"

"I learned," Father Kovacs said with a weary shake of the head, "that crude words often contain great wisdom."

Now Peter was intrigued. "Please go on, Father."

"As you know, I had to substitute again today in biology. You were on hand yesterday. You witnessed the—how shall I put it?— *discussion* between Terry Wisniewski and Sally Schneider. Well, today they were talking once again when they arrived, but this time much more civilly. It almost sounded like they were having a respectful dialogue."

Peter tipped an imaginary hat. "Perhaps you taught them something after all."

"Perhaps." Father Kovacs was quiet a moment as he summoned his memory. "I was prepared to deliver a lecture on dangerous bacteria. I had my notes, my thoughts. I had everything in order this time. But every time I looked out at Terry, he kept shifting in his chair, like his seat was poking him or he had ants in his pants. Finally, I said to the fellow, 'Mr. Wisniewski, do you have a question?' And he blurted out, 'My dad and I had a conversation about sin last night.' I thought to myself, 'Well, here we go again. I can't keep the lesson to biology.' These kids—they want to talk about religion. So I told him to continue. And he said, 'My dad said sin is like defecating in your own cistern.'"

Peter was glad he wasn't nursing a cup of tea. Otherwise, he would have sprayed a mouthful all over his desk. "That's one way of putting it, I suppose."

"'Charming,'" Father Kovacs said. "That was my response. Then the boy said, 'My dad said this is particularly rough on your family and guests.' The other students started giggling, of course, and Sally piped up and said, 'That's gross.' She and Terry began quibbling, with him saying something to the effect of, 'Yeah, but it's true.' I saw that his father had a point, so I asked Terry what his father's recommendations were for purification. I tried to frame it in biological terms and substituted bacteria for sin. He answered that his father's cure was the same as mine: Jesus has purified us of our sins. But his father couldn't talk anymore on the subject, apparently, because he gets emotional when discussing Christ's sacrifice. I told him, 'Perhaps his understanding has greater depth than mine,' and I meant it. I was standing there in front of my students, and all I could think was that Mr. Wisniewski's description of sin, however coarse, will remain with the children for some time, judging by how captivated they were by the conversation. Mine? It will be forgotten—if it already hasn't been."

Chapter 35

As spring wore on, the days grew longer, the weather warmer, and the students more distracted. Sandra could relate. On a Wednesday afternoon in May, she found herself thumbing through the box of records next to the turntable in the gym, unable to remember what album she'd set out to find. Her students had gone home for the day, leaving her alone in the partially lit gym, but she wanted to be prepared for her next dance lesson.

Her mind, though, was elsewhere. With her first year of teaching nearly in the rearview mirror, she couldn't help marveling at how quickly the time had passed. She'd arrived at St. James with few expectations, which had seemed wise back in August during her prep weeks before the first day of school. It was always better to be cautious about the future, she'd told herself, lest reality not live up to fantasy. But her first year as a teacher had left her wholly, wonderfully drained. And it wasn't even finished yet.

Her students, fellow faculty members—almost everyone at St. James had been friendly and supportive and had contributed greatly to her education. She'd found a way to inspire her young charges in the classroom without straying too far from the curriculum, and, perhaps more astonishingly still, she'd managed to introduce her other great love—dance—to a growing number of students. In the process, she'd come to see herself as a conduit between the older faculty members, who were often more skeptical of new methods and ideas, and the students, whose rebellious generation seemed intent on rethinking everything.

"Sandra, what are you looking for?"

Sandra gasped and whirled around to see Bobby Jones a few feet behind her. Dressed in blue jeans and an olive-green bomber jacket, he looked like the embodiment of cool. Even Sandra, who liked to think she'd outgrown the pop culture thrust upon her in her youth, couldn't deny his magnetism. All that was missing was a pair of aviator glasses.

"Sorry to surprise you," he said in a tone that reminded her that he had manners and a sensitivity that belied his persona.

"That's okay," she said. "I just didn't hear you coming."

He shifted his weight to his right foot. "What are you looking for?"

Sandra laughed. "That's the funny thing. I forgot." Then it hit her. "Oh yeah. It's a blues piece. Just wanted to have it ready for tomorrow's class."

"Which one?" Bobby asked.

"'I Got a Feeling' by Otis Spann. It's a punchy West Coast swing with a beat that will be easy for the students to follow." Sandra thought a moment. "You wouldn't happen to have time for a dance, would you?"

His face lit up with a smile. "Are you kidding? I'd love to dance some West Coast."

"Wonderful!" Sandra hurriedly flipped through the albums, and this time she found the LP, with its familiar blue-tinted cover photo of Otis playing the piano, near the back of the stack. She removed the album from its white sleeve, placed it on the record player, and turned to Bobby, suddenly aware that the dimly lit gym felt awfully romantic.

Perhaps noticing the same thing, Bobby appeared tentative as the record came to life with a plucky piano pickup. On the downbeat, an upbeat blues groove took hold that oozed the kind of chin-thrusting swagger that made the piece so irresistible.

Sandra, sensing Bobby's reticence, gave him a gentle push. "Come on, Bobby. Give me a lead I can work with."

He looked momentarily shocked by the remark before a mischievous smile overtook his lips. "You got it, teacher."

And just like that, the two were flying across the court. Sandra keyed in on Bobby's lead, which was suddenly firm and definitive— precisely what she needed to follow him with confidence. Taking a cue from him, she opted for a less-cluttered style with beautiful lines and crisp, rhythmic moves. She felt free to express herself in her dancing, and the uninhibited expression set loose a kind of sensuality that was as much art as it was growing affection for her partner. Something about Bobby aroused in her a passion she no longer feared. With every bluesy guitar riff and snare fill, she felt emboldened to perform more suggestive movements. She was no longer willing to hide what Otis was singing about: a good little feeling deep down in her soul. Enticing, sultry, it couldn't be denied.

At the song's conclusion, she gave into Bobby's spontaneous embrace and for a brief moment felt his heart beating against hers. But, no longer liberated by the music, she found herself retreating to a guarded demeanor. Bobby, too, stepped back, smiling awkwardly. The dance had been thrilling. In its afterglow, they both took a moment to catch their breath.

After some small talk and nervous laughter, Sandra found the courage to mention the school dance, which was only a few weeks away. Then she showed Bobby the practice schedule for her class. "Do you think you could help demonstrate?"

He hesitated. "Maybe. We'll see."

"Okay," Sandra said, trying in vain to sound casual in response to his hot-and-cold personality. Why did he always have to be so elusive?

"Can I help you with those?" Bobby asked as he motioned to the box of records.

"Sure," Sandra said. "I was planning on dropping them off in my classroom. Would you mind?" She hated how reserved she suddenly felt. It was as though their dance had already been forgotten and a barrier had been erected between them.

"Not at all." Bobby scooped up the records and followed Sandra out of the gym.

As they walked through the courtyard toward the main building, Sandra searched for something to say. "So . . . how was your day?"

Bobby's eyes flashed brightly. "Pretty spectacular, actually."

"Really? What happened?"

"Well, Mrs. Weaver invited me to conduct a master class for her best singers. But it was a ruse. I showed up to a surprise party."

"That's wonderful!"

"I gotta say, it's nice to be appreciated. Since the spring concert, they haven't needed me. I kind of missed volunteering."

"Who was there?" she asked.

"Everyone. The choir. The orchestra. When I walked in, they broke into Wayne Newton's 'Danke Schoen.'" He laughed. "You could tell the kids were a little embarrassed. You know, it's not Led Zeppelin. But they sang their hearts out. Then they got to do some contemporary stuff. The Beach Boys' version of 'Papa-Oom-Mow-Mow.' The Beatles' 'With a Little Help from My Friends.'" He grew quiet. "I was floored. It meant a lot to me."

They entered the main building and walked in silence to Sandra's classroom. After dropping off the records and locking up, they made their way to the parking lot. Sandra bit her lip, searching for something to say. Why did it suddenly have to be so awkward? She wished they could be back out on the dance floor.

Bobby finally broke the ice. "Thanks for the dance. You were amazing."

She blushed. "So were you."

He turned toward his motorcycle, which was propped on its kickstand nearby.

"Bobby?"

He stopped and turned to face her again. "Yeah?"

"You deserved that party. Your volunteer work is much appreciated."

Now he appeared to be the one blushing. "Thanks. So long."

She groped for a reply but could only nod tentatively and repeat his words. "So long."

Chapter 36

On the following Monday, after the last of her students had left the classroom, Sandra retrieved her gradebook from her briefcase and began the preliminary work of determining final grades. With the exception of the next day's quiz and one assignment due later in the week, the work was finished, the heavy lifting over.

She thought back to the first day of school, seemingly a lifetime ago, when Jenny O'Donnell had behaved so shyly and Danny Corvino so crudely. Both students, and all their classmates, had come a long way. Jenny flourished despite the loss of her mother, gradually opening like a blooming flower, and Danny softened, revealing a sensitive side he'd hidden from his peers. Poetry had unmasked them, and the power of the English language had given them both a voice to communicate their innermost thoughts and feelings.

Sandra leaned back in her chair and swiveled toward the windows, staring at the sunny afternoon unfolding outside. A ribbon of cobalt-blue sky stretched in every direction above Hideki Fuchida's glorious landscape of ornamental trees, exotic perennials, and winding pathways. The fact that St. James was on the chopping block seemed unbelievable. She was still finding her footing, still exploring a career she knew would take a lifetime to master, but she couldn't imagine doing so anywhere but here, among such a vibrant community.

"Knock, knock."

Sandra flinched, surprised by the intrusion, and turned toward the doorway, where Mathilde Weaver stood with a smile. The diminutive music teacher was balancing on one foot and had one hand on her hip and the other on the door jamb. "Got time for a visit?"

"Of course," Sandra said. "Come in."

Mathilde entered and took note of Sandra's sundress. "You look lovely."

"Thank you," Sandra said and glanced down at the bright yellow dress that fell just below her knees. "I hope it's not too much."

"Not at all. It's good to see you embrace something splashy once in a while. You always dress so conservatively."

Sandra felt her face burn red. "I prefer not to draw attention to myself, but this spring has been so lovely. I felt like participating—if that makes sense."

Mathilde grinned. "Absolutely."

Sandra caught her taking in all the plants scattered around the classroom. "You like?"

"If I didn't know better, I'd think you were teaching horticulture. It looks like a greenhouse in here."

Sandra laughed. "I don't know which I'll miss more, the students or their plants. This place will feel awfully empty without them."

The comment froze both of them.

"Then again," Sandra finally said in a quiet voice, "it's possible none of us will be back here again."

Mathilde put her hands on her hips and frowned. "I don't like to think about things I can't control. Let's assume we'll be back. Will you do the same lesson?"

Sandra appreciated her colleague's determination to remain optimistic. "That's a good question. On the one hand, I feel like the students learned a lot from the experiment. Especially the boys. We all benefit when young people become more nurturing."

"On the other hand?"

"On the other hand, I love how spontaneous it was. It wasn't part of any curriculum. It grew out of a classroom discussion. Who knows how the conversation will go next year?"

"Right," Mathilde said. "Every class is different. Every new group of students brings with it a new kind of energy, a new focus, a new paradigm. What animates one group doesn't register with another. Maybe next year your room will be full of ant farms."

"Oh goodness," Sandra said, chuckling. "I hope not."

"I definitely prefer the plants," Mathilde said. "They're more . . . *romantic.*"

Something about the way Mathilde said the last word caught Sandra's attention. Was she hinting at something?

"How's the dance program going?" Mathilde asked.

Sandra tried to shift gears. "Oh, wonderfully. We're having a year-end dance party this Thursday afternoon. You should stop by. Some of the kids have made quite a bit of progress"

"I'll plan on it." Mathilde was quiet a moment. "Will Bobby Jones be participating?"

"I'm not sure," Sandra answered guardedly, suddenly feeling she was being led somewhere.

"He was such a wonderful help to me this year," Mathilde said without prompting. "And the Christmas concert! I'll never forget his performance. He saved the day!"

Was she being set up? Sandra was pretty sure where this was leading but decided to play along. "He did indeed. He's been a godsend to the ballroom dancing program. I think it would have failed without him."

Mathilde nodded. "He has such a kind heart, such a generous spirit. And what a talent!" She gave Sandra a sly grin. "He's also quite the gentleman. And very handsome."

"So I've noticed, although I don't know that he's noticed *me.*"

Mathilde's eyes widened. "Are you kidding? How couldn't he? You're a sight to behold."

Sandra attempted a smile, but it quickly faded.

"Do you know the Blooms?" Mathilde asked.

"We met at the school concert, if memory serves."

"Well, Rachael and Jonathan are having an afternoon picnic and evening party next Saturday at their beach house on the Cape. Rachael asked me to extend a warm invitation to you and Sister Consuela. They'd be delighted if you both could attend."

Sandra smiled to herself as she closed her gradebook and stood. She wasn't sure what Bobby had to do with the party at the Blooms' beach house unless . . . *That's it!* Bobby, no doubt, had been invited as well. It was clear that Mathilde had been talking with Rachael. Sandra could almost see the two conspiring together over lunch at a diner in downtown Lawrence. Perhaps Mathilde had raised the issue. Or perhaps Rachael was the matchmaker. They'd probably discussed Bobby's dashing good looks, his awful experience in Vietnam, his tortured soul—and decided she was the tonic he needed.

Sandra had to admit to herself that she wasn't opposed to the idea. She'd found herself drawn to Bobby ever since their first dance, but she wasn't sure Bobby felt the same. They'd shared a few moments that revealed their powerful connection, but whether he'd want to do anything about it was another matter entirely. She could only guess at what was in his heart, for he kept his feelings hidden.

"Rachael says they've totally updated their beach house," Mathilde said, perhaps sensing Sandra's indecision. "The place hadn't been decorated since the thirties, I guess, and needed a major facelift. Now it has modern décor, plus an old upright piano for singalongs."

As it happened, Sandra had already planned on spending most of the summer on the Cape, where her extended family had already made arrangements to rent a property. There was no reason to say no.

She felt her shoulders relax as she smiled at Mathilde. "I'd love to attend. And please count my sister in. I'll call her tonight and let you know if there's a conflict."

"Wonderful!" Mathilde turned on her heel. "See you at the dance party!"

~~~

Vice Principal JD Long was about to leave for the afternoon when Maria Donatello intercepted him in his office doorway.

"You have a visitor," she said with an arched eyebrow.

JD looked past Maria at the student standing behind her: Phil Major. The wiry kid with slumping shoulders and a prominent Adam's apple had become somewhat of a legend since setting the record for the rope climb in Coach Sanders's conditioning class. Now here he was, hands stuffed into his pockets, looking as sheepish as ever.

"Caught smoking again?" JD asked.

Maria maintained her deadpan expression. "Actually, Phil has come of his own volition." She tilted her head slightly as she gave JD an amused look. "I'll leave you two gentlemen to it."

JD invited Phil into his office and then returned to his desk. "So," he said, settling back into his chair, "what can I do for you, Mr. Major?"

Phil tentatively slid into the chair opposite JD and cleared his throat. "I just wanted to say thank you, Vice Principal Long, for everything you've done for me."

JD was taken aback. When he'd first spied Phil standing behind Maria, he'd assumed he'd be doling out one last round of punishment—no small feat during the last week of school. Phil was a senior and on his way out. JD would have to get creative. But thankfully Phil hadn't been caught smoking in the bathroom or cutting class.

"Well," JD said, fumbling for a response, "I'm glad I was able to help." He paused a moment to sort through his emotions. "Have you thought much about what you're going to do now that you're about to graduate?"

Phil nodded. "Me and Mike are going into business together."

"Mike Morgan?"

"Yup."

Mike, just like Phil, had earned a unique reputation at St. James. But unlike Phil, he had no athletic aptitude. It was his ultra-dry sense of humor, understated but always at the ready, that regularly left his classmates in fits of laughter. From what JD understood, he'd become a gym mascot of sorts. By all accounts, conditioning class was more entertaining whenever Mike was present. His drawings—hilarious caricatures of the trainers straining with stacks of weight—had been used to wallpaper the weight room. JD had studied most of them, not to mention the reactions of the students and teachers to each portrait. The hands-down favorite showed Coach Sanders attempting to demonstrate proper squat technique. In the drawing, the handsome coach had just lost his balance and was tumbling to the floor with a heavy stack of weights. The expression on his face—one of terror and disbelief—captured the emotions of a competent coach whose demonstration had gone terribly, comically awry. Human emotion and the nuanced expressions it produced were Mike's specialty, and his talent hadn't escaped the notice of Laurel Nord, whom JD had heard in the lunchroom more than once marveling at Mike's drawings. She'd urged him to take her art class, where he'd apparently had great success.

"What kind of business?" JD asked.

"Woodworking," Phil said.

JD swelled with pride. He'd recognized Mike's talent early on and had encouraged him to take woodshop. Unlike some students, present company included, Mike had seemed a perfect fit, not just someone in need of academic redirection.

"I've always been pretty lousy at it," Phil explained. "But not Mike. He makes these amazing leaves out of wood. Maple leaves from maple wood. Oak leaves from red and white oak. Birch leaves from birch. Cherry leaves from cherry wood. They're really something. So I got to thinking. My neighbor owns a gift shop downtown. Maybe he might sell 'em. Mike was cool with the idea, so I talked to my neighbor. We've already sold several dozen."

JD shook his head in delight. "Amazing!"

"We're calling ourselves M&M Wood Specialties of New England. Mike is the designer and builder. I'm the promoter, I guess you'd say. Mike says he hates thinking about business stuff. You know, finding customers, setting price points, marketing stuff. But that stuff comes naturally to me. I like trying to figure out what people want, what motivates them, and all that. Right now it's just a cottage industry, but we got plans to go into it full-time as soon as we graduate."

"What about home décor? Don't you need to know something about how people decorate their homes?"

Phil nodded. "I've been reading up on all that. Right now, a ton of Asian products are flooding the market. But people around here want something from our part of the world, you know? Something that says New England. That's where Mike and me come in. We sell homegrown art, not fancy imports."

JD had gone from tickled to astonished. "Where'd you learn all this, kid?"

"I just pick up stuff," Phil said with a shrug. "It's fun."

"What about finances? If Mike's the artist and you're the salesman, you still need someone with business sense to run things. Otherwise, you won't make a profit."

"Yeah," Phil replied with a chuckle. "I'm no good with money. Neither is Mike. When it comes to finance and accounting and all that, we're a freakin' disaster." He laughed again. "But I've been watching how things operate around here. Mrs. Donatello runs a tight ship. I've seen how her administrative team works. You and Father Ryan . . . well, how can I put this? When it comes to the bottom line and keeping this place afloat, you two probably don't know much more than Mike and me. Am I right?"

All JD could do was laugh in agreement. The kid had no idea how right he was.

"Well," Phil continued, "hopefully I can put everything I learned during my detention time to good use. I look at Mrs. Donatello and her team like mechanics. They keep the engines running and in tip-top shape. Without them, nothing gets done."

"It's a good metaphor," JD said. "But you'll need more than a conceptual framework. You'll need training."

Phil ran a hand through his short hair. "Yeah, I figure I'll take a class or two at the junior college. Learn some accounting tricks. Heck, maybe you can write me a letter of recommendation when I apply."

JD stood and shook the young man's hand. "I'd be glad to, son."

Phil started for the door. "I hope we make you proud, sir."

Not one to wear his heart on his sleeve, JD choked back a tear. "You already have, Mr. Major."

Chapter 37

Peter had just hung the last of the streamers in the gymnasium for the dance party and was collapsing the stepladder when he heard the staccato sound of high heels striking the tile floor in the front entryway.

A second later, Maria Donatello burst through the double doors. "Did I miss it?"

Everyone laughed.

"No," Peter said, propping the stepladder against a wall. "The party's just about to begin."

The students in the dance class and their faculty supporters had gathered in the drafty gym for one last celebration before the end of the school year. Ostensibly the students were marking their progression from neophytes to budding young dancers, but Peter felt something else in the air, a kind of letting go, or healing ritual. With the school's future still in doubt, the tension at St. James had reached a fever pitch in the final week of school. Catharsis was needed, and the transcendent power of dance offered a way through the confusion and angst. Cheerfulness, given all they'd been through over the course of the school year, was the same as defiance.

Peter offered his hand to Maria as she approached. "Ever danced with a priest before, Mrs. Donatello?"

Maria laughed, her eyes crinkling at the corners. "I don't know that I have, Father."

"Well," he said loud enough for everyone to hear, "what say we cut a rug?"

The students laughed and cheered, lifting their voices to the rafters, and Sandra, who had been sorting records near the turntable, dropped the needle on an LP. A second later, the sitar-guitar intro to Stevie Wonder's brand-new hit "Signed, Sealed, Delivered I'm Yours" echoed across the court.

Peter grabbed Maria's free hand and danced an ecstatic triple-time swing in the jitterbug style. He could feel the groove in his bones and for two minutes and forty-two seconds, the length of the song, lost himself in the music.

> Ooh, baby!
> Here I am!
> Signed, sealed, delivered—I'm yours!

Eight steps instead of four, leading into an underarm turn, and then—bam!—an inside turn. Wild abandon had never felt so good. Peter knew just how to move, when to step and how to guide Maria, who was smiling ear to ear. He felt like he'd stepped back in time and was in Oahu, waiting to be shipped out, waiting for the war to engulf him, finding escape in the music, on the dance floor, in a whirl of sweat and ecstasy. He could only imagine what the students thought: a Catholic priest burning up the hardwoods with the school administrator.

As the song faded, the students unleashed a full-throated cheer of approval, and Peter, never one to miss a beat, clasped Maria's hand and took a bow, all smiles.

A second later, Sandra dropped another record on the turntable, and Wilson Pickett's "Mustang Sally" droned forth like a big rig rounding a bend in the road.

Peter guided Maria toward the bleachers so they could catch

209

their breath.

"What do you think will become of this place," Maria asked over the music, "if the diocese sells the property?"

Peter heaved a heavy sigh. "I wonder. I suppose whoever buys it will bulldoze the buildings and start fresh . . . maybe with an office complex or a small shopping center."

Maria gasped and covered her mouth. "That would be awful."

Peter gazed out at the dance floor and spotted his nephew dancing with Jenny O'Donnell. He was amazed by the transformation of both. Bobby, no longer a bitter man trapped in his own disillusionment and grief, was playing the role of the protective older brother. And Jenny, long having stepped out of her shell, looked confident and radiant. Her artistry and sensuality, it seemed to Peter, shocked even her as she followed Bobby's lead on the dance floor.

The mood in the gym changed with the next song, Ben E. King's "Stand by Me," Bobby and Jenny had retreated to the bleachers to share an animated conversation, but it ended when Danny Corvino tapped Jenny on the shoulder. Peter saw her face flush as she accepted his invitation to dance. The song was a rumba, and far from shrinking from the task, Danny and Jenny demonstrated it to perfection while the playful bass line and haunting chorus of "Stand by Me" evoked in Peter something akin to nostalgia.

"They dance beautifully together," Maria said in astonishment.

Peter nodded, certain he was witnessing the beginning of something more than impetuous infatuation, more than young romance. "They say rumba is the dance of love."

As he listened to the song's lyrics, Peter realized it wasn't nostalgia he was feeling; it was déjà vu. The first verse had been about overcoming fear and loss, and the second verse continued that theme:

If the sky that we look upon

210

Should tumble and fall,
Or the mountains should crumble to the sea,
I won't cry, I won't cry.
No, I won't shed a tear.
Just as long as you stand, stand by me.

"The Psalms," he whispered under his breath, caught by the sudden epiphany. Ben E. King was riffing on Psalms 46, which contained similar imagery and a similar theme:

God is our refuge and our strength,
An ever-present help in distress.
Therefore we fear not, though the earth be shaken
And mountains plunge into the depths of the sea . . .

Perhaps Jenny's growth and newfound strength came from her faith, Peter thought. And perhaps Danny was attracted to her now that she radiated God's love. They looked like more than two individuals dancing. They looked like a couple.

Peter was still smiling at these thoughts when Sandra's final selection—a waltz—began playing. It struck him as a fitting piece to close the ballroom portion of the dance. Bobby strode toward her, took her hand, and the two glided gracefully across the hardwoods to Andy Williams's dreamy performance of "Moon River."

Moon River, wider than a mile.
I'm crossing you in style someday.
You dream maker, you heartbreaker.
Wherever you're going, I'm going your way.

Some of the more daring students joined them, but most gave the couple a wide berth, seemingly awestruck by their silver waltz, which they made look easy. Elegant. Smooth. Their performance opened a window into another era and left Peter longing for the past.

After the song drew to a close, the students cheered once more. Then they gathered around Sandra, who had signaled her desire to address them.

"I hope everyone enjoyed the class," she said. "It's my wish that music and dance will always hold a special place in your hearts. Seniors, whether you're thinking about going to college or entering the work force, do so with the confidence and joy you display on the dance floor. This is your time to shine! Undergraduates, I hope that God smiles on us all and grants us another year together. Everyone, it's been an absolute pleasure."

Sandra changed records one more time, and the selection that followed—all seventeen tracks from the Beatles' *Abbey Road*—signified the transition from the past to the present. Still less than a year old, the music was combustible, revolutionary, frightening to some. Peter found it brash but intriguing and couldn't deny the power of its primal rhythms and rough-edged melodies. The new style of dancing was improvised and personal, and though the students danced in pairs, they moved separately, in harmony but not in unison. During slow songs, they swayed together, holding one another as closely as they dared under Sandra's watchful eye.

Peter wasn't sure how to respond to "I Want You (She's So Heavy)," a schizophrenic tune that veered between lumbering dirge and discordant frenzy. But he couldn't help but tap his foot along to "Here Comes the Sun" and its cheerful chorus. As he watched Jenny and Danny bounce to the spontaneous rhythms animating them, he could almost see the future. Perhaps they'd marry, raise a family, and grow old together. And perhaps they'd return one day to thank their English-teacher-turned-dance-instructor for a memorable introduction to the miracle of dancing. The world would be theirs to shape, and they'd make the transition to adulthood with a steady backbeat as their soundtrack.

"Times are changing," Maria said.

"They are indeed," Peter said with a wistful smile. "I hope we can keep up."

Chapter 38

Peter breathed in the salty sea air like an oenophile inhaling a heady red wine at the dinner table. He and Jonathan were lounging peacefully on their Adirondack chairs on the Bloom family's beach house deck. Above them, the night sky full of twinkling stars seemed to stretch outward forever. Below, the soothing surf glowed in the moonlight.

"Another school year in the books," Peter said.

"Not just *any* year," Jonathan countered.

Peter smiled but said nothing. He and the Blooms had beaten the others to the beach house and were all too happy to enjoy a quiet Friday evening. Rachael was already curled up with a novel inside. Bobby would arrive the next morning, followed by Mathilde and, a few hours later, by Sandra and Sister Consuela. By Saturday evening, the house would be overflowing with guests. With the Blooms' permission, Maria had even invited Antonio and Kathleen Federici. Jonathan had agreed it was the least they could do after Antonio's generous offer of help. Peter only wished the timing of the offer could have been better.

"What are you feeling?" Jonathan asked.

Peter didn't need long to search for an answer. "Gratitude."

"*Gratitude?*" Jonathan repeated in a voice tinged with disbelief.

Peter smiled sadly. "I can't say no to God's plans, whatever they may be. Every day is a new opportunity, another chance to show our gratitude for God's grace."

"You sound like you're ready to say goodbye to St. James."

"I don't know that I'll ever be ready, but I suppose that's the whole point. It's not really a leap of faith if you can see where you're going to land."

Jonathan raised his gin and tonic. "Mazel tov."

Peter clinked glasses with him. "Cheers."

Jonathan leaned back in his chair, his dark silhouette almost disappearing into the inky backdrop. "Do you ever wonder how a Jew and a Catholic priest became best friends?"

"Not for a second," Peter said. "Our friendship is nearly as old as we are."

"Sure, but friends outgrow one another all the time. Boys become men. Their faiths harden."

"I suppose. I guess I just don't view our faiths as that different. We both view this earth as the handiwork of our creator. We both see faith and love of God as our greatest blessing. We know everything good in our lives comes from God."

"Yahweh or Jesus?" Jonathan asked.

Peter didn't fall for the trap. "Judaism and Christianity are co-heirs to the Kingdom of Heaven. As long as we do the Lord's work, every day has meaning and purpose. I believe in the Nicene Creed, the love of Christ, the Trinity, the Holy Mother, and the saints. You believe in the discipline of the Torah and the law of the Prophets. We each have a relationship with God. We pray. We interact with the community of the faithful."

"Are we two sides of the same coin?"

Peter paused a moment before quoting the Torah or, as it was known to his faith, the Old Testament. "'Do not seek revenge or bear a grudge against anyone among your people, but love your neighbor as yourself. I am the Lord.'"

"Leviticus," Jonathan said.

"'Love the Lord your God with all your heart, and with all your

215

soul, and with all your mind.'"

"The Gospel of Matthew."

Peter paused to listen to the waves lapping at the beach just beyond the deck. "I've never been much of a theologian. But yes, I'd say we're two sides of the same coin. The positive results of a life lived according to these two truths are empirical in nature. You can see the exciting and satisfying outcomes in people's lives, which are almost always paid forward. It's a mystery that can't be fully understood or adequately articulated. My faith attributes it to the Holy Spirit, the source of infinite creativity. Perhaps yours would attribute it to the love of God Himself. But these are semantics, no? We're discussing the same thing."

Jonathan took another sip, then set his drink on the small table between them and rested his right hand firmly on his chair's armrest. "These Adirondacks have a long history."

"They sure do," Peter said and stared at the finish on his armrest. It had been worn smooth from years of use.

"Our parents used to sit in these very same chairs," Jonathan said. "Seems fitting they left them here for us and the next generation."

Peter nodded. "We were lucky to have such great parents. My parents taught me generosity, but so did yours. Your father gave our family the root stock for our own little orchard. He taught me the art of grafting and caring for trees." Peter remembered Ed Bloom with great affection. "When I think of your father, I always think of the Book of Isaiah: 'There shall come forth a shoot from the stump of Jesse, and a branch from its roots shall bear fruit.'"

"That's nice," Jonathan said in a peaceful tone. "I like that."

~~~

After breakfast the next morning, Peter was back in his chair and basking in the morning sun beside Jonathan on the deck. Blue skies. A slight onshore breeze. He could feel contentment seeping into his bones. Instead of a gin and tonic, he was nursing a strong cup of coffee, courtesy of Rachael, who seemed to have the magic touch. She was rummaging through supplies in the kitchen, and Peter found the clatter of pots and pans colliding and cupboards and drawers banging shut wonderfully comforting.

"You finished with the arts and leisure section?" Jonathan asked from his chair.

Peter extracted the section from the morning newspaper he was reading and handed it across the table to Jonathan. "Be my guest."

Peter had been staring at an article on the front page for the better part of ten minutes but had yet to finish it. It was an update on the fighting in Vietnam's A Shau Valley. The state of the campaign wasn't as concerning as one small detail, a mere aside, mentioned about three-quarters into the story. The fighting, it seemed, had crossed the border into Cambodia.

The war struck Peter as something without definition or clarity. Like an amorphous octopus with too many tentacles to count, it was everywhere and nowhere, a shadowy struggle in jungles too dense for daylight to penetrate. The participants—the US military, the South Vietnamese forces, the NVA, the Vietcong—seemed to be waging different wars, with each fighting for different reasons. Was this a civil war or a war for independence? A fight to contain communism or to stop colonialism?

Peter gave up and turned to the sports page, but the news there wasn't much better. The Boston Red Sox, behind new manager Eddie Kasko, were mired in third place in the American League East, well behind the first-place Baltimore Orioles.

"Do you think the Sox will ever win a World Series?"

Jonathan looked up from his reading. "In our lifetime?"

Peter motioned to the features section, now spread open in Jonathan's hands. "Anything interesting?"

"Just reading about Tanglewood."

Since the 1930s, the Boston Symphony Orchestra had performed each summer at Tanglewood, perhaps Massachusetts's most beloved music venue. Its current conductor, William Steinberg, had been hired the previous year.

Peter wondered if Bobby would perform there this summer. He gazed out at the surf and spotted his nephew, clad only in a pair of red shorts, trying to catch a medium wave. From the beach house, Bobby cut an impressive silhouette against the late-morning sun.

"Look at Bobby," Peter said with a shake of his head. "What a physique! It's hard to believe we were ever that lean."

Jonathan shifted his rangy frame in his Adirondack and then patted his ample stomach. "These days I look like an orange on a toothpick."

Peter laughed and then reached for the thermos of coffee on the table and topped off both their mugs. A second later, he heard Mathilde's Volkswagen Beetle pulling onto the driveway's hard-packed sand. He glanced at his watch and saw it was ten o'clock.

"Right on time," Jonathan said.

Peter hoisted himself up from his chair and followed Jonathan through the house to the front door. Rachael was already greeting Mathilde in the driveway by the time they joined them.

The music teacher's sunny cheeks shone from beneath her wide-brimmed straw hat as she stepped from her car. "What a glorious morning!" she declared in a cheerful voice.

Mathilde and Rachael exchanged hugs.

"Can we help with anything?" Peter asked.

"Yes, please." Mathilde pointed to a box of supplies in the passenger's seat. "Do you mind carrying those inside?"

"Not at all." Peter opened the door, leaned over to pull the box free, and tried not to grimace under its weight as he carried it inside.

Jonathan grabbed Mathilde's overnight bag and followed suit.

Rachael was right on their heels. "Once you're done helping Mathilde, gentlemen, I have a list of chores for you."

Chapter 39

The coolers had been stuffed with ice, and the extra chairs had been retrieved from the shed and dusted with damp rags. Two hours had passed since lunch, and Peter was happy to be nearly finished with Rachael's list. While prying apart the dining room table to add two extension leaves, he and Jonathan exchanged glances. Rachael and Mathilde could be heard talking in the nearby kitchen.

"I was hoping Sandra and Sister Consuela would show up at three o'clock," Rachael said. "That would give Sandra and Bobby more time to get acquainted. But it's already three-fifteen."

"Let's not worry," Mathilde said. "There's still time for them to walk the beach together—if Bobby can ever pull himself away from his surfboard."

As if on cue, Peter spied Bobby entering through the sliding glass door on the deck. He'd donned sandals and a white T-shirt with a surfing logo on it and had slung his beach towel over his shoulder.

"Bobby!" Peter said loudly enough to be heard in the kitchen. "How was the water?"

"Cold!" he answered with a mock shiver. "But I sat out in the sun to warm up between runs. The waves weren't bad for this beach."

Rachael appeared in the entrance to the kitchen, hands on hips, apron at the ready. "You're just in time, young man. We need some muscle in the kitchen."

"Having trouble with the pickle jar again, honey?" Jonathan quipped.

Rachael threw him a sideways glance. "Very funny, dear."

Peter patted Bobby on the back as his nephew dutifully headed toward the kitchen. "Go get 'em."

Peter and Jonathan finished with the table leaves and set the table for a grand Cape Cod seafood feast. Then, before the women could enlist them in more chores, they escaped back to the deck.

They were about to take up residence in their favorite chairs when Peter spotted two people on the beach walking toward the house. He recognized their silhouettes immediately. Sister Consuela, even out of habit, projected the same stout form and walked with the same energized gait. Her younger, more petite sister struggled to keep pace.

Peter signaled as they approached, and they waved heartily in return.

Sister Consuela took the wooden steps two at a time and was the first on the porch. "Father Ryan!" she said as she accepted his handshake. "It's so strange to see you in casual beachwear."

Peter laughed and made a show of giving Sister Consuela, dressed in cotton pants and a short-sleeved blouse, a double-take. "I should say the same to you. Welcome, both of you."

Rachael and Mathilde, dressed in matching aprons, joined everyone on the deck, but Rachael stayed only briefly—long enough to give each sister a hug and a warm welcome.

Then she opened the screen door once again and excused herself. "Time to liberate my kitchen help."

A moment later, she reappeared with the freed prisoner, who was still proudly wearing his apron.

Sandra's face lit up at the sight of Bobby. "Has he been a good helper?"

Mathilde's lips quivered as she tried to keep a straight face. "He was most helpful carrying heavy items and opening jars."

Everyone laughed, even Bobby.

"What do I smell cooking?" Sister Consuela asked.

Rachael, never known to waste an opportunity, took her by the hand. "I'll show you, Sister." She turned to Bobby. "I hereby release you from your duties, young man. Perhaps you and Sandra can enjoy some beach time before the five o'clock cocktail hour."

Bobby took the suggestion in stride. "Sounds good to me. But don't make Sister Consuela work too hard, okay?" He grinned and handed his apron to Rachael. Then, before Sandra could get too big of a head-start, he slipped off his sandals and followed her down the sandy planks to the beach.

Peter watched them all the way to the surf and then turned and smiled to the only other person remaining on the deck. "She really is a talented matchmaker, your Rachael."

Jonathan nodded. "You're lucky you're a priest. She'd have married you off by now if you weren't."

~~~

Sandra felt sweet relief when she reached the chilly surf, having just outsprinted Bobby across the hot sand. She waded into the cool ocean ahead of him and let out a gasp when a small wave partially submerged her.

"That's cold!" she exclaimed as Bobby tromped through the water toward her.

"You get used to it," he said with a reassuring smile. His deep tan skin shone under the New England sun, every sinewy muscle dappled with ocean spray.

They frolicked in the water until Sandra was ready for a break, at which time they took up residence on a towel on the hard-packed sand just beyond the receding tide.

Bobby shook the sand off his feet and leaned back on his elbows. "So what are you going to do if the merger goes through?"

Sandra frowned. "Apply for the same job all over again, I guess."

"You're smart and on your way up. They'd be crazy not to hire you."

She tried not to bask in the compliment. "What about you?"

He paused to squint up at the sun and then turned toward her. "I don't know. I guess I could volunteer at Notre Dame, assuming they need help. I really enjoyed working with the choir. And your dance class was a blast."

"There were so many surprises," she said, already feeling nostalgic, "and so many bright kids. Thank you for sharing your time and talent with us. Without you, the dance class might have folded. And poor Mathilde. She would have been lost without you at the Christmas concert."

"I was glad to help."

Sandra glanced down the beach, which seemed to stretch on forever, and felt inspired to move. "You want to go for a walk?"

"Sure," Bobby said and stood up.

"Let's just stay close to the water," Sandra said. "My feet can't take the hot sand."

"Sounds good to me."

They wandered north, covering perhaps a mile or more, and Sandra found herself so engrossed in conversation that she felt time and distance melt away. She reminisced about her first year of teaching—the excitement of new relationships, the growth of the students, the success of the dance class—and wondered aloud if every year would be so invigorating. Bobby reiterated how much he'd appreciated the surprise party the choir had thrown him.

"I'm sorry I disappointed you that day," Bobby said.

She waved it off. "You came through in the end. That's what counts."

"I really did have fun," he said.

Sandra, unable to ignore the gratitude welling up inside her, instinctively hugged Bobby. Much to her delight, he hugged her back. She could feel his heart pounding against hers, and when he stepped back to gaze into her eyes, she realized her life would never again be the same. She'd found the love of her life.

Then it hit her. "Oh my God! What time is it?"

Bobby gazed out at the sun, now arcing toward the western sky, then glanced at his watch. "It's five-thirty. The cocktail hour's almost over."

They shared a giddy laugh and turned to jog back the way they'd come. When they slowed to a walk about a quarter mile from the beach house, Sandra grabbed his hand, determined not to let go.

Chapter 40

When Peter spotted Bobby and Sandra on the beach, he thought he detected something different about them. Then he noticed it: they were holding hands.

He nudged Jonathan. "Rachael can put another notch in her belt."

Jonathan shook his head in wonderment. "She really knows her material, doesn't she?"

Standing beside them at the deck railing were Antonio and Kathleen Federici, the last of the guests to arrive. They had a full house now, and Peter was glad they'd inserted the extra leaves into the dinner table, even if Rachael had eventually made them cart it out onto the deck—with the settings already in place—so they could eat outside in the salty air.

"Remember the new English teacher I told you about?" Peter asked Antonio. "The one who started a dance class after school?"

"I do. Is that her?"

"It is."

Antonio squinted into the distance. "Who's she walking with?"

"My nephew," Peter replied. "Bobby Jones."

Patrick, nursing a drink next to Kathleen, looked out of his element with no cabana to preside over. "Are they an item?" he asked in his working-class British accent.

"They are now," Jonathan quipped.

Before they could call for Rachael, she was slinking through the sliding door with a sly smile. "I saw them from the kitchen window. I knew they were meant for each other."

"You always know, dear," Jonathan said.

By now they were nearly within earshot.

"Now don't make a fuss," Rachael said and ushered Mathilde, just now stepping onto the deck, back inside.

Peter noticed Maria, who had arrived by herself, holding back a laugh. "Maybe we should gather at the table."

"A fine idea," Antonio said.

They didn't have far to go. The table took up a good portion of the far side of the deck, and it took some time for everyone to squeeze into their seats.

When the young couple had joined them and everyone was seated, Peter kept the prayer short, lest the food get cold and he invoke Rachael's wrath. "Bless us, O Lord, and these, Thy gifts, which we are about to receive from Thy bounty. Through Christ, our Lord. Amen."

Jonathan was the first to dig in, but Peter, after crossing himself, wasn't far behind. Before he knew it, he was staring down at a plate piled high with clams, boiled potatoes, corn on the cob, and the main dish that had everyone salivating in anticipation: fresh lobster. He'd wash it all down with a glass of Roero Arneis, one of a handful of Italian white wines Jonathan had picked out with Antonio in mind. The man was from Piedmont, after all.

Still embarrassed by his overindulgence at the Federici home a few months earlier, Peter promised himself that he'd go easy on the wine this time.

"This all looks amazing," Bobby said in a reverent tone.

"We couldn't have done it without you," Rachael quipped, earning a smattering of laughs.

"Hey, I opened a *lot* of jars."

Peter smiled. It was good to see his nephew playfully interacting with friends and family like he had in years past, before his tour in Vietnam. Susan would be thrilled and relieved to know that her son was back on his feet again, ready to risk happiness, even if it meant leaving behind once and for all the war and those who had fought and died at his side.

At the other end of the table, Antonio, his face alive with a joyful, almost lustful smile, raised his glass. "I'd like to offer a toast!"

"Hear! Hear!" Jonathan announced.

When everyone had raised a glass, whether of wine, beer—or, in Maria's case, unsweetened iced tea—Antonio spoke. "Long live St. James High School and its magnificent staff and faculty. May the teachers continue to motivate and lead their students to greater and greater heights, and may the students strive to achieve what they were destined to accomplish and, ultimately, leave our world greater than they found it."

The table fell silent, and Peter, glancing at the others, could see that he wasn't the only one confused by Antonio's toast. Still, they sipped from their glasses and returned them quietly to the table.

"But Mr. Federici," Sandra said to the man she'd met only moments earlier, "St. James is closing. Haven't you heard?"

Antonio let go a hearty laugh and then, as though struck by a painful thought, turned to Peter with a sober expression on his ruddy-cheeked face. "Do you remember what you said, Father, when we dined at my home?"

Peter searched his memory but came up empty.

"You talked about what it would mean to break up St. James. The faculty. The students. You said the community would suffer a great loss."

Peter nodded. "Yes, I remember saying that."

"You said more than that, Father. You talked about your vice principal. Your gardener." Antonio motioned to Sandra across the

227

table. "Your new English teacher here."

Sandra's cheeks pinked.

"You talked about synergy and the unique atmosphere at St. James," Antonio went on. "Your words . . ." He paused, then picked up his wine glass and sipped. Peter realized that Antonio had momentarily lost his voice. He returned his glass to the table, cleared his throat, and started over. "Your words, coming on the heels of my mother's death, gave me something I haven't felt for some time: hope! Hope for the future. Hope for our community, our children. Every wealthy man with even the tiniest sliver of a conscience is in constant search of a way to pay back the world for what he has gained, and I've found that way in you, in your school. You saved me, Father, and I'd like to return the favor." Antonio turned to Maria. "Would you like to tell them, or shall I?"

Maria smiled coyly. "This is your moment, Mr. Federici."

Antonio returned his gaze to Peter. "Father Ryan, sometimes it's enough simply to have faith that everything will work out, God willing. 'Consider the lilies.' Isn't that what Jesus told his disciples? We're not meant to spend our lives worrying about what is to come."

Peter's mind raced. "Are you saying—"

"I'm saying St. James will be around for a long, long time, Father. You had until the end of June, correct? Well, according to the calendar, it's still June."

Peter gaped at him. "But . . . how . . . ?"

"Funny story: I recently met a man with an obsession for ancient Roman statuary that rivals my own. A dashing gent from the Old Country. Hardly speaks a word of English. Anyway, long story short, he saw my collection and absolutely had to have it."

Peter suddenly realized where Antonio was going. "Your Roman statues?"

"His offer was very generous. I refused him at first, of course, just as I've refused several other offers over the years. But then I thought of you, Father, and your school, and the community you so love, and it seemed to me I'd stumbled upon the perfect solution. How could I say no? I met with the archbishop yesterday to work it all out, and our lawyers finished drawing up the paperwork last night. The archbishop received the cashier's check this morning." He offered an almost bashful smile. "I asked him to let me be the one to break the news."

Peter stared in disbelief. The words felt like a punch to the gut. "Not your statues! You sold them? But they were so precious to you."

Antonio smiled serenely at him and once again held his glass of wine aloft. "Dust to dust, Father," he said in a low, resonant voice. "Besides, all funds ultimately belong to God. We happened to direct them where they were most needed. Trust me, when I'm old and on my deathbed, I'm not going to be thinking about those statues. I'm going to be thinking about a priest and his beloved school. I'm going to be thinking about where my treasure is."

"'For where your treasure is,'" Peter murmured, recalling the verse from the book of Matthew, "'there will your heart be also.'" He glanced at Maria, and her smile said it all. "You knew about this?"

"I learned about it just this morning, Father."

The others sat in stunned silence until, one by one, smiles overtook their dumbfounded expressions.

"To St. James!" Bobby exclaimed.

"To Mr. Federici's treasure!" Sandra added.

What followed was a joyful feast—one so overflowing with ebullience that Peter scarcely remembered what passed from his plate to his palate. As the others traded stories and reveled in laughter, Peter caught sight of Patrick, the stoic centurion from the New Testament, quietly enjoying his meal. When all had seemed lost, Antonio's right-hand man had counseled faith.

All around him, Peter felt buttressed by people of a deep, abiding belief, and for a brief moment he wondered who belonged to the flock and who had been called to shepherd them to safety. He was their priest, certainly, but any notion of an inflexible hierarchy had long since left him. He had as much to learn as anyone.

After dinner, Antonio struck up a bar from *South Pacific*'s "Some Enchanted Evening," and some of the guests, by now well-lubricated, joined in during the chorus.

"Why don't we go inside," Kathleen suggested. "Jonathan and Antonio can play some show tunes, and the rest of us can sing along."

Peter seconded the idea, although he was careful to leave his glass at the table. He followed the others inside and smiled at the sight of Jonathan plunking out a few chords on the very upright he'd learned on as a boy. Now a renowned concert pianist, Jonathan still had the same flare from his youth, both hands flying over the keyboard, shoulders hunched as he communed with his instrument. Antonio joined him a moment later for some piano four-hands, and the others sang along with gusto. Bobby and Jonathan took the tenor line, Sandra soprano, and Rachael and Mathilde alto. Peter, meanwhile, shared the baritone with Antonio.

Peter glanced over his shoulder and spotted Maria grinning from the couch, where she was looking on in amusement.

"Wonderful!" she hollered over the singing.

Patrick, who was leaning against a nearby bookshelf, nodded in agreement. "I don't know much about music, but even *I* recognize four-part harmony when I hear it. Bravo!"

Selections from *Guys and Dolls*, *My Fair Lady*, and *Oklahoma!* followed, among other songs. Just when Peter felt his voice begin to tire, the others, too, seemed to lose their enthusiasm. Slowly, in ones and twos, they drifted away from the piano until only

Jonathan and Antonio remained.

While the two men carried on, Sister Consuela led a kitchen cleanup crew. Peter thought about retiring to the deck but stopped in his tracks when he saw Bobby and Sandra sitting in the Adirondack chairs. The young couple held hands while staring at the stars.

Maria sneaked up beside him. "They make a lovely couple, don't they?"

Peter nodded silently, too tired—and too happy—for comment. Since his youth, he'd been a great lover of words and elocution, but at the moment, he felt content to let the evening speak for itself.

Chapter 41

Sandra felt as though she'd just lowered her head to her pillow when the old alarm clock beside her nightstand unloosed an urgent, merciless ring. She groped for it in the darkness, shut it off, and turned on the lamp beside it. It was 4:45 in the morning—an ungodly hour even for a schoolteacher conditioned to waking up early five days a week—but she threw off the covers and shuffled to the pedestal sink in the tiny bathroom on the other side of her family's rental cabin.

At the previous evening's celebration, she and Bobby had made plans to watch the sunrise together, and now, less than six hours after saying goodnight to him, she was slipping on a windbreaker, ready for their rendezvous.

A tiny part of her worried he might not show, just as he hadn't appeared at dance class that fateful day so many months ago. But she knew he was past that now. *They* were past that. The awkwardness. The hesitation. Any such barriers between them had finally crumbled. She'd known they shared a powerful chemistry the moment they'd met, even if she'd tried to keep her feelings at bay, and she sensed he'd felt the same way. Something undeniable smoldered between them, and it was no longer a question of when they'd pursue their feelings for each other. The time was now.

She rolled open the sliding glass door and stepped outside into a cool breeze. The sand, so hot beneath her feet the day before, felt cool under her toes the second she left the boardwalk and hit the beach. Stars twinkled from every corner of the sky, but the moon was already

232

retreating to make room for the first rays of sunrise.

Sandra took a left on the beach and headed north. Soon she was able to make out a dark-but-familiar silhouette approaching her. The figure paused and then picked up the pace, and an eternity seemed to pass as they closed the gap between one another, each step accompanied by a heart-pounding euphoria. When she could finally see Bobby's face—the crooked grin, the thick sideburns and unruly hair—she leapt into his arms, and the two shared their first kiss. The passion between them left her knees weak.

"I'm so glad you came," she said, unable to contain her joy.

"Me too."

Their lips met once more, and when she pulled back to stare into his deep brown eyes, she felt instantly lost in his gaze. It was as if their souls were entwined in a dance, and for a moment she was transported back to the gym at St. James, to their silver waltz on the squeaky hardwoods, surrounded by her students, all eyes on them, the drafty space sizzling with an electricity that couldn't be denied. Sandra had dated only sporadically in college—and not at all in high school. She'd never felt moved to step off the educational path long enough to lose herself in what would surely be a fleeting romance. But this was different. She could get lost here, in Bobby's arms, without losing herself. She could give in to the romantic wave washing over her without losing her identity or dignity. It was the difference between a childhood crush and a once-in-a-lifetime love. She was safe with Bobby Jones.

Bobby exhaled. "Wow."

"Yeah," she said, barely able to catch her breath.

"You wanna take a walk?" he asked when they'd regained their composure.

She took his hand in hers. "Let's."

They continued north, all the while searching the eastern horizon for the first light of day. Other than a stray gull foraging in the low tide and another floating in the air currents overhead, they had the beach to themselves as they wandered out toward an exposed sandbar. On the way, Sandra waded through knee-deep water before finally gaining higher ground.

"It's glorious," she said as the sun inched above the eastern horizon.

Not much more than a faintly glowing pink-orange orb at first, it soon brightened the sky around it, and with each passing minute, took on a fiercer hue until finally it was too bright to stare at for more than a second or two at a time.

"Every single one is different," Bobby uttered softly.

"Every single one what?"

"Every sunrise."

She thought for a moment. "I suppose you saw your fair share in Vietnam."

He nodded. "Not like this one. And I'll never see one like it again."

She glanced down at her feet in the sand, unsure what to say.

"You wanna go for a swim?" he asked, his voice brightening like the sun behind him.

"Sure."

She unzipped her windbreaker and tossed it onto the sandbar. Next, she removed her sweatshirt and jean shorts so that only her one-piece bathing suit remained. When she looked up, she saw Bobby gazing at her with his lips slightly parted, his eyes moist with tears.

"What's wrong?"

"Nothing," he whispered. "You're just . . . breathtaking."

She blushed.

Before she could divine a response, he tore off his sweatshirt and T-shirt and turned toward the surf. As he did, she spotted several tattoos on his golden-brown back, each one the name of someone she'd never met. She didn't have to ask who these men were, for she knew it the moment she saw the black letters scrawled into Bobby's skin.

Suddenly she understood the defensive walls he'd erected, the constant balking, the faraway look in his eyes when she tried to make a connection at school. Bobby Jones was a wounded warrior, a proud man who'd lost a piece of himself in the jungles of Vietnam. Whatever pressures the average person faced in day-to-day living were trivial in comparison to the grief he relived every moment of every day.

He turned to beckon her into the water, but stopped and stared at the tears streaming down her face. He seemed confused, but then a shadow of recognition passed over his face and he sprinted back to her, high-stepping the knee-deep water.

He took hold of her shoulders as soon as he reached her. "What's wrong? Are you all right?"

"Your back," she said, still crying. "The names of the men on your back. I'm so sorry. I know it hurts you badly. It hurts me too."

She felt her body trembling beyond her control, and all she could do was sob into his shoulder as he tried to comfort her. His scent and touch—even the sound of his voice as he tried to soothe her—seemed powerless to stop the quaking. The tension she'd stored away since meeting Bobby was pouring from her soul, and for a moment she was a child again, sitting cross-legged on the living room floor, the black-and-white TV on, her father skulking nearby like a ghost who, even when he was in the same room as her, was never fully present.

She'd heard her father speak the truth of his heart a few times—but only when caught in one of his nightmares. It was a bloody sound, deep and frightful, emanating from somewhere unreachable. In those moments late at night, she'd stand outside her parents' bedroom and listen to her mother's soft voice, every word a helpless plea to retrieve the lost man. During those dark nights, she'd come to hate war, to hate men of war, even the one living in her own home, impersonating her father. But now, as the sun continued to climb the sky, she could feel that anger and hurt receding into the shadows, replaced by blinding light.

She gazed up at Bobby. "I'm sorry."

"Don't be," he said, wiping away the last of her tears. "I'm touched. I really am." He looked up at the sky, seemingly struggling for the right words, and then returned her gaze. "What you just did . . . to react like that to someone else's pain . . . I can't tell you how much it means to me. It sounds stupid, but for the first time since the war, I feel like I'm not alone."

She gave him a sad smile. "It doesn't sound stupid at all. And you're right. You're not alone. You never were."

He turned away, but not before she saw a lone tear roll down his cheek. Without another word, they gathered their things and continued walking hand-in-hand along the low tide.

Finally, after several minutes of silence, Sandra squeezed his hand. "What happened to those men?"

It was a dangerous question, but she felt compelled to ask it. More importantly still, she felt *safe* to ask it. And to her great relief, he answered without hesitation, recounting the moment he'd led his company into an ambush. Eager for his baptism of fire, he'd instead run headlong into the reality of war, which proved more savage than heroic, more chaotic than orderly. The earth had exploded. Trees had been shredded into splinters. And men had gone down. These men, some of them disfigured beyond recognition, had been his family, and the jungle his adopted home. The grisly encounter had left him feeling like a fool, a man betrayed by his own naïve ambition.

The greatest injustice: while they'd gone home in body bags, he'd gone home without a scratch. Every waking breath was a reminder that his good fortune had come at their everlasting expense.

236

"But you know that's not true, right?" she asked. "You could have just as easily been killed and someone else spared."

"I know," he whispered. "I've just never been able to accept it. Until now."

They continued walking north, and Sandra thought of her father, who had died in his sleep during her junior year in college. She liked to think he was finally lifted from the battlefield and born anew in heaven.

"When my father died," she said, "my mother didn't allow me to push away my grief. She told me to lean into it. She said there's no shortcut to healing. Just like any injury, it takes time to heal."

"Your mother sounds like a wise woman."

Sandra smiled. "She'd have to be. Look at my sister."

Bobby laughed, and slowly, as the morning bloomed all around them and the beach became populated with beachcombers and birdwatchers, the heaviness lifted. Soon Sandra was reliving her first year at St. James, and the two were giddily recounting their first dance together. Bobby, it turned out, was a great storyteller when not weighed down by his grief, and he recounted tales of his childhood and school years. He even added a few comedic anecdotes from his tour in Vietnam, which, it turned out, hadn't been all horror. He'd made beautiful friendships there, even if some of them had been tragically cut short.

Eventually, they turned in their tracks and retraced their steps. Their footprints, still fresh in the wet sand, looked playful in the morning sun, and Sandra felt her spirit lighten with each step.

When they were within hailing distance of the Blooms' beach house, they spotted Father Ryan waving to them from the deck.

"You ready for breakfast?" Bobby asked.

She turned toward him and smiled, suddenly feeling ravenous. "I'm ready for anything."

Chapter 42

Peter drained the last of his cup of coffee just in time to greet Bobby and Sandra at the top of the short set of stairs to the sun-bleached deck. The sky was blue in every direction, and the sun had already begun to warm the beach. As for the two young people standing before him, Peter saw the light radiating from their shining faces and knew something marvelous had happened.

Perhaps sensing the same thing, Jonathan took Bobby by the arm and guided him toward the sliding glass door, peppering him with morning pleasantries.

Peter turned toward Sandra to search her face for clues, but Sandra, with her hypnotic blue eyes dueling with the sky for primacy, was already tearing up as she wrapped him in a hug that felt as joyful as it did purgative. He could smell the sea in her dark hair and feel the trembling in her limbs as she bore deeper into his arms, seemingly determined to convey what could not be said with mere words.

When she finally stepped back, the tears were gone, though her eyes remained glassy, like tiny oceans glistening with hope. She raised her chin and spoke in a hushed voice. "I met Bobby Jones today, Father."

Peter immediately understood the anguish that Sandra was trying to shed. He was the priest, and therefore the rock, and she'd come to him for solace, to be seen, to be loved as God loved her, however imperfect, however incomplete. They stood silently a moment, hands still locked, and then he led her to a private corner of the deck, where

238

their words could be theirs only.

"He told you about the war."

She nodded.

"About the men he lost."

Another nod.

"But you knew it already, no? Maybe not the names, nor the circumstances. But you understood his pain. It's partly what drew you to him."

Sandra's mouth dropped. "How did you know?"

Peter chuckled. "I know a loving heart when I see one. And my guess is you've seen someone else fight the same battles inside. Perhaps an uncle or a grandfather. Or someone closer."

"Now you're scaring me, Father," Sandra said, tilting her head toward him and narrowing her eyes.

"I don't mean to. But in my line of work, there are no new stories. Just new wrinkles. Maybe a new character or two. A new backdrop. But the stories, they're the same."

A mystified grin replaced her frown. "Nothing new under the sun, eh, Father?"

"That's what the preacher says."

She was laughing now. "It will probably sound crazy, but I already know I'm going to spend the rest of my life with Bobby. We're going to raise a family, plant a garden, grow old together—all of it."

"It's not crazy at all. You two are meant for one another. And your empathy for my nephew is lovely to behold. It shows the strength of your love for him. But remember, this love does not belong to you. It comes from the Holy Spirit, and the fact that it resides in your heart is wondrous and beautiful. Keep it there, Miss Alvarez. Keep it always."

"*Sandra!*" she said with an exasperated smile.

He chuckled. "Sandra. Now go find your man. He's probably

missing you already."

~~~

The Federicis arrived a few minutes later, along with Patrick. Maria, too, made the walk from her nearby beach cabin and was kicking the dust from her sandals just as the group gathered for breakfast. Rachael, still bubbling with joy at the sight of Bobby and Sandra together, served homemade cinnamon rolls, a huge bowl of strawberries and cream, freshly squeezed orange juice, and perfectly brewed coffee. Small talk and barely restrained grunts of pleasure marked the meal's consumption. Afterward, as the others leaned back from the table and patted their full stomachs, Peter found himself rhapsodizing aloud.

"This morning," he began, "surrounded by so many beautiful souls, I'm reminded that my life is one of abundance."

Antonio, who'd brought with him a thermos that surely contained more than just orange juice, raised his spirited hand high. "*Saluti!*"

Everyone reached for something to toast.

"Cheers!" Bobby said, leading the chorus.

Peter waited for the others to still and then continued. "Good food and drink. A roof over your head. A community to nurture you. Such things nourish more than the body; they sustain the spirit. But sometimes"—he felt his voice catch in his throat—"sometimes when I'm surrounded by so much goodness and beauty, I find myself wondering why God has seen fit to bless me in such a way." He paused a moment, overcome by his good fortune. "As some of you know, I haven't always been so lucky. I've seen what mechanized death looks like. Man's inhumanity to man. And I know, right now, on the other side of the world, the same hell on earth that I witnessed is happening all over again. God willing, the fighting will end in Vietnam. But it will resume somewhere else. And the poverty and destruction it brings will be the torment of untold millions, just as it always has." He shook his head. "But here we are. Blessed. It's this awareness of the world as it is that brings my heart so much pain—and so much joy. For every war, there is a peace. For every injustice, recompense. For every ugliness, there is undeniable, unyielding beauty."

Peter turned to Antonio. "You say I saved you, Mr. Federici. The feeling is mutual. For me, St. James is a beacon of hope, the antidote to all that is broken in the world. In our halls and classrooms, we strive for something more than knowledge; we strive for grace. We know in our hearts that salvation is possible, that 'the kingdom of God is in our midst,' even if most people cannot see it. You made an extraordinary sacrifice in parting with your Roman statues—all to save some little Catholic school most of the world has never heard of."

Antonio raised an eyebrow. "Maybe not yet, Father, but perhaps someday the world will know of St. James High School."

Maria, seated beside Kathleen, took hold of her hand and held it affectionately. "Thank you both."

Kathleen wiped away a tear but said nothing.

"You all know the parable of the vine," Peter said.

Jonathan nodded from the other side of the table.

Peter smiled at his old friend. "Jesus said, 'I am the true vine, and my Father is the gardener. He cuts off every branch in me that bears no fruit, while every branch that does bear fruit he prunes so that it will be even more fruitful. You are already clean because of the word I have spoken to you. Remain in me, as I also remain in you. No branch can bear fruit by itself, it must remain in the vine. Neither can you bear fruit unless you remain in me."

"'I am the vine,'" Sister Consuela said, taking over the narrative, her tone as authoritative as ever, "'you are the branches. If you remain in me and I in you, you will bear much fruit; apart from me you can do nothing. If you do not remain in me, you are like a branch that is thrown away and withers; such branches are picked up, thrown into the fire and burned. If you remain in me and my words remain in you, ask whatever you wish, and it will be done for you. This is to my Father's glory, that you bear much fruit, showing yourselves to be my disciples.'"

"Amen," Antonio said, propping his hands on his belly as he leaned back from the table.

As everyone sat quietly digesting the allegory, Peter gazed out at the incoming tide. A sailboat, not much more than a speck in the distance, teetered on the waves and then disappeared in the glare of the morning sunlight. All around them the Cape was coming to life, and Peter, already brimming with a lust for all that was creation, felt his cup overflowing with abundance.

Made in the USA
Middletown, DE
01 March 2021